rs of

Christmas Wish

"Carolyn Davidson wonderfully captures gentleness in the midst of heart-wrenching challenges, portraying the extraordinary possibilities that exist within ordinary marital love."
—*Publishers Weekly*

"Judith Stacy is a fine writer with both polished style and heartwarming sensitivity. Fabulous!"
—Bestselling author Pamela Morsi

"Nobody does it better than Theresa Michaels. She is an incredible storyteller who...touches your heart over and over again..."
—*The Literary Times*

One Christmas Wish

Carolyn Davidson
Judith Stacy
Theresa Michaels

MILLS & BOON®

All the characters in this book have no existence outside the imagination of the author, and have no relation whatsoever to anyone bearing the same name or names. They are not even distantly inspired by any individual known or unknown to the author, and all the incidents are pure invention.

First published in Great Britain 2001 by Harlequin Mills & Boon Limited, Eton House, 18-24 Paradise Road, Richmond, Surrey, TW9 1SR

ISBN 0 263 83302 X

101-1001

Printed and bound in Spain by Litografia Rosés S.A., Barcelona

CONTENTS

Dear Reader,

Christmas is a time for families, for giving and receiving gifts, and for reaching out to those who are in need. Sometimes the neediest among us are those who possess much, but have few with whom to share their wealth. When I thought of the Tanner clan and the abundance of love they had to offer, I knew that Morgan Brady would find within their midst a family to call his own. How to draw two needy people together became the issue I faced in writing this story. Misunderstanding and distance provided the conflict, and Christmas, that most glorious of all days in the year, became the reason for Morgan to work at overcoming the obstacles standing in his way.

Anna Tanner, torn between her love for adventure and the nurturing family she leaves behind, discovers a man who claims her heart, yet seems to be set on a different road than she. And then there's Jamie—a child who also lays claim to Anna, wishing on the Christmas star in order to make his dream come true.

I love Christmas—the decorations, the traditional baking and cooking, the music, the stories, and most of all the gathering of family as the day approaches. Whether family be yours by blood ties or those of friendship, there is a need within each of us that causes us to seek their presence. And so we assemble with those we hold dear, celebrating the birth of One whose name is synonymous with love. May your holiday season be rich in all of those things that really matter. May you embrace the traditions you cherish, even as you pass them on to the next generation.

Merry Christmas, everyone!

Carolyn Davidson

Wish Upon a Star

Carolyn Davidson

For all the wonderful Christmas mornings that will
forever live in my memory...
For the flurry of holiday baking...
the cookies and fruitcake
that filled our home with marvelous aromas
as the season of miracles approached...
For the carols sung and the Christmas story we
learned almost by heart throughout those magical
days of preparation...
For the glitter of tinsel and the rustle of
tissue and wrapping paper...
The secrets hidden in the closet...
And the favorite ornaments that held a special place
in our family's history...
For all of this, I will always be grateful...
Thank you, Mother and Daddy,
for leaving such beautiful memories behind.
I speak for all of your children,
but especially for myself.
With love and gratitude, I dedicate this book to you.

And to the man who makes my Christmas
mornings a time of joy...
To Mr. Ed, who loves me.

Prologue

Dallas, Texas
December 20, 1897

Her mouth was soft beneath his, her lips unmoving, in his experience a sure sign of either a disinterested or an unawakened woman. And although her eyes were wide with surprise, she appeared far from disinterested. There was a certain clinging element to her, a lissome melting of her slender curves against his, as though she were drawn to his larger, firmer, muscular frame.

Morgan Brady sensed the quickening in his loins that preceded arousal.

He should have spoken first, but something about her had pushed him beyond his normal reticence, and he'd drawn her from the doorway and into his arms. Certainly he'd surprised her with the summons to his study, having always conducted his business with her at the dinner table or in the nursery. Now, he could only surmise he'd shocked her with his unexplained intimacy. And why he'd been so impulsive, so spontaneous, was beyond his comprehension. Morgan Brady was not an impetuous man.

Anna Tanner's attire was understated, as always. Dressed

neatly in her dark garb, brown hair looped and pinned at her nape, she looked the epitome of respectable womanhood—rather, of *nannyhood,* and that thought quirked his lips at one corner. He felt the breath of a sigh as her lips parted and her hands pressed against his chest.

He'd wasted half the kiss with dissecting Anna and his attraction to her, and it seemed only prudent that he offer her the courtesy of his full attention. Accordingly, he encircled her waist with both his hands and drew her body to rest against him.

''You're a lovely woman, Anna,'' he murmured. ''I fear I've been distracted from my purpose in this meeting.'' Their lips brushed briefly and he felt her tremble, sensed the surrender to his will he'd hoped for.

''Do you wonder why I asked you to come to my study?'' he whispered. His mouth parted as he murmured the rest of his message against the soft curve of her lower lip, ''I wanted to tell you that I have plans for your future.''

At her shocked inhalation of breath, he took advantage of her surprise and meshed his lips with hers once more. This time the hint of arousal he'd noted became a full-blown threat to his composure, and with a daunting lack of caution, he slid one hand lower, resting his palm at the lowest possible position he dared, just beneath the small of her back.

She stiffened, only for a moment, and then, as his tongue teased the inner surface of her lips, she sighed and slid her arms around his neck, obeying his unspoken command, and forming herself against his needy frame. She trembled and her mouth opened to his coaxing. Morgan was delighted with her response.

Anna Tanner would make a delightful addition to his life. As a mother to Jamie, she would be incomparable, and as his hostess and bride, she more than fit the bill he had been composing in his mind for the past two years. A spot in his plan he'd had little success in filling, although he'd scanned the most eligible women in Dallas, and found them wanting.

Anna was different.

He leaned back from her just a trifle, playing his trump card. "Anna," he said, only a trifle breathlessly, "I have a proposition to offer you."

She inhaled sharply, jerking from his embrace, and stepped back. Her arms fell to her sides, and he watched as her face lost its color. Her shoulders squared and her head tilted upward as soft gray eyes met his gaze.

"Sir?" It was one word, spoken curtly, and he rued his haste, surmising that her reluctance was due to his unfortunate choice of words.

At the doorway a commotion caught his eye and the same word was spoken again, this time in a frantic fashion. "Sir!" Harley, his almost imperturbable butler stepped hesitantly over the doorsill. "Mr. Brady, you're needed immediately."

Morgan lifted his head, his own reply harsh and impatient. "Come in, Harley." And then as the florid-faced butler approached with haste, Morgan turned toward him. "I gather what you have to say is an announcement of some major import?"

Harley nodded with vigor. "The police are at the door. A message from the bank, sir. You must go immediately. There's been a break-in."

A curse erupted from Morgan's throat and his mind switched from his private life to the bank he owned and was responsible for. "Yes, all right." He looked down at the woman before him, the woman he hoped to make his wife within the next week.

Daddy? It's all I want for Christmas. Can Miss Anna be my very own mama? Jamie's words rang in his head and Morgan forced himself to put aside the agreement he'd hoped to solidify tonight. Instead his mind absorbed the message brought by his butler. The message that demanded he leave

Anna standing in the middle of his study, her eyes confused, her mouth rosy and damp from his kiss.

He reached to her, his hands grasping hers between his palms. ''We'll continue this in the morning, Anna. At breakfast.'' And then he left, snatching his hat and coat from Harley's hands, donning them even as he made his way through the big front door.

It closed behind him and he hoisted himself into the waiting carriage.

Morning could not come too quickly. Anna Tanner was exactly what he wanted, what Jamie needed. The bright star just above the horizon caught his eye and he thought of Jamie's wish. And of his own need.

Anna Tanner would very nicely fit the bill, very nicely indeed.

Chapter One

December 21, 1897

She was home. Well, almost home, anyway, now that she could see the outline of the town just ahead. The train whistle blew loudly and she winced, then visualized Homer Pagan snapping open his pocket watch to check the time of arrival of the afternoon train from Dallas. The cars jolted, then slowed as they neared the depot and the familiar sights of Edgewood came into full view.

Anna peered from the window, watching as trees and meadows gave way to the houses and gardens that clustered at the edge of town. There, just beyond the hotel was Pip's Emporium, and across the street was the sheriff's office and the barber shop. The Golden Slipper looked almost deserted, although there were no doubt a few regulars inside. A pair of wagons waited next to the depot platform. Perhaps one of them might belong to a neighbor, she thought hopefully, and she could hitch a ride to the ranch.

The train came to a halt with a mighty whooshing of steam and a shout from the conductor. ''Edgewood!'' he called out, as if the name were not painted boldly on the sign just outside her window.

Anna got wearily to her feet. She'd missed the late train, and sitting up all night in the railway depot in Dallas had not been conducive to slumber. She'd found herself dozing off several times, but keeping her eye on her baggage and watching for disreputable characters had been incentive enough to stay awake most of the night.

During the trip from Dallas she'd leaned her forehead against the window once she'd been settled in place, and found herself jostled every time the train lurched. Now her head ached dreadfully, probably due to the tears she'd shed, most of them unnoticed, thankfully. Her veil was full, and she'd worn it before her face, only lifting it to wipe her eyes.

She'd shed enough tears over Morgan Brady. Her jaw firmed as she considered that decision. No matter that she'd lost her heart to the man. He could have couched his *proposition* in terms more palatable, but in making her such a blatant offer, he'd forever put paid to any hope her tender heart might have harbored in his direction.

She would survive. She would return home, to the comfort of her family. Morgan Brady would have to look elsewhere for a woman to warm his bed, and he most assuredly would not have much difficulty doing that very thing, if Anna Tanner knew anything about womankind in general. The man was both rich and handsome. The fact that she had cast her eyes in his direction had been a mistake of gigantic proportions. He would never know that he'd delivered a telling blow to her heart with his gesture.

I have a proposition to offer you. I have plans for your future. His voice rang in her ear as if he were close at hand, and she looked around quickly, then laughed at her own foolishness.

Morgan Brady was miles away, neatly ensconced in his home in Dallas, probably uncaring that his prey had slipped from the house in the darkness. He'd found out soon enough, she'd warrant, when Harley, the butler, let him know that his second rig had been put into service late last evening. And little he would care. Perhaps he would snap his fingers and wish her well.

Her chin rose as she stepped on to the platform. Jamie would carry on, of that there was no doubt. A pang of sorrow vibrated in her breast as she thought of the child she'd left behind to mourn her leaving. Her shoulders straightened. It couldn't be helped. Children have short memories, she determined stoutly.

Gathering her wits about her, she waited as the conductor placed her baggage beside her. With a small salute and a nod, he bid her good day and was gone. Men hurried back and forth, unloading barrels and crates. Amid the hubbub, Anna caught sight of Pip Sawyer, the redheaded owner of the general store and smiled as she called out instructions to the men who did her bidding.

"Put all my supplies on the wagons," Pip told the youngest Comstock boy. He nodded and directed the lads with him to do as she instructed, and they set to with a will. Pip Sawyer was nearing middle age, but youthful and vibrant nonetheless, and Anna had considered her an extended part of her family for years.

She lifted a hand to hail her. "Pip. Over here," she called.

"Anna?" Pip's voice rose in a note of surprise. "What on earth are you doing here? I thought you were celebrating Christmas in Dallas with your employer's family."

Anna grimaced, thankful for the netting that covered her face. "I was, but I changed my mind. I decided I needed to be at home instead."

Pip strode closer, peering intently at her. "Why on earth are you all covered up like that? Are you ill?" She lifted a hand and touched Anna's cheek through the veiling. "You don't seem to have a fever."

Anna laughed aloud. Depend on Pip to get to the heart of the matter. There was no lollygagging around with her. "I'm not ill, and no, I don't have a fever. To tell you the truth, I've been missing my folks and I thought the veil would hide my red eyes.''

''Well, you'll be home before you know it, girl,'' Pip said cheerfully, reaching to hug Anna tightly. ''Angelena's still in town with the buggy. I'll warrant she'll give you a lift to the ranch.''

''Angelena?'' Anna asked eagerly. The thought of seeing her sister-in-law was a gift she hadn't expected. ''Does she have the baby with her?''

''No.'' Pip shook her head. ''Wes kept her at home. Angelena came in to pick up her order from the catalogue, and I asked her to stick around and watch the store for me. She sent to Dallas for a pair of boots for Wes, and I think they're in one of these crates.''

''I'll go on to the Emporium then,'' Anna said quickly. ''One of the men can pick up my baggage later on.''

''I'll keep it in the station, Miss Anna.'' Homer Pagan, the stationmaster, stepped from the depot, and Anna shot him a look of gratitude. ''Just send somebody by later to get it.''

She set off down the street eagerly. For ten long months she'd been in Dallas, away from her family. Angelena had been heavy with child when Anna left, her brother anxious for the birth. Now they had a beautiful little girl. At least according to the family letters she'd received, everyone claimed she was the picture of her golden-haired mother. Anna had not seen her niece. But she would remedy that lack before another day passed, she decided.

She opened the door and stepped into the Emporium, inhaling the familiar scents of leather, dried apples and wood smoke from the potbellied stove in the middle of the floor. A checkers game was in progress and the two men bent over the board barely noticed her presence. Behind the counter a slender woman held up a piece of material, then folded it carefully. She looked up as Anna approached and a smile lit her face.

"Anna! Where did you come from?" Angelena scooted from behind the walnut counter and embraced her sister-in-law with enthusiasm.

"From Dallas." Anna's words were soft, accompanied by a smile that wobbled around the edges.

"Well, for heaven's sake, lift that veil and let me look at you," Angelena told her. "Wes said just yesterday that he was wishing you were here to spend Christmas, and now you've arrived. He'll be so pleased."

And full of questions, too, Anna thought glumly. Her brother had always been adept at reading her expressions, ever in tune with her moods. If he caught a whiff of what had sent her scurrying from Morgan Brady's house last evening, he'd have a royal fit and probably be on the next train to Dallas.

"Will you have time to take me out to the ranch?" Anna asked.

"I'll make time," Angelena said. "Wes can hold the fort until I get home." Her voice lowered in deference to the men who were bent over the checkerboard. "I left a bottle for the baby, in case I was overlong. He won't mind. In fact," she said with a wide smile, "he'll be tickled to death to hear that you're home for Christmas."

Anna forced a smile, her fingers clamped tightly to her reticule. "Do you suppose we can pick up my baggage from the depot?"

"I don't know why not," her sister-in-law answered. "I'll be ready to leave as soon as Pip gets her wagons unloaded."

December 22, 1897

Morning chill, carrying more than a hint of cold weather to come, greeted Morgan as the train slowed to a stop. Stepping from the relative warmth of his Pullman car to the frost-covered platform, he tugged his hat down over lowered brows and scanned his surroundings. Edgewood, Texas. A typical small town, and just about what he had expected. A Texas community where law and order thrived, it seemed, with folk scurrying around doing whatever small town folk do at eight in the morning. The street was wide, with covered sidewalks that stretched along either side of the road. Beneath an overhang were various establishments whose windows were decorated for Christmas; even the window of the newspaper office contained a large picture of the nativity scene.

Beyond the *Edgewood Gazette* were lined up a hotel, a building labeled Sheriff's Office and a barber shop. Just across the street was a watering hole called The Golden Slipper, a rather incongruous name for a dusty town such as Edgewood promised to be. Grasping his single piece of luggage, Morgan set off for the hotel, his stride long, his mission certain.

Finding Anna Tanner in a town this size would be nothing short of simple. Certainly the woman must even now be within his reach, and at that thought his mouth softened. He'd give a bundle to have her within his reach. First off, to scold her roundly for leaving his house in the middle of the night.

His honest heart amended that thought. Not really the middle of the night, but certainly after dark, when a woman should be at home, safe and sound where she belonged. And *his* woman had chosen that time to pack her bags and order up his buggy to take her to the train station. And it had taken a full day of setting things in order before he could set off in pursuit.

She deserved a scolding, he decided, and then he'd forgive her, once he'd explained himself fully. She would fall into his arms, properly grateful for the opportunity to become Mrs. Morgan Brady of Dallas, wife of a prosperous banker. And then, and then…

His mind reflected on the pleasure offered by that soft, rosy-hued mouth, the warmth of that lithe body she'd pressed against his so fleetingly.

With any luck at all, he should be able to locate Anna,

explain his intentions and take her with him, aboard the Pullman, back to Dallas tonight. If not tonight, then surely tomorrow, giving Jamie his Christmas wish, and fulfilling the plan he had only begun to set into motion two days ago.

The hotel was quite splendid for a small town, Morgan decided, stepping up to the front desk, where a neat, businesslike lady presided, a handkerchief pinned to her bosom.

''What can I do for you, sir?'' she asked nicely. ''You're a stranger in town, I take it. Just get in on the morning train?''

Such informality set him back a bit, but he recovered nicely. ''Yes, ma'am. I'm Morgan Brady, of Dallas, and I'm here for a day or so.'' Perhaps asking after Anna might not be the thing to do so swiftly. He'd bide his time.

''Breakfast is being served right now, if you'd care to partake,'' the woman suggested, eyeing him with a measuring gaze. ''Dallas, you say?''

At his nod, she turned the registry in his direction and proffered a pen for his use, then watched closely as he scratched his name in bold letters. ''That'll be a dollar a night,'' she told him, ''breakfast included.''

''Sounds reasonable,'' he said agreeably. ''Will you send my bag up to my room?'' The thought of breakfast sat well, he thought. There was no point in starting off hungry.

She nodded and Morgan turned from her, toward the dining room just across the lobby. A tall man approached through the wide front doors, purpose in his stride, his carriage erect, hat pulled low over his forehead. There was about him something familiar, and Morgan searched his memory, but to no avail.

Once seated at the table, he waited impatiently as his waitress approached, coffeepot in hand, and smiled at her as she filled his cup and took his order. Just beyond her, the man who had followed him paused, scooping his wide-brimmed hat from his head. He searched out the tables, and his head dipped in acknowledgment as his gaze touched upon a man at the next table to where Morgan sat. Its occupant raised a hand in greeting, and his words rang like an alarm bell in Morgan's ear.

''Mornin', Sheriff Tanner. We'll get you some coffee, pronto. I suspect Angelena already fed you though, didn't she?''

Sheriff Tanner? A relative of Anna's? No wonder the man had looked so oddly familiar. He had the straight nose, and even his hair was the soft brown of Anna's.

The imposing figure moved with economy, marking his goal and making straightway toward it. ''Just coffee,'' he said in an aside to the waitress and then looked fully at the man he'd apparently come to meet.

His voice was deep, mellow and yet carried a note of authority. ''Not Sheriff Tanner, not anymore, August. When you took over the job, you got the title with it. I'm just Farmer Tanner these days, and I tell you, son, that's just fine with me.''

Surely the name was not common in this area, Morgan thought, watching as the waitress approached with his meal. Chewing a piece of bacon, he listened. Eavesdropping had never been a failing with him, but this was too good to pass up. Anna was getting closer all the time.

''Wanted to talk with you about a couple of things, Wes,'' the younger man said, then got involved in small town happenings, his questions met with sharp, concise answers. A sense of regard for Wes Tanner began growing at a rapid pace as Morgan listened. Well-spoken, intelligent and respected, if the glances shot in the man's direction reflected the general attitude of the town.

It was time to move. Morgan drank the last of his coffee, rising as the two men left their table. He stepped quickly through the lobby and lifted his hand to touch Wes Tanner's shoulder. With a smooth, swift movement his quarry spun to face him, and Morgan stepped back.

"I beg your pardon, sir. I couldn't help overhearing your conversation in the dining room. You're Wes Tanner?"

Cool eyes surveyed him, and Morgan met the gaze with assurance. Tanner was not a man he wanted to cross. A mere tilt of his head acknowledged Morgan's query.

"I'm looking for someone, Mr. Tanner. I thought you might help me."

"How's that?"

"My name's Morgan Brady, from Dallas. I'm looking for Anna Tanner. Would she be your sister?"

"You're looking for Anna?" His brow raised and his eyes narrowed. Wes Tanner was no man's fool. "Why do you want to see my sister?"

"She left Dallas rather unexpectedly."

"Yeah," Wes said softly. "I heard."

"She spoke to you?" Morgan asked, wary of the steely glint in the other man's eye.

"No, she talked to my mother, and a little to my wife." Wes slapped his hat atop his head and tugged the brim low over his forehead. "I'm not sure she'll be interested in seeing you, Mr. Brady. She seemed pretty upset over something."

"I assumed she was, or she wouldn't have left without any word," Morgan told him bluntly. "There seems to have been a misunderstanding of some kind. I've come to sort it out and get things settled."

"What do you want with my sister?" Wes asked bluntly.

"I think I'd rather address the issue with her, if you don't mind, sir," Morgan said quietly. "If you'll tell me where to find her, I'll make my way there and get this thing settled."

"She planned to go visit with my wife this morning," Wes said. "But I'm not tellin' you how to find her there, at my house. You'll have to go on out to the homeplace and take your chances. She won't be too long, anyway." Wes stepped back, his stance wide, his fists at his sides.

"I think I need to know just what your intentions are,

Brady. Anna's been my responsibility for a lot of years. You'd better be on the up-and-up with her, or you'll answer to me. Not to mention my father.''

Morgan gritted his teeth against the words that begged to be spewed forth. Never in his life had he been judged any less than a gentleman. And now, to have this man question his moral fiber was enough to make him lose his temper. ''I have no intention of sullying Anna's reputation, Mr. Tanner. She has been in my home for almost a year, and I have done nothing to harm her. I'm certainly not going to begin now. Especially in her hometown, with her family surrounding her.''

''Then I'm sure you won't mind telling me what your plans are where she's concerned,'' Wes said with deceptive softness.

Morgan felt a moment's sympathy for any man who would be foolish enough to face Wes Tanner in a fight. The former sheriff would be a formidable foe. ''I believe I told you that I would rather speak to Anna privately. If you'll give me directions to your parents' home, I'll go there and wait for her.''

Wes hesitated, then nodded, and lifted his hand to point to the road running east, out of town, giving instructions tersely.

''We're so pleased you came home for Christmas, Anna.'' Angelena's kitchen was warm, the windows steamy, the air redolent with the scent of cookies cooling on the buffet and chicken stewing on the back of the stove. An altogether wonderful place to be, Anna decided.

''I was lonesome,'' Anna said simply, nudging the floor with her toe to keep the rocking chair in motion. In her arms her niece yawned widely, then closed her blue eyes. Anna watched in awe as the small mouth opened and closed, a sigh expressing the baby's content. ''I think I wore her out with the patty-cakes and peekaboos, didn't I? Or is it just her usual nap time?'' She bent to kiss the flawless skin on the baby's brow. "I don't know how I stood it, not seeing this child all this time."

Angelena stepped closer, one hand resting on the downy curls. "She's usually crawling from one room to the other, and by this time of day, she's about worn herself out. I'm not surprised she's gone to sleep." She wrapped one finger in a golden curl as though she could not resist the temptation. "She's been a pleasure to the whole family. Your brother is downright dotty over her."

"And so he should be," Anna said. "He's a lucky man, having you and Joy Marie."

"Have you ever thought about having a child of your own?" Angelena asked hesitantly. "About getting married, I mean? Wes said you could have had several offers, but you didn't seem interested."

Anna looked up into Angelena's soft gaze. "I never found a man I could love, I suppose. Maybe I compared them all with Wesley and my father, and none of them measured up."

"Never? No one even came close?" Angelena asked, pouring two cups of tea.

Anna was silent. She did not have it in her to lie to her sister-in-law. And as a vision of Morgan Brady filled her mind, tears misted her eyes. "I thought I might have found someone, but it didn't work out."

"Let me take the baby," Angelena said. "She can sleep in her cradle while we talk. I think a cup of tea would do us both good."

Anna gave over the child and watched as Angelena settled her, then walked back to the table. "Come join me," Angelena invited.

They sipped silently at their tea, Anna adding sugar to hers, then stirring it far beyond necessity.

"I don't want to pry, Anna. But I know what it feels like to love a man without being loved in return. I'm willing to listen if you want to talk."

Anna looked up quickly. ''You mean Wes?'' She shook her head in denial. ''I know my brother loves you. He absolutely dotes on you.''

''Ah, but it wasn't always that way, and you know it. Remember when he announced that we would be married and didn't even let me in on the secret? Do you really think that Wesley loved me then?'' Angelena smiled softly. ''It took him a while, but I knew he was worth the wait.''

Anna nodded. ''I'd almost forgotten all the hassle. It seems now that you've always been together.''

''I know. It seems that way to me, too. But Wes married me—'' Angelena halted, and bit at her lip. ''Your brother married me because he wanted me in his bed, Anna. And I needed him. It was about as convenient a bargain as could be.''

''Well, the man I thought I loved wasn't interested in marriage,'' Anna said bluntly.

Angelena hesitated. ''What exactly was he interested in?'' Her cheeks took on a rosy hue and she shook her head. ''I'm not prying, Anna, honestly. It just seems that you're not very happy, and I'm willing to listen.''

There was no help for it. She'd held the hurt inviolate for almost two days, and Angelena's words opened the floodgates. Tears trickled down Anna's cheeks, and she brushed at them with little effect. ''I came home because my employer—'' She halted. Just what had he done? Kissed her? Suggested that she assume a new position in his house? Neither of which she could confide to her sister-in-law without labeling the man a reprobate. And somehow, she could not bring herself to name him that.

Angelena's eyes opened wide and her cheeks flamed, this time with obvious indignation. ''What did he do? Oh, Anna! Tell me he didn't hurt you.'' Her hands reached to Anna and clutched at her arm. ''Did he make advances?''

"I don't think I want to talk about it," Anna said quietly, even as her tears flowed.

"Did he force himself on you?"

Anna looked up quickly. "Oh, no. Not that. Just...kissed me and held me. He didn't hurt me. Morgan Brady wouldn't ever hurt a woman."

Angelena's head tilted to one side and her eyes probed. "What did he expect of you? Did he actually make you an offer of sorts?"

Anna shook her head. "Not in so many words. But he said he had a proposition for me. He had plans for my future."

"Maybe he wants to marry you," Angelena said quietly.

Anna's laugh was bitter. "I doubt it. He could have any woman in Dallas. Why would he want his son's nanny?"

Angelena sighed deeply. "Surely you've looked in a mirror, Anna. You're lovely. Any man worth his salt would be able to appreciate you."

"I think you may be prejudiced," Anna said with a sad smile. "It's too late now to worry about it anyway. I've left and that's that. After Christmas I'll make plans. For now, I'm just going to enjoy my family."

"You love him, don't you?" Angelena's words were sad, and her eyes filled with tears as she leaned across the table to brush at Anna's cheek.

"Yes," Anna admitted. "I've loved him for months. He's a good man." The tears overflowed, no matter that she pressed her lips together, and she blinked furiously as they trickled down her cheeks. The giving of her heart had been a gradual thing over the months of her employment with Morgan Brady. He, with his tender concern for his small son, his consideration of the houseful of servants he employed, and the proud elegance of form and face bestowed upon him by his ancestors, was, without a doubt, the man she had only dared dream of.

In a word, Morgan Brady had stolen her heart with absolutely no effort on his part, only by being there, for almost a year now. And then he'd ruined it, ruined the dreams she'd harbored, ruined the joy she'd found with his son. In fact, ruined her opportunity to live in Dallas, where theaters and museums filled the hunger in her heart for those things she had yearned for in her early years.

His words rang again in her head. *I have a proposition to offer you.... We'll talk about this in the morning.* And then he'd been gone, taking with him her innocence. Oh, not the stuff of which virgins are made, but her girlish thoughts of kisses and hugs and warmth and desire. Of necessity, Anna's daydreams always ceased their existence at the sight of a bed and what might take place on such a surface. Her mother had only hinted at those particular pleasures, her cheeks rosy, her eyes sparkling as she'd postponed such a conversation until the appropriate time.

"I haven't even seen Wesley yet," Anna said, eager to change the conversation. "I thought I might catch him home this morning. In fact, I didn't even eat breakfast, just harnessed up the buggy and headed here. I kept getting odd looks from Mother yesterday, and I knew I was in for some hard-shelled questioning this morning if I stuck around."

"Does she know where you went?"

Anna nodded. "I left a note. Besides, I told her last night that I had promised to come spend a little time with you and the baby."

"You only missed Wes by half an hour or so. He had to go into town to meet with August Rhinehold this morning. But he'll be home before long. I gave him a list of things I still need for my baking. I'm out of lard, and my flour bin is about empty."

"Well, you tell Wes that I'm home, and looking forward to spending Christmas with my family. That's all he needs to know for now, and I'll come up with the rest of the story in a day or two." Anna rose from the table and donned her cloak, then pulled her gloves into place. "I'm going to head for home. I think I need to talk to Mama, and it looks like we might get some snow. Wouldn't that be fun? It hasn't snowed for Christmas in years."

Chapter Two

The snow began midmorning, big soft flakes that seemed to catch everyone in town by surprise. Morgan looked up at the sky, thankful for the sturdy cowboy-style boots he'd chosen for this trip, instead of the leather oxfords he'd taken to wearing in the city. Perhaps incongruous with his suit, they nevertheless suited his purpose as he considered buying a pair of denim pants at the nearby general store.

According to the directions Wes Tanner had given him, he had some traveling to do, and perhaps renting a horse was not out of the question. A buggy might do as well, but if the inclement weather continued, he might be better off on horseback. He stood outside the Emporium, gazing upward to where its name was engraved on a sign overhead. It was but a general store, yet the fine carving of its name and the heavy walnut doors guarding its portals bestowed a certain amount of prestige upon the establishment. A bell sounded as he opened the door, and several pairs of eyes turned in his direction as he walked inside.

At the counter, a woman with red curly hair noted his coming and a smile lit her face. "Good afternoon," she said cheerfully. "I'm Pip Sawyer. What can I do for you, sir?"

Which seemed to be the general greeting he'd received

wherever he'd gone this morning. He stepped closer, aware of her admiring glance, yet not sensing a flirtatious manner in her smile. "I think I need a pair of trousers to ride in. Something with a thirty-four inch waist perhaps."

She raked his length with a sparkling gaze. "And very long, I think, in the legs." A series of shelves held men's trousers and she scurried to search among them. "Blue? Maybe denim?" she asked, holding up a pair for his approval.

"Is there somewhere I can try them on?" he asked, looking around for a likely spot.

"Just my office, behind the curtain there." She waved her hand at the far side of the store and Morgan nodded, taking the trousers from her and crossing the room.

"Pip, I need a few things for Angelena," a low voice said from behind him, and Morgan turned on his heel to face the man who spoke. "You still in town, Brady?" Wes drawled, pushing his hat back with one finger. "Thought you'd be hot-footin' it out to my folks' place by now." His gaze took in the denim pants Morgan held. "Sorry we don't have any fancy riding britches for you. Edgewood doesn't run to much beyond plain old denim."

"I'm sure these will serve the purpose," Morgan said easily, aware of the touch of sarcasm in Wes Tanner's voice. Morgan stood his ground, allowing Anna's brother a target.

The men near the potbellied stove were silent, their eyes casting interested glances at Morgan and Wes. It was beginning to feel like an arena, Morgan decided, and he might very well be designated as one of the prime attractions.

A movement behind the counter caught his eye, and he breathed a sigh of relief at the interruption. "Angelena doing a lot of baking?" the red-haired Pip asked brightly. "How you going to get a twenty-five pound sack of sugar home with you, Wes?"

Wes gave up the staring contest and turned to Pip. "I've got the buggy," he answered shortly, and walked toward the long, walnut counter. ‘‘Might as well pick me out a new dress for my wife, while you’re huntin’ around for the stuff on my list, Pip. And something for the baby. Maybe a doll?’’

Sounded like the man was a bit late with his Christmas shopping, Morgan thought, turning away and ducking as he went into the room Pip had called her office. In one corner a small cot held a sleeping child, a boy from the looks of it, his thumb in his mouth, his cheeks rosy. A pang of loneliness struck close to his heart as Morgan bent over the child, thinking of the sturdy lad he’d left in Dallas.

Jamie had called to him out the door. ‘‘Promise you’ll bring her back, Papa. Bring my Miss Anna back to me. I nee-eed her really bad,’’ the boy had howled, before the housekeeper had hauled him inside the house.

‘‘I’m doing my best, Jamie,’’ Morgan said beneath his breath, tugging his boots off, then dropping his trousers in order to try on the new denim pants. They fit, a bit stiffly to be sure, but some time in the saddle would take care of that. He folded his suit trousers and donned the Western-style boots he’d worn. He held the curtain to one side, surveying the store. Wes Tanner had gone, and the men around the stove once more tended to their checkers game.

‘‘Sir, I’m over here,’’ Pip announced as he allowed the curtain to fall in place. Carrying his coat and trousers, he walked to the counter.

‘‘I’ll need a short coat, maybe warmly lined,’’ he said. ‘‘I don’t want to wear my overcoat to ride in.’’

‘‘I have just the thing, and it’s only four dollars,’’ Pip said. ‘‘I’m sure I have your size. They just came in.’’ She rummaged through a shelf where bulky jackets were folded, lifting one from the pile. ‘‘Black leather, lined with fleece.’’ She peered closer at the garment. ‘‘Size 44. Does that sound about right?’’

‘‘I think that will do,’’ Morgan said, reaching for the coat and shrugging into it. ''I'll just take my things back to the hotel and search out a horse for hire.''

''Down at the end of the street, right on the edge of town, sir,'' Pip said quickly. ''The livery stable has some fine horse-flesh. Bates Comstock will fit you out nicely.'' She eyed him closely. ''You're heading for Gabe Tanner's place?''

''Yes, ma'am, I am.''

''Anna was in here yesterday, sir,'' Pip said. ''Are you the gentleman from Dallas?''

Morgan smiled. ''It seems so, ma'am.'' He slid his hand into the pocket of his new denim pants and drew forth his leather purse. ''How much do I owe you?''

''Five dollars will do it,'' she answered, holding out her hand for his money. And then she hesitated, holding the coin within her palm. Sharp eyes surveyed him from stem to stern, and Morgan stood his ground, waiting. ''Folks in town think a lot of Anna Tanner.''

Morgan nodded. ''I agree with them wholeheartedly. She's a fine lady.'' The woman facing him was taken aback at that, he decided, but not for long.

''We wouldn't appreciate it if your visit made Anna unhappy,'' she told him, her eyes narrowed in warning.

He could not resist. His hand went out to clasp hers, and she stiffened, her gaze widening as she allowed his touch. ''I have every intention of making Miss Anna happy. In the long run,'' he added quietly, ''I've come here for that express purpose.''

She nodded. ''All right. You got your directions, right? The Tanner ranch is smack dab east of town.''

He nodded. ''Wes Tanner told me where to go.'' And he smiled. Perhaps the man had not expressed himself fully, but certainly Morgan had gotten the message from Anna's brother. He'd better be on the up-and-up, or his hide would be forfeit.

His trip to the hotel was made in short order, and clad in his new clothing, he set out for the livery stable. The snowflakes were falling more rapidly, having abandoned the lazy approach to settle into a steadily mounting ground cover. They'd melted at first, then began piling into satisfying mounds where the wind blew them into small drifts. He felt exuberant, his spirits lifted by the freedom of the clothing he wore, excited by the prospect of riding out after the woman he'd chosen.

And he was only the least bit hesitant as he considered his task of persuading her to his plan. He'd take her aside, he decided, speak to her without her family present, assure her of his respect and esteem. This time, his desire for her would not get out of hand. He'd treat her as propriety demanded, no matter that her rosy lips tempted him to taste of their bounty. There would be time for all of that later, once he'd put his ring on her finger.

The livery stable was warm, the scent of horses and hay one that appealed to Morgan as he stood in the doorway. A husky man approached, calling out a greeting.

"Yessir, what can I do for you?" For the fourth time today, or was it five now, Morgan heard the words and grinned widely at the friendly nature of this town.

"I need to rent a horse, something sturdy enough to hold me." He looked down at his considerable length and laughed aloud. "Also try to make it a gelding, with a lot of patience. I haven't ridden in several years. I've been using a buggy to get around in, so I'm a bit out of practice."

"No problem there," the livery man replied. "My name's Bates Comstock. I've got a horse to suit about any rider. I'll fix you up."

They walked the length of the stable, and Bates chose a tall chestnut from the end stall, leading him to the middle of the aisle. "What do you think of this one?" he asked, his prideful look not allowing a word of doubt to be uttered. "I'll brush him down a little and find you a good-size saddle." He looked at Morgan more closely. "Whereabouts you heading?"

"I'm looking for the Tanner ranch," Morgan said easily. "I have business there."

"With Gabe? You gonna buy yourself some horseflesh?" And at that, Bates studied his customer carefully. "Or is it the other Tanner place you're headin' for? Young Wes has a farm just outside of town, but some north of Gabe's ranch."

"No, I'm not heading out to see Wes Tanner," Morgan told him. "I believe Miss Anna Tanner lives with her parents."

Bates lifted his eyebrow. "I thought Miss Anna was working for some big shot in Dallas. You're sure she's back in town?"

"Yes, I'm certain of it," Morgan answered.

"Well, that's easy enough then. Just take this road east and you'll find old Gabe's place without any trouble at all. Got a nice sign over the gate, and about quarter mile or so of road up to his front door."

That made three set of instructions so far. He shouldn't have much trouble finding the place, Morgan decided, swinging his leg over the saddle. He tested the length of the stirrups and pronounced them good. Then, reins in his right hand, he ducked his head as he rode from the stable.

The snow fell in a soft, drifting curtain, and the road ahead of him wore almost an inch of white. Everywhere in town, he'd noted the air of excitement as folks contemplated the sky, voicing their approval of the weather change. It seemed they regarded it a special gift, this promise of snow for Christmas. For a man on a mission, it might just be an impediment in his travels.

Morgan tugged his hat lower, shielding his eyes from the blowing wind, hunching in the saddle as white flakes formed patterns on his new leather coat. The town behind him, he scanned the gentle hills of the countryside. A far cry from the hustle and bustle of Dallas with its busy downtown and affluent areas. Yet his surroundings lent an air of peace that was missing at home. A sense of well-being filled him, and he wondered, just for a moment, what life would be like, here where each day followed another without the constant busyness he was used to.

He smiled to himself. He'd last about a week, maybe, in this atmosphere. There was within him the need for adventure, for power, for the satisfaction of knowing he could change lives and make improvements in the city he'd chosen to call home. His diversified investments had allowed him to be in control of more than just the bank he owned.

And yet he had been unable to control one small woman, had missed the opportunity to solidify a simple arrangement with her. Marriage and a mother for Jamie on his part. Security and a good life for her. And Anna Tanner in his bed, his conscience reminded him. A definite plus on his side of the ledger, given her response to his brief foray on her innocence just two days since.

He shook his head, breathing deeply of the crisp air, putting thoughts of those moments with Anna aside. His daydreaming just might have cost him, he thought, looking ahead. Hopefully, he had not missed the turnoff to the Tanner ranch. It was unlike him to be so lost in thought, and he scanned his surroundings once more.

A set of tracks caught his attention, veering onto the road from a narrow lane off to the north, and he lifted his head, peering through the falling snow. Somewhere up there a buggy, or perhaps a surrey, traveled this road, for the tracks were too narrow for a heavy farm wagon.

He bent his head, focusing on his path directly ahead, mentally calculating the distance he had come. Probably just a bit more than halfway, he thought, since his pace was hampered by the weather. And then the skid marks caught his eye, the wheels of the vehicle he followed slipping to the edge of the road, then back, where the light conveyance had slid almost to the ditch.

''Fool driver needs to watch what he's doing,'' Morgan muttered to himself, envisioning the vehicle overturning.

But it hadn't overturned. Only a hundred feet or so ahead of him, a black buggy sat forlornly at the edge of the road, one wheel askew. Before it, a woman made her way to where a dainty mare tossed her head. She reached for the harness, then slender, gloved hands caressed the mare, fingers spread wide against the forehead and against the long jaw.

''Can I be of service?'' Morgan asked, his gaze focusing sharply as the woman turned fully to face him. ''Anna?'' His whisper was hushed with amazement. What a stroke of good fortune, to find her so easily. And to find her at his mercy, he amended silently.

He slid from his mount and strode to her, his hands lifting to fasten on her shoulders. She stared at him, eyes luminous, skin pale, as if all color had fled at his approach. ''Mr. Brady? Whatever are you doing here?''

''Looking for you,'' he answered boldly. ''I came in on the morning train.'' And at the memory of his long, sleepless night, he felt a resurgence of the anger he'd managed to stifle over the past hours. It spilled over, chilling the tone of his voice, glaring at her from his dark eyes as he demanded his due.

''What were you thinking of, leaving my house that way? I told you we'd talk in the morning, and when I got home you were gone. No explanation for your actions, just a very unhappy little boy weeping over his oatmeal because his nanny left him.'' His hands tightened their grip and he bent closer.

Anna looked up at him, her mind racing as she considered his words. The very arrogance of the man, expecting compliance, hunting her down and then squeezing her shoulders between his huge hands as he berated her. She shivered, recognizing her peril in this moment. They were isolated, and she was at once exhilarated, yet strangely fearful.

"Anna?" His use of her name was a command, and she stiffened, rejecting his demand for her submission.

"I came home to be with my family," she said firmly. His eyes were almost black in the eerie light of their surroundings, searching out her soul with a probing gaze. Caught in the midst of a freak snowstorm, isolated by the side of the road, they faced each other as wary strangers. And at that thought she swallowed a senseless chuckle of mirth that begged to be given birth. Only two days ago she'd been held in his arms, his mouth taking possession of hers. How could she consider him a stranger?

And yet he was. For no longer did he wear the guise of patient father and understanding employer. Now he glowered at her from beneath his hat brim, his jaw taut with annoyance and anger, his eyes flashing a message of frustration.

"I'm not at your beck and call any longer," she said, attempting to sound reasonable. "I have my family to protect me."

"I thought I was offering my protection, back in Dallas," he said, his hands sliding down from her shoulders to grip her arms through the heavy cloak she wore. His fingers held her firmly, and she endured it, aware that his greater strength would not allow otherwise.

"Protection?" she asked, her teeth clenching as she recalled the thrust of his tongue against her own, the heat of his body that had lured her into his embrace. "I suppose that's one word for it."

"What other word would you choose?"

"*Seduction,* perhaps," she said, tossing her head and succeeding only in losing the protection of her hood. His fingers tightened their grip and then, as if he rued his use of force, he released her, reaching behind her to tug the hood back in place over her hair.

His eyes were dark, his jaw firm, and yet his lips curved with a faint smile as if he contemplated the word she had spoken so smartly. *Seduction.* Backing from him, she found herself pressing against the shoulder of her mare.

He watched her closely, noting her retreat, and his smile became a teasing grin. ''Seduction certainly would enter into it, eventually,'' he agreed. An element of humor coated his words, and she was once more balanced on the edge of falling beneath his spell.

It would never do. She'd submitted to his touch, enjoyed his kiss, even as it sent shivers of apprehension down her spine. But that was then, in the warmth of his study back in Dallas. Now she stood in the midst of falling snow just outside of Edgewood, and having made the break from his presence, she might as well let him know that his pursuit of her was a vain attempt.

''I will not be seduced to your will, sir.'' She turned from him and loosened the mare from her harness.

''What are you doing, Anna?'' His voice was harsh, his anger coming again to the forefront.

''I'm going home, Mr. Brady.'' With a quick movement he would not have suspected her capable of, she hiked herself over the mare's back and sat astride the placid horse. Bending over its neck, she retrieved the reins from either side of the mare's head and looped them in her hands. He looked down the length of her limbs in astonishment, where slim ankles and rounded calves gripped the side of the horse, watching as her heels dug in, signaling the mare into movement.

And then he stood back as horse and rider disappeared into the falling snow.

''I'll be damned,'' he muttered, astounded at the turn of events. The genial young woman who had graced his home for almost a year was gone, and in her place was an independent creature he barely recognized. She had no right to change so abruptly, and almost before his eyes, he thought irately.

Now, she'd left him standing beside the road, his horse pawing at the ground, and himself staring like a simpleton after her. She was gone, out of sight, and he thought for a moment of the danger inherent in such weather. Surely, she knew her way. Certainly, she would be safe. He shook his head. It would never do, allowing her to ride off alone, without protection. But in her present frame of mind she would not welcome his offer of safe passage, should he make it.

He mounted quickly and followed her tracks, determined that she not ride in solitary fashion. He didn't increase his pace, only needing the assurance that she find her way home, and that he could do at a distance. The hoofprints in the snow turned from the road and he followed, riding beneath an overhanging sign that announced he was on the property of Gabe Tanner. After mere moments he spied a large frame house, its white paint blending into the snow, offering a picture of pastoral beauty to his gaze.

Tall trees marked the road he traveled, leading to the house and he drew his mount to a halt, leaning forward to watch as Anna slid from her mare. She gave the reins to a youth who reached to hug her, then walked to the house, disappearing from his view.

He could either follow her and face the other members of her family, all of whom were no doubt even now being regaled with the tale of his miserable treatment of her. Or he could cut his losses and return to the hotel, even consider wiping clean the slate of this whole affair.

What affair! He'd had barely a tempting hint of the woman's charms, a kiss—well, two, if he were pressed as to the actual number. Then why did her scent linger in his memory? Why did the pressure of soft breasts against his chest and the slender lines of her body haunt his dreams? He was a fool, that's why. With a city full of beauties to choose from, he'd listened to a four-year-old boy whom he'd allowed to send him on a wild-goose chase to this godforsaken town in East Texas.

He turned his horse around, noting the cessation of falling

snow. Flakes drifted past his face, the last of the flurries, if the sunlight peeking through clouds overhead was any harbinger of things to come. By the time he reached the outskirts of town, the small drifts were puddles and the air was fresh with a crisp breeze. It seemed that his meeting with Anna was but a dream, a moment out of time. He closed his eyes. Her scent lingered, the sweet, womanly aroma she exuded, that lured him, tempted him and promised to linger in his mind.

Somehow, some way, he vowed, Anna would be his.

Chapter Three

Lamplight reflected on Rosemary's spectacles as she bent over the shirt she was mending. Anna watched from the couch, inhaling the scent of wood smoke from the fireplace, her gaze flickering over the library table that held family treasures, then returning to the woman who was the lodestone of this home and family. Gabe Tanner's stalwart strength empowered the success of his ranch, brought order to the complex details of running such an operation. But it was the energetic, loving woman he'd had the good sense to marry who drew his family into a cohesive unit.

And, Anna realized, Gabe was wise enough to acknowledge the fact. They'd been wonderful parents to her and Wes. From the moment they'd brought the pair of them into their home. Indeed, their early years with the man who had fathered them both, Nate Pender, were all but wiped from her memory, for his abuse had not touched her fragile flesh, only that of the sturdy boy who had protected her. Wesley, her brother, a man she would gladly spend her last breath to defend, should ever the occasion arise. Now they were both Tanners by adoption, and blessed to be part of a loving family.

"Mama?" Jenny, the family pet, dark-haired and petite, called from the doorway and Rosemary lifted her head to offer silent response. ''Mama, I need my new dress ironed for the program at church. If I bring it down to the kitchen, and if I sweep the floor real good in the morning, will you do it for me?''

''I'll do it for you,'' Anna said quickly, rising from the couch. ''Go get the dress, sweetie, and I'll put the irons on the stove to heat.''

Rosemary looked up at her eldest daughter. ''You may have to poke up the fire a little, Anna. Stick in another chunk of wood.'' After less than a moment's hesitation, she rose, gathering up her mending. ''Matter of fact, I can do this in the kitchen. I'll join you.''

''Just like the old days, Mama?'' Anna asked with a grin. The nights they had worked together in the kitchen were numerous, sewing, ironing, baking or helping the younger children with schoolwork around the long table.

''You've been my right hand, Anna,'' her mother said, walking the length of the hallway to the kitchen door. Rosemary settled herself in the rocking chair near the window. ''I've missed you terribly this past year.''

''And I've missed you,'' Anna replied. The fire flared to life as she poked within the depths of the cookstove, and the split wood she added caught the flame. She considered her words before she spoke again. It would not do to cause hurt to the woman who had been more than a mother to her.

''I love the city,'' she said slowly, reaching for the set of sad irons that she would use on Jenny's dress. She placed them on the stove lid and stepped back from the heat. ''There's something about the hustle and bustle of people and stores and the places to go that makes me feel—'' Her pause was alive with the words she hesitated to speak.

''Awake? Aware of the world around you?'' Rosemary supplied, looking up at Anna over the tops of her spectacles. A gentle smile rode her lips and her hands were still, holding the needle aloft, the mending forgotten for a moment.

"Yes." Anna nodded, pleased that her mother understood. "The whole city of Dallas is filled with urgency, Mama. There's so much to see and do, and the newspapers are full of news from around the world." She lifted her hands in a helpless gesture. "I can't begin to explain it. When Morgan speaks at the dinner table about some new building being erected or new housing, it's exciting. What he does affects lives."

"Morgan?" her mother asked quietly. "I wasn't aware you spoke so informally with your employer, Anna." She lifted the shirt to her mouth and bit at the thread, then scrutinized the tear she had mended. Her gaze held that same element as she glanced up at her daughter. "I heard that he came into town today on the morning train."

Anna felt the flush rise in her cheeks and turned quickly to the stove, lifting an iron to test it. "Yes, he did."

"And have you seen him?" Rosemary asked quietly.

Anna hesitated. Had she seen him? Her shoulders still felt the imprint of his hands. Her body held the electric awareness of his nearness, as though he could be drawn from thin air should she close her eyes and visualize him here. And at that thought, her heart yearned for just such a thing to happen. How could she have tossed aside her opportunity to speak with him, allowed her pride to garnish her speech with such harsh tones?

"Yes, I've seen him," she answered. "I spoke to him on the road just before I got home from seeing Angelena this noontime."

"Why didn't you invite him here for dinner?" Rosemary's words were edged with reproach. The hospitality of the Tanner ranch was well-known.

"We didn't part on good terms," Anna admitted. "We had a falling out, in fact."

"Today?"

Anna shook her head. ''No. Well, yes, today, too. But in Dallas to begin with.''

Rosemary folded the shirt she held, carefully buttoning the buttons. ''You're angry with him?''

''*Disappointed,* I think would be the better word.'' Anna drew a chair from the table and perched on the edge of its seat.

From the doorway, Jenny watched warily. ''Can I bring my dress in, Anna? Or are you talkin' about something important?'' The plaid dress was red and green, its skirt full, its sash long, and Jenny carried it with pride.

''Oh, let me see,'' Anna said brightly, holding out her hands. ''You did a beautiful job on this, Mama,'' she told Rosemary.

''I'm learning,'' her mother said dryly. ''Jenny wanted me to make it instead of picking something from the catalogue or from the shelves of the Emporium. I've never been much of a hand at sewing, but it came out rather well, I thought.''

She looked up at her youngest daughter. ''You need to be in bed, Jenny. Your dress will be ready.'' The child nodded agreeably, although her face expressed the longing to stay with her elders.

''Good night,'' she said, bending to kiss Anna, then her mother. Her footsteps sounded in the hallway and Anna turned back to Rosemary.

''He spoke to me the night I left Dallas.'' Her hesitation was long, and Rosemary looked up expectantly.

''He made a suggestion I could not accept,'' Anna said finally.

''He wants you as his mistress?'' Rosemary's tone was sharp, her cheeks crimson.

''Please, Mama.'' Anna rose quickly and paced to the window. ''I don't want you to interfere in this. And no, he did not mention that word. But I assumed that was what he meant. Perhaps,'' she said slowly, ''I was wrong. I don't know. He said he had a proposition to offer me. And then he was called away. A break-in at the bank or something.'' She turned back to face Rosemary. ''I left. I couldn't face him again.''

She crossed to Rosemary's rocking chair and knelt at her mother's feet, bending to rest her forehead on the familiar lap where she'd spilled out childhood woes over the years. ''He kissed me, and held me in his arms.''

''Did you—'' Rosemary halted abruptly as though she thought better of the question she had formed in her mind.

''Did I respond?'' Anna asked, knowing the bent Rosemary's thoughts would travel. ''Not at first—I was so surprised, and then…I couldn't help myself. When he pulled me against him, I felt like all my insides were on fire and my bones wouldn't hold me up, and I was afraid I might be willing to do whatever he asked of me.'' She looked up, her eyes filling with tears. ''Do you think I'm terrible?''

Rosemary smiled, her hands wiping the salty drops from Anna's cheeks as they fell. ''No, but I do think you may very well be in love with the man, dear. And although that's good in one way, if he doesn't have your best interests in mind, it may bring you heartbreak. And if he does that to my daughter, I may have to seek him out and deal with him myself.''

Anna shook her head vigorously. ''No, I don't want anyone to interfere. This is my problem, and I'll work it out. Besides, he may be on the train to Dallas tonight. I told him I would not be seduced, and then I rode the mare back here.''

''Your father said someone followed you back, Anna. He saw the tracks in the snow down the lane when he went to get the buggy.''

''He did?'' Anna shook her head. ''If so, I didn't see him. But then, that would be typical of Morgan Brady. He's a gentleman.''

''Is he, now?'' Rosemary said, her blue eyes seeking the answer as she searched Anna's face.

Anna sniffed, and Rosemary provided her with her handkerchief. She blew noisily, wiping her nose and blinking away the remnants of tears. ''Up until the past days, I'd have said so,'' she admitted.

''Perhaps, if you really believe that, you need to speak with him again. Why don't you go to town in the morning? Give him a chance to explain fully what he was offering you. And then decide if it's what you want,'' Rosemary told her. Her mouth twisted in a half smile, and her eyes sent a message of love that was unmistakable. ''I don't want to have to track him down, sweetie.''

December 23, 1897

''What do you think of this Brady fella?'' Wes Tanner strode into his father's barn, his face set in firm lines.

''Well, good morning to you, too,'' Gabe said dryly.

Wes stood in the winter sunlight, glaring toward the man who mocked him, then shrugged, acknowledging the reprimand. ''Good morning. Now, answer my question. Have you talked to Anna?''

Gabe turned from the horse he was grooming and faced his son. ''Rosemary thinks Anna's made some hasty judgments about her employer. Whatever the problems are, the man followed her here from Dallas to set things straight.'' He tugged on the lead line of his mare, drawing her closer, then with long strokes he worked through the horse's mane, using the other side of his curry comb.

He shot a glance at his son. ''From the looks of you, I'd say you've got your own ideas.''

''Anna talked to Angelena.''

Gabe looked up expectantly. ''What did she tell her?''

Wes blew out his breath in an exasperated sigh. ''She won't tell me.''

''So you're assuming the worst?'' Gabe grinned. ''Women kinda have this thing about them, son. They like to keep secrets. Just give her a few days and she'll spill the beans. There's something about a dark bedroom and doing a little huggin' and kissin' that'll make a woman tell you what's on her mind.''

Wes smiled and his mouth softened. ''About that time, I'm not much for talkin'.''

''Well, Rosemary's not real worried about it. She's willing to give the man a chance to do what he came here for.''

''And what's that?'' Wes asked belligerently, reminded of his sister's vulnerability. ''What if he—'' He broke off, snatching his hat from his head. ''I don't want anything to happen to Anna. I couldn't stand it if he hurt her.''

''Do you think Rosemary would let him?'' Gabe asked mildly. He turned with the mare, leading her to the stall where fresh straw awaited. ''If you're gonna hang around here, grab a pitchfork, son. I never did enjoy workin' while somebody watches.''

''No, I'm going up to the house to see Mother, then I'll head on into town. The thing is, he doesn't seem a bad sort. Citified, but still, he looks you straight in the eye.''

Wes's stride was long as he approached the house and took the steps in one leap. ''Mother?'' he called, opening the door.

''I'm in here,'' Rosemary answered. ''Why aren't you home, helping Angelena get ready for Christmas?''

''I wanted to see you, and Anna,'' he added, looking around as if his sister might be hiding in the corner.

''You've missed her, I'm afraid. She left for town right after breakfast.''

''She's going to see Morgan Brady?''

''I wouldn't be surprised.'' Rosemary scanned him, from the top of his bared head to the hand that crunched his hat brim, down to his wide-spread stance and back to where consternation colored his features. ''You look like a man set on trouble, Wesley. I hope you're not planning on interfering with your sister's business.''

''If she needs me, I'll be there,'' he said quietly.

''So will I,'' Rosemary told him. ''But we need to give her a chance to work things out for herself.'' She stepped closer and looked up into the face of this man who had become her son at the age of twelve. ''Promise me, Wesley Tanner. You'll keep your hands off, unless she asks for your help.''

His jaw clenched as Rosemary's penetrating gaze raked him. There was no help for it. He'd never been able to deny her anything she asked. And this was no time to begin. ''All right,'' he said grudgingly. ''But I won't be far away.''

And with that she would have to be happy, he thought. His horse waited patiently at the hitching rail and Wes was in the saddle with one powerful movement. The road to town was short, easily taken in half an hour or so, maybe less if his gelding had his way.

''Anna?'' The voice was deep and familiar, as smooth as the flavor of fine wine.

Morgan Brady was behind her and she hesitated, her heart doing a quick leap within her breast, her mouth trembling as she sought words to speak. For this moment she had driven the buggy to town, its wheel repaired by her father and Bennie, one of the hired hands. Because of the man who faced her, midway between the bank and the barbershop, she had walked the length of this sidewalk, searching him out, yet fearful of asking his whereabouts. It would not do that she should go to the hotel and seek his direction. Propriety must be observed, and yet Rosemary's advice had propelled her into action right after breakfast.

The night hours had dragged, with memories of Dallas and the home she'd left so precipitously filling her mind. Jamie, his precious face tilted up to hers as she read to him, his pudgy hands holding a paintbrush as he laboriously splashed color on big sheets of paper. The sweet weight of his body as she rocked him, singing lullabies in his ear, inhaling the scent of boy and fresh air combined.

Another face, one she'd only recognized as *beloved* in the past days filled her thoughts. Dark hair, eyes that seemed to penetrate beneath the surface of the words she spoke, understanding the yearnings of her heart.

The knowledge of her gradual attraction to the man was a pain to be borne, she'd long since decided. Morgan Brady was not for the likes of Anna Tanner, nanny and teacher of his son. For she'd seen the articles in the paper, telling of several lovely women, each in turn being escorted by Morgan Brady to the social events of the city.

And then he'd approached her, Anna, the nanny who was so convenient, so handy, just down the hallway from his own suite of rooms. And she'd almost fallen into his trap, nearly been swept up in the web he sought to weave around her willing body and soul. *If that was his intent.*

Surely he wouldn't have followed her here if his intentions were not honorable. She had clung to that hope as she paced the length of Edgewood.

"Anna?" He repeated her name, and his voice was strident. She turned to him, there on the sidewalk where the whole town might be privy to their meeting. His hands clenched into fists and he thrust them into his pockets, as though they fought a battle with his will.

"Where can we talk? Is it proper for me to take you to a private parlor in the hotel?"

She hesitated, a moment too long it seemed, for his reaction was swift. He reached for her, gripping her wrist and hauling her behind him. She scampered to keep up, breathless as she held her hood in place with the other hand.

"Proper or not, I need to speak to you without listening ears, Anna," he growled, hustling her up the single step to the hotel lobby, then slowing his pace as they approached the desk. "I'd like to have access to a private parlor, ma'am," he said boldly, holding his hat before him as he faced the woman behind the desk.

Mrs. Westcott eyed him carefully, turning her glance to encompass Anna before she answered his demand. ''I suppose that can be arranged,'' she said finally, stepping from behind the tall, oak partition to escort the couple to a door at the far side of the lobby. She opened it with a flourish and stood aside. ''May I send in some tea?''

Morgan shook his head. ''No, we just need a bit of seclusion to discuss some mutual business.'' His gaze was stern as he silently bid the woman to remove herself, and it was with obvious reluctance that Mrs. Westcott left, closing the door softly behind herself. Morgan strode across the room as the latch clicked, his hand reaching to set the lock, guaranteeing the element of privacy.

Anna took a deep breath. They were as isolated now as they had been that evening in his study. Outside this room the other occupants of the hotel and its employees went about their business, all unaware of the two people facing each other within these walls. Emotion charged the very air she breathed, permeating not only her own scattered thoughts and heartfelt feelings, but unless she missed her guess, those of the man facing her.

A man she'd managed to fall in love with.

Now he was free to set loose his anger upon her if he chose. And probably it was no more than she deserved. Yet it was not simply anger seething from his dark eyes she decided, but frustration and hurt pride.

Morgan's gaze swept her form, his jaw taut, his mouth firm, and when he spoke the words were shards of arrogance. ''You had the last word yesterday, Anna. Today it's my turn.'' He took her cloak from her, tossing it over a chair, and unbuttoned his own leather jacket.

She tilted her head proudly, searching her mind for the phrases Rosemary had spoken. *If he doesn't have your best interests in mind, it may bring you heartbreak.* And so it might, Anna thought. She clenched her hands into fists, then jammed them into her pockets, lest they betray her and reach for the man whose narrowed eyes watched her.

But even as she met his challenge, lifting her gaze to his, those dark orbs swept her length, softening as they fed on her feminine form, returning finally to rest on her face. A ruddy hue rose to his high cheekbones and one long hand lifted, his index finger nudging her chin yet higher. He captured it, enclosing it with his palm, holding her gaze.

"I almost left town last night, you know." His words stunned her with a sense of loss, and then his eyes softened. "But I've never been a quitter, Anna. I was about to head in your direction again this morning."

"You were coming to the ranch?" she asked, absorbed with the presence of the man who touched her, whose warmth set small fires blazing wherever his fingers brushed her skin. He nodded, his eyes intent on her, his gaze a caress.

"Ah, Anna," he whispered. "I was not going to touch you. But you tempt me so." He shook his head, a teasing gesture, as that enticing finger of his drew a pattern up the tilt of her chin to touch the fullness of her bottom lip. He pressed against it, as if judging its firmness, then brushed it softly.

"You have a beautiful mouth, Anna," he whispered, the words guttural, barely discernible. Her hands slid from her pockets and she leaned just a bit closer, the better to hear, her gaze tangling with the sultry depths of his.

His fingers defined the line of her upper lip and she was tempted to touch them with the tip of her tongue, to taste the male flesh that dared to pleasure her with such disregard for propriety. His other hand swept to enclose her face, and she blinked, captured by the frame of his palms, aware only of his touch as his head dipped closer.

His lips were warm, firm against hers and his hands no longer held her face immobile, but tangled themselves in her hair, loosening it, pulling free the pins that held it fast. Her palms met the hard planes of his chest, and then she was drawn against his body. One muscled arm gripped her firmly around her waist, the other wrapped in the long length of her dark hair, free now from its confinement.

Gone was the gentleman from Dallas, and in his place was a man bent on persuading Anna Tanner to his way of thinking. His murmurs reached her ears and she strained to catch the words he spoke. He needed her, needed to take her home with him, he muttered darkly. But then she already knew that. Without her in the house, Jamie was no doubt more than a little upset. Of course Morgan needed her.

And then he whispered a threat that brought forth a gasp of astonishment. Something about his bed and wanting to see her there. She shivered as images of that masculine room where he slept invaded her mind. She'd peeked in the door just once, taking note of that haven of male solitude, with its tall windows and mahogany furniture.

And an enormous bed against one wall.

It was there he planned on taking her, if her ears were in working order. And it was exactly that threat she must guard against. She pressed her palms flat against his chest, whimpering against the firm pressure of his mouth.

"I won't be seduced this way," she whispered, aware that her lips were being suckled by his, and her protest was being ignored in the frenzy of his kiss.

"Morgan!" She breathed his name and it sobbed between them.

"Well, hell's bells," he grunted harshly, lifting his head, glaring at her from glittering eyes. His mouth was damp, his nostrils flaring and her heart leaped in her chest as she recognized the desire he made no attempt to disguise.

He bent his forehead to touch hers and inhaled deeply. "Hush, don't tremble so, Anna." His hands moved from her back, his fingers untangled themselves from her hair, and he smoothed it away from her face. ''I won't hurt you. I'll never hurt you.'' He peered down at her and his mouth twisted wryly. ''There's something about you—''

''Miss Anna?'' A fist pounded on the door, as a husky voice called her name. ''Miss Anna! This is Sheriff Rhinehold, ma'am. I don't want to be causin' a fuss, ma'am but Mrs. Westcott is kinda worried about you. Bein' alone with a strange man and all.''

''Oh, my word!'' Anna broke away from Morgan, stumbling backward, her hands cool against her heated cheeks. ''I can't believe I—'' She turned to the door, tripping over a chair.

The doorknob was in her hand and she rattled it with futile movements. Only when Morgan stepped behind her and clasped her fingers within his own did she remember the lock he'd so firmly set in place.

''Let me,'' he said softly, pulling her against his tall form, his hands freeing the lock and opening the door partway. Moving her to one side, he gave her the time she needed to calm her breathing, then scan the floor in search of her hairpins. They lay scattered across the carpet and she bent to retrieve them.

Her fingers were swift, attempting to repair the damage he'd wrought, though she felt frustrated without the aid of a mirror. She listened as Morgan spoke soothing words to August Rhinehold, hoping he would keep the sheriff for a few minutes. Smoothing her hair into place, she wound the long length into a presentable form, and placed the pins quickly, then moved to where Morgan stood before the door.

''Is there a problem, Sheriff?'' she asked brightly, peering past Morgan's shoulder.

''That's what I'm askin' you, ma'am,'' August answered, one hand on his gun.

Chapter Four

The woman had disappeared. Out the big double doors of the hotel and onto the sidewalk, only to vanish by the time Morgan was able to get past the sheriff, who had blustered mightily, with all his righteous indignation in full force. He'd done his best to look upright and decent, soothing the man's feathers as best he could.

Now Anna was gone, and with one black buggy looking about like the next, he couldn't even tell if the vehicle heading east belonged to her or not. There was no way around it. He'd have to make his way to the Tanner ranch. And this time he'd walk up to the door and announce himself.

He took time out to dress warmly, donned his leather coat and spoke briefly with Samuel Westcott before he left. He paid for another night's lodging, thinking of the child he'd left in Dallas. This was the last night he could stay, the last chance he had to persuade Anna to his purpose. Tomorrow was Christmas Eve, and come hell or high water, his Pullman car would be hooked on the late train to Dallas, and he'd be on his way. Unless… And never had that word assumed such great prominence in his plans.

Unless the dual persuasion of his own presence and that of Jamie would convince Anna of his plan.

He walked to the depot and spoke to the gentleman there, wrote out his detailed message to Harley and paid the fee required. Then sent a fervent prayer upward.

Bates Comstock greeted him nicely, saddled the chestnut without comment and accepted Morgan's coins in payment. ''Watch the weather,'' he called after him. ''Snow looks likely. We don't get it often in these parts, but you got to look out for it when it hits.''

The Tanner ranch was quiet, not a soul to be seen when Morgan rode up to the hitching rail near the back porch. Looping his horse's reins over the rail, he fastened them securely, then headed for the door. He rapped smartly and waited impatiently, shifting from one foot to the other.

The door swung open before him and he found himself face-to-face with a woman who could only be Rosemary Tanner. ''Come on in,'' she told him. ''I've been wondering how long it would take you to find the place.''

Anna's fingers deftly rearranged the length of her hair, coiling it at the back of her head, for the third time in one day. The haphazard arrangement she'd managed in the hotel would never pass muster once she got home, she'd decided. The pins pressed between her lips were a deterrent, but she managed to mutter past them. ''I've never been so embarrassed in my life. And I stood there and let him do it.'' One pin slid from place and she glared down at the floor where it lay, as if it were somehow responsible for her dilemma.

''He took your hair down?'' Angelena's eyes widened with dismay and her hand patted the baby's back with an increasing rhythm. ''Right in the middle of the hotel?''

Anna shook her head, then retrieved the last pin and stuck it in place. ''No, of course not. Not exactly, anyway. We were in the private parlor Mr. Westcott keeps for special occasions.''

''He actually put his hands in your hair and took out your

pins? He had his hands on you?'' Angelena sat down on the sofa, then got to her feet again. ''Here, you hold the baby,'' she said, handing her daughter to Anna.

Anna took the transfer in stride, sitting down at the table to dandle Joy Marie on her knee. The little girl reached for the buttons on her dress, her mouth pursed, her eyes intent. Soft nonsense sounds flowed together, and then Joy Marie chortled, squealing as she grasped one decorative button in her tiny hand. Anna laughed aloud at her antics. ''Seeing this angel was worth the trip home.''

Angelena waved at her distractedly. ''She'll wrinkle you if she gets the chance. She delights in chewing on buttons. Put her down if you like.''

''No, I'll hold her. I've just gotten to meet her, and she needs to know her aunt Anna loves her.'' Now that she'd managed to escape the questioning looks of the townspeople and make her way to Wes's farm, not to mention putting her hair back in order, she was ready to take a deep breath.

Angelena sat on the chair facing her and leaned forward. ''I can't believe you went into the private parlor with him, Anna. And if he has honorable intentions, why didn't he ask you to marry him, once he got you there?''

Because he was too busy kissing me. ''I think he was getting around to it. And then there was so much fuss, and I was so mortified, I just got in the buggy to go home.''

''What did Rosemary say?''

Anna lifted Joy Marie, propping her against her shoulder, and rocked with an automatic motion, unwilling to meet Angelena's gaze.

''You didn't tell her, did you?''

Anna shrugged. ''I changed my mind and came here instead. She'll find out soon enough. I guess I needed to talk to you.''

''To me?'' Angelena sat back in her chair. ''I'd have thought you'd go to Rosemary.''

It was hard to ask such a personal question, Anna decided. She and Angelena had not been close, had not known each other well enough before she left for Dallas. But Angelena herself had mentioned it yesterday. Now Anna was about to ask her for details she might not be willing to share. "When you married Wes, you said he didn't love you. But you loved him." She halted, unable to pry further into her brother's marriage.

Angelena was silent for a moment, and then she smiled. "Is that what's bothering you? Do you think Morgan doesn't really care for you?"

"It has entered my mind," Anna said dryly. "I know he wants to get me into his bed. I'm bright enough to figure that out. But I'm wondering if this whole issue has been because he needs a mother for Jamie."

"And is that so bad?" Angelena asked. "Marriages have been formed for worse reasons. Look at your mother and Gabe. They got married so that you and Wesley would have a home."

"Really? Are you sure of that?"

Angelena nodded. "Wes and I got married because he wanted me in his bed, Anna. It was just that simple. No, I don't think he loved me then, but I loved him, and that was enough for me." She smiled and her eyes reflected the happiness she made no attempt to conceal. "He loves me now. And Gabe loves your mother. You know that."

"How do you know about—you know—my mother and my father?"

"Wes told me."

And if Wes said it was so, then it was. Anna took a deep breath.

"Mr. Brady followed you here, Anna. That isn't the act of a man set on seduction, no matter that he's been downright foolish in his pursuit of you."

"He's not foolish," Anna said quietly. "But he certainly isn't acting like himself."

"Do you love him?"

Anna stood and carried the sleeping child to her cradle, depositing her with care and pulling the quilt to cover her. She looked down at Joy Marie through a mist of tears. "Does it show?"

Angelena stood beside her, Anna's cloak in her hands. "Yes, it shows. And I think you need to do something about it. Talk to the man."

Anna's embrace was quick, and then, cloak in place, she stepped onto the porch, glancing up at the sky, where clouds gathered. "It looks like more snow. Maybe we'll have some on the ground for Christmas."

"Hold your horses, Wes." Gabe faced his son squarely, smack-dab in the middle of the street, in front of the Emporium, where business was brisk. Two days before Christmas, heavy clouds overhead looking like a storm was coming, and half the town looking on as the two men stood face-to-face.

"The man needs to state his intentions," Wes said harshly.

"I have a notion he will, probably would have if August hadn't stuck his nose in where it didn't belong." Gabe managed a smile as he thought of the fiasco in the hotel that was the subject of much discussion. "I understand Anna shot out of town like a rocket, and Morgan Brady was not far behind."

"Well, I'm giving him one more day, and he'd better make things right."

"Go on home, son," Gabe told him. "Get your family a Christmas tree. That's what I'm about to do. Rosemary's got the boys and Jenny busy stringing popcorn and I haven't even chopped a tree down yet. Guess I'd better follow my own advice." He lifted a hand in farewell, then sought out his horse at the hitching rail.

Wes watched him go, then followed his example, riding

cross country toward the north. Gabe was right. It was time to get a tree, and help Angelena with the decorating. Anna was going to have to make her own choices.

Morgan stepped past Rosemary, into a kitchen filled with warmth and the scent of fresh bread. So this was Anna's home, and this—he eyed the woman standing before him—this was her mother. He swept his hat from atop his head.

"I'm Morgan Brady, ma'am. Your daughter's employer. I've come from Dallas."

"So I hear. Well, you're just in time for dinner, Mr. Brady," she said, taking his hat and hanging it on a hook beside the door. "Won't you take off your coat and have a seat while I finish setting the table?" She turned from him, and he accepted her invitation, settling himself in the closest chair.

"The children are in the parlor, getting it ready for the Christmas tree," Rosemary told him, returning to him with a cup of coffee. She placed it on the table before him and stepped back. "Gabe promised to cut one this morning, but I think he went to town first. I fear our eldest son has been making noises about confronting you, sir. He's fearful of your intentions toward his sister."

Morgan's hackles rose abruptly. "Really? He's still questioning my motives?"

Rosemary's smile was a surprise and most contagious. It was all he could do not to respond to her good humor. "Yes. I'd say questioning your motives was a good description of his mood."

"And you, Mrs. Tanner? How do you feel about all of this?" He picked up his cup and sipped from the dark brew.

"I have the utmost confidence in my daughter's judgment, Mr. Brady." Pot holders in hand, Rosemary bent to remove her roasting pan from the oven. "I hope you like meat loaf," she said, placing it on top of the stove and lifting the lid.

"It smells wonderful," Morgan told her, sniffing appreciatively. "So does the bread. Did you bake this morning?"

Rosemary nodded. "Three times a week. We have a large family, and the hired hands usually eat their dinner with us. Not now, of course, with Christmas so close. Gabe has pared down the work outdoors to rock bottom, just the everyday chores so that they can be at home with their families."

"I haven't sat in a kitchen for a long while," Morgan told her quietly. "This brings back memories of my childhood, when my mother did the cooking."

Rosemary glanced at him in surprise. "Who does it now?" And then she flushed and smiled. "You have a cook, I suppose. And a housekeeper?"

"Didn't Anna tell you about her home with me?" he asked.

"Yes, but only so far as your son was concerned. And she mentioned the lovely room she was given as her own. But mostly we've heard about Jamie in her letters." She lifted the meat from the pan and centered it on a large platter. "I've only heard about you to any extent in the last day or so, since she's been home."

"And what has she had to say about me, Mrs. Tanner?"

"That you're a gentleman." Rosemary plunged a fork into the pan of boiling potatoes and then moved the kettle from the stove, draining the water off into the sink. Steam rose and she backed away. "I hope Gabe gets here soon. It's not like him to miss dinner."

"What else did Anna have to tell you?" Morgan persisted. Somehow it seemed important to know what words she had used to describe him. *Gentleman* was a fine beginning, but surely she'd had more to say than that one phrase.

Rosemary poured milk into the pan of potatoes, added a lump of butter from the dish in the center of the table and set to work with her potato masher. He watched her, willing her to speak, aware that she considered carefully what she would say.

"She told me she was disappointed in you."

Well, that was enough to take the wind out of his sails, he decided glumly. Of all the things the woman could have said, such a remark was the last thing he'd expected to hear.

"Disappointed in me." He repeated her words slowly and then lifted one booted foot to rest it upon his other knee. His fingers stroked the fine leather. "In what way?"

"To be very frank with you, Mr. Brady, I'd rather not discuss the matter. I think it's something you need to speak to Anna about. Perhaps make yourself more clear."

His pause was long, long enough to allow Rosemary time for dishing up the various vegetables she'd prepared for this midday meal. She carried the heaping bowls to the table and then turned to the kitchen door.

"Ma'am? Mrs. Tanner?" Morgan was on his feet, fearful that she would leave the room, with his question unspoken. "What subject are we talking about here?"

Rosemary turned back, her skirts swishing. "Why the subject of your intentions, of course." Her blue eyes narrowed and her gaze probed his skillfully. "I'd be interested to know myself just what they are, Mr. Brady."

And then she was gone, her voice trailing back over her shoulder as she spoke to the children she'd mentioned earlier, the ones preparing the parlor for a Christmas tree. They followed her back down the hallway only moments later, their voices rising as they vied for her attention, three young boys and a small girl.

"Wash up quickly," their mother said, and they obeyed, scurrying past him, their eyes wide as they took stock of the visitor, silent as they assumed company manners. And then they sat in their apparently appointed places, the three boys on a long bench, the girl, Jenny was her name, according to a whispered aside from one of her brothers, across from them on a chair.

They had all bowed their heads, Morgan hastily assuming

the same posture, when the back door opened. With a rush of cold air, a man he could only assume was Gabe Tanner entered the kitchen. One gloved hand held the trunk of a tree, a massive object, fully ten feet long.

''You're beginning without me,'' he stated, dragging the tree inside the room and then closing the door. Immediately the scent of evergreen filled the kitchen and Morgan found himself inhaling deeply, the aroma pungent and welcome.

''I love the smell of Christmas, Gabe,'' his wife said, crossing to his side to take his hat and coat. She lifted on tiptoe to kiss his cheek. ''I knew you'd bring home a beauty.'' And then she nodded in Morgan's direction. ''We have company for dinner.''

Morgan rose quickly, extending his hand. ''Morgan Brady, sir. I've heard of you. It's a pleasure to meet you.''

Gabe hesitated, his face somber, his words noncommittal. ''I'm sure.'' He accepted Morgan's hand, his own gloved, and the handshake was brief. ''You'll excuse me while I wash up,'' he said shortly.

The boys nudged each other as Morgan sat next to Jenny, where Rosemary indicated his place would be. Jenny, on the other hand, seemingly oblivious to her father's demeanor, leaned toward the visitor and spoke in an undertone. ''I like to have company for dinner. Mama always finds something good for dessert when we have a guest.'' Her eyes gleamed with good humor and a dimple appeared in her cheek.

''You're quite a young lady,'' Morgan said quietly. ''How old are you, Jenny?''

''I'm six,'' she told him. ''Almost six and a half.'' She leaned closer. ''Are you my sister Anna's friend?'' Her eyes seemed anxious as she awaited his reply.

He nodded. ''I hope so, Jenny. I'd like to be your friend, too.''

''She just came home you know. Are you gonna take her away again?'' Her dimple disappeared.

Now, how he was supposed to answer that one was a conundrum, Morgan thought. He was rescued from attempting the impossible by Gabe's arrival at the table. Standing behind his chair, he slanted a quick glance at his sons, then the visitor, and finally his daughter. Rosemary received the benefit of a lingering look, and Morgan took heart. Any man willing to acknowledge his tenderness toward the woman he'd married, and in front of a total stranger, must have a soft spot somewhere in his makeup.

The words of a blessing fell upon the food and those about to receive it, and then Gabe's chair was pulled back from the table and occupied. Food was passed between the adults and Morgan found himself spooning out potatoes and vegetables onto Jenny's plate. Strange that he'd so seldom eaten dinner with his own child. A pang of regret dealt harshly with him as he considered the many hours he might have spent with Jamie, if his own household were run in the same manner as this.

Gabe cleared his throat and Morgan's attention left the child beside him. "I understand you spoke to my daughter this morning at the hotel."

And what he was supposed to reply to that remark was a mystery, but he did his best, hedging just a bit. "Yes, we spent a few moments together."

"So I heard," Gabe said. He filled his fork and thrust it into his mouth, each movement filled with untapped anger, if Morgan were any judge of such an emotion. Gabe's jaw worked as he chewed and then he turned the full force of his dark eyes on the visitor.

"In the private parlor, I understand."

Morgan nodded agreeably. "It seemed the best place to hold a private conversation."

"And did that conversation involve laying hands on my daughter?"

"Gabe!" Rosemary's single word of warning brought her a sharp look from her husband.

"I'll deal with this," he said crisply, then turned back to his victim. "August Rhinehold is our sheriff and has the reputation of being an honest man. He tells me that Anna was *disheveled* when she left the hotel. Do you think that's a fair description?"

Morgan stifled the urge to grin, aware that his very health might depend on his reply. "I don't think I'd use that word, exactly, sir." His pause was long as he considered his reply. "She may have been somewhat—"

"Would you pass the meat loaf? Mr. Brady," Rosemary asked, smiling widely. "How do you like the potatoes? I use a little garlic to give them extra flavor."

"They're very good," he told her, lifting the platter of meat, allowing her to help herself. He offered it in turn to the three boys across the table, and received three identical refusals, their eyes round, their mouths compressed, as if they awaited the falling of the sky any moment.

"I'll have some meat loaf, sir," the pixie beside him said pertly. "I like my mama's cooking, don't you?" She moved her plate a bit closer and Morgan was profoundly grateful for her interference.

"You were saying, Mr. Brady?" The respite was over, and Gabe was on him.

"Anna was somewhat upset, having the sheriff interrupt our visit," Morgan said quietly. "I'm sure she felt she was the center of attention when we left the parlor, and perhaps that was what Sheriff Rhinehold noticed."

"I'm sure you're right," Rosemary said brightly.

"I'm not." Gabe reached for a slice of bread, stabbing it with his fork, and Morgan wondered at the ferocity of his gesture. "I thought she might have come home, but I assume she's not here." This last was delivered in Rosemary's direction.

''Perhaps she went to see Angelena. She was there yesterday, too.''

''I can't seem to catch up with her for very long,'' Gabe said. ''But I think it would be wise for us *all* to wait here until she comes home.''

''She can help us decorate the tree,'' Jenny suggested, wriggling in her chair. ''I can't wait until we get all the candles on it. And the popcorn and the pretty glass balls.'' She turned to Morgan. ''My sister always helps with the tree. And my brother, Wesley, always lifts me up and lets me put the angel on top.''

''Tradition is very important in this family,'' Rosemary said. ''Do you have special rituals at your home?''

Morgan considered the thought. ''We go to church on Christmas Eve together, but I'll have to admit that Jamie usually goes to sleep and I end up carrying him up to bed. And of course we open our gifts in the morning and have breakfast together.''

''Do you have a big dinner, with lots of people there to eat it?'' Jenny asked.

He shook his head. ''No, I always give my staff the day off.''

''What's your staff?'' Jenny asked innocently. ''Why does it need the day off?''

''Those are the people who work for Mr. Brady,'' Rosemary said quickly. ''The woman who cooks the meals and one who cleans the house.''

''Why doesn't he just get a wife like papa did?'' Jenny grinned, delighted at having solved the staff problem so neatly.

''It's not quite so easy,'' Morgan told her, beguiled by the child. ''I have a big house and I need people to take care of it for me.''

''Perhaps a wife is what you need, now that Jenny has mentioned it,'' Gabe said, his voice soft, his eyes shooting sparks.

Morgan opened his mouth to toss back a rebuttal to that

suggestion and was interrupted by the opening of the door, and the arrival of the young woman who had been at the forefront of his mind for four days. The woman he'd brought very close to ruination only this morning.

Her cheeks were rosy with cold, her eyes blinking snowflakes from her lashes, and with a chorus of voices she was greeted by her brothers and the small sister who obviously adored her. Voices rang out, telling of the planned tree decoration, and Rosemary rose to bring a plate from the warming oven. Gabe stood, holding Anna by her shoulders and dropping a kiss on her forehead.

To which she responded by bursting into tears.

Chapter Five

The bench took a tumble, three boys standing as one. Jenny moaned mournfully and Rosemary shot like greased lightning from her chair and down the length of the long table. Gabe responded with a snarl of anger, hugging Anna against his chest, then setting her away to peer into her face.

"What's happened? Who hurt you?" And as if that query could only have one possible answer he turned his attention to Morgan, his fury a viable entity.

Rosemary uttered his name, softly spoken, but a command nonetheless, and Gabe gave over Anna to her mother's embrace. Two dark heads blended as Anna's forehead rested against Rosemary's shoulder, her body calm now, as if the storm of weeping had never been.

"I'm fine, Mama. Really. It's just been such a day already, and only half over."

"We have company, Anna." Rosemary's words brought stiffness to Anna's spine, elevated her head to an upright position and caused her hand to grope into Rosemary's pocket.

"I need your hankie," she murmured, even as she drew forth a formidable example of women's small vanities. As large as a dinner napkin, but daintily crocheted around the edges, it was a handkerchief fit to control the most virulent of sneezing fits, Morgan decided. Trust the dependable Rosemary to come well equipped.

"Thank you," Anna said. "I didn't mean to collapse. It's just that I've missed you all so dreadfully, and to see everyone sitting around the table, I finally felt like I'd come home." She turned, a look of apology on her face as she prepared to greet the guest. Her eyes were great pools of tears, as gray as storm clouds, and her gaze was filled with astonishment when it collided with Morgan's.

"Hello, Anna," he said. "Your sister is a bit upset. You might want to assure her that your tears are happy ones." He stepped back and Jenny climbed upon his chair, her head on a level with that of her sister. Anna moved quickly, her arms circling the child, and they exchanged hugs, then kisses. Finally Jenny took the hankie from Anna and carefully wiped the residue of tears from her sister's cheeks.

"Are you happy?" she asked soberly. "I don't want you to be sad, Anna. It makes my chest hurt if you get sad."

How Anna could have left this family was beyond his comprehension. They surrounded her with love, even her three brothers rounding the table to hug her in unison, lifting their voices to talk of the tree they would decorate after dinner. At a word from Gabe, they all returned to their seats, albeit reluctantly, and the meal was eaten quickly.

Then, Rosemary nodded and the family rose from the table, the boys descending on Anna once more. She was drawn to the side of the kitchen to admire the tree Gabe had cut, then hauled from the room to the parlor.

She glanced back over her shoulder at him, and Morgan sent her a smile of understanding, his heart aching as he thought of the child he'd left behind in Dallas. How Jamie would enjoy this. He'd have done better to bring him along, he thought ruefully. Jamie's eyes would be like saucers, his attention fragmented between the boys and Jenny and the excitement of Christmas.

And if Anna were to be his bride, if they were to have a family, Jamie might share in this same circle of love not only in Dallas, but on occasion here in Edgewood. And that prospect was worth whatever it took to convince both Anna and her family that his intentions were honorable.

How had she not noticed him? How could she have come in the house and not felt his presence, there beside Jenny? Anna, swept along by the tide of siblings, cast her thoughts back to the man who watched her. Whose strength and courage had brought him here to face her family, knowing that Gabe thought the very worst of him, that Rosemary probably was tempted to give him what for.

''Bring the tree, Papa,'' Adam called from the parlor. ''We have the stand from last year. It might fit.''

''And if it doesn't, we can take it apart and make it fit,'' Seth added.

''Come see the glass balls, Anna,'' Jenny commanded, opening a box on the couch. ''We got some new ones from Auntie Pip's store. Mama said I have to be very careful and somebody bigger than me has to help.''

Daniel stood to one side of the doorway, and Anna smiled in his direction. So tall for his age, so sober and thoughtful, he was her soul mate. Always aware of her moods, he was her brother in a way that none of the others could touch. Twelve going on twenty, she thought, with eyes like Rosemary's and the look of Gabe. A Tanner through and through.

''I've missed you, Anna,'' he said quietly, and his eyes lit with the glow of love as he smiled for her benefit. They were infrequent, were Daniel's smiles, and cherished because of their rarity.

''Me, too,'' she whispered, and knew he understood the unspoken message.

''I've missed you, too, Anna.'' Her heart clenched in her breast as Morgan stood behind her. His words were soft, barely discernible, his hand but a whispering caress against her shoulder. He'd brought her anxious moments today, been the source of her aggravation as she left the hotel and braved the curious eyes of the townsfolk.

He'd faced her family without her in their midst, with no buffer between himself and Gabe Tanner. For that he deserved top marks, she thought, for Gabe was a formidable presence. She'd warrant that Rosemary had not left him unscathed either, and her mouth lifted in a smile as she considered that thought.

"You're smiling," he said softly. "Because you're glad I'm here? Or because you're relieved that I lived through the past hour of my life?" His tone was amused, but she felt the tension in the touch of his hand, the catch in his breathing.

"I didn't doubt your ability to face down Gabe. It was your meeting with Mother I worried about." She turned her head, just enough to see his face. "I'm pleased that she didn't skin you alive."

"Were you really concerned? Or are you just teasing me?"

It mattered to him. It really mattered whether or not she felt for his well-being. And her spirits lifted, her heart infused with the pleasure of his presence in her home.

The memory of his touch in the hotel, and the thrill of his kiss in Dallas were treasured bits she'd tucked away for safekeeping, proof perhaps of his desire for Anna Tanner. Maybe in Dallas, she thought, she'd been simply handy, convenient. But his trip to Edgewood gave new meaning to the words he spoke, the glances he turned her way.

Rosemary stood in the parlor doorway. "Step back boys and let your father put on the tree stand, and then we'll all have a hand at decorating," she said. Gabe was at her heels, dragging the magnificent pine tree by its stump, and Anna winced as she thought of the mess she would sweep from kitchen and hallway when this project was complete. She paused by Rosemary's side.

''I'll take care of cleaning up while Father sets the tree in place.'' As her mother's mouth opened to utter a protest, Anna shook her head. ''Please, Mother.'' With reluctance Rosemary agreed silently, and Anna left the room.

Once in the kitchen, she smiled as her imagination proved to be on target. The bits and pieces of needles and dried grass from the tree lay scattered across the wide-plank floor, and she crossed to the pantry where the broom was stored.

''I'll do that,'' Morgan said from behind her and she spun in place, unaware he had followed her. ''I learned how to swing a broom years ago,'' he told her.

She gave it over, enjoying the teasing light in his eyes, seeing an unfamiliar side of the man, far removed from the employer she'd come to know. ''I didn't know you were so talented,'' she said, watching as he began at the back door, gathering debris and forming a neat pile.

''Just do your own work and leave me to mine,'' he ordered, sweeping closer to where she stood. And then, as she made no move to attend his words, he halted, leaning the broom against the back of a chair. ''So long as you're close at hand, I need to say something,'' he said quietly. His fingers touched hers, his palms enfolding the narrow length of her hands in his own.

And then, in a gesture that touched her with its simple message, he brought their clasped hands to his mouth. His lips touched her fingers, the backs of her hands and then, with a smooth movement he turned her palms upward and buried his mouth there, breathing against her skin. ''I suppose this isn't the proper place or time, Anna. But I made a terrible mess of things in Dallas when I began this the other night.''

She caught her breath, her eyes misting with tears, her heart scrambling to beat in a proper sequence. Morgan Brady was in her home, in the kitchen, in fact, and unless she missed her guess he was *not* about to ask her to be his mistress. With almost all of her family only twenty feet away, he was kissing the palm of her hand and making an offer.

"Anna?" From the doorway, Jenny fluttered her hands and looked from one adult to the other. "Can I come in? I wanted to help you, and Mama said I might. But if you don't want me to, I'll go back to the parlor."

Morgan chuckled beneath his breath and looked up at Anna. "It's all right, sweetheart," he murmured. "I'll get back to this later."

She nodded, beyond speech, as Morgan released her hands and took up the broom once more. Jenny, a relieved smile wreathing her face, wrapped her arms around Anna's waist.

"I just want to spend a lot of time with you, 'cause I'm afraid you'll go away again, and I won't see you for a long time."

"That's all right," Anna said, her voice back in commission once more. "I need your help. We have this whole table to clear and take care of. Then we'll all go back and work on the tree together."

And so they did, all three of them, laughing, teasing, and unless Anna missed her guess, Morgan managed to endear himself to the child with his attentions to her and his ready wit. The table was cleared and the oilcloth washed. The left-overs put on the back of the stove, in case someone was still hungry during the afternoon. Then the dishes were washed, dried and put into the kitchen dresser.

"How many times have you done dishes in the past few years?" Anna asked him as she rolled down her sleeves and buttoned her cuffs. His fingers brushed hers aside and he completed the task, his hands warm against her wrist, his fingertips slow against her skin.

"You have beautiful hands," he said, ignoring her query. "I've noticed them before, when you were reading to Jamie, your hands holding the book, your fingertip pointing to the words as you spoke them.'' His index finger ran the length of each of her digits and a shiver of delight traveled her spine.

''And to answer your question, I always clean up after myself if I go into the kitchen late at night and look for something to take the edge off my appetite.'' He released her hand and turned to Jenny. ''Are we ready to decorate now, sprite?''

Jenny took his hand and led him to the parlor, filled with importance as she showed him the proper procedure for placing the angel on top. He felt a moment's hesitation when the child asked him to lift her so that she could complete that part of the tradition and he glanced at Gabe, unwilling to trespass.

''Go ahead, Mr. Brady. Wes usually helps out, but he's probably knee-deep in greenery right now. And Angelina's no doubt got stars and snowflakes ready to hang.''

''If you don't mind, I'd just as soon you called me by my name, sir,'' Morgan said, then waited for the older man's decision. With a nod, Gabe agreed, and Morgan felt that one more obstacle had been set aside.

''All right, Morgan. Let's get that angel in place. I think Jenny is about out of patience.''

It was done as the child instructed, and within an hour the tree was covered in strings of popcorn, blown glass balls of various sizes and colors, and of course, candles. Each of them perched on the end of a branch, carefully located so that the flame they would produce would not set fire to the tree. A bucket of sand, and another of water stood nearby. The children nodded solemnly as they were given instructions in case of any sign of disaster.

They'd probably heard the same words every Christmas, Morgan thought, yet they listened quietly. Anna's parents had done well, he decided. And then he looked again at the woman he yearned to take as his own.

He was glad this whole fiasco had come about. That she had run off from Dallas, that he had been obliged to hunt her down, even that his moments with her had been unproductive up to this point. If he could just keep his hands from her person, concentrate on his purpose in being here, he'd have things under control and his Pullman car would be on its way to Dallas on time.

Not touching her was the problem. Now that he had a store of memories to draw from, it was becoming more and more difficult to refrain from it. He'd been distracted all afternoon, watching her movements, admiring the toss of her head, the gentle curves of her body beneath the simple dress she wore.

That she had been right beneath his nose, so to speak, for the better part of a year before he took notice of her face and form was more than he could fathom. She'd been the nanny, the woman who cared for Jamie, a satisfactory employee, but no more than that. Until the day he'd been expounding upon a new development at the dinner table and had found her to be a rapt audience. He'd been surprised by her enthusiasm and charmed by her avid attention to his words.

Since that time he'd watched her, measured her for the position of wife to himself, and mother to his son, and in his own plodding, methodical way, had prepared for the revealing of his plan.

If he'd kept his hands to himself, if her mouth had not lured him, her slender body not fit so well against his own taller, more stalwart form, he might have delivered the words in proper fashion, instead of stammering and making such a botch of it. And yet, he could not regret the mess he'd made of things that night. For it had brought him here, and upon consideration, this was the better place to begin their future.

Rosemary began a carol, and the other voices joined in, Anna's melodic alto carrying the harmony. She glanced up at him and smiled, her eyes glittering in the candle glow. He took the hint and added his own deep voice to the blend. Jenny sang with vigor, oblivious to the melody, but enthusiastic nonetheless.

"Can we sing 'Silent Night' next?" Seth asked quietly as the song came to an end.

Rosemary smiled, nodding her head, and began the first verse. Morgan stumbled through the second and finished triumphantly with the final lines of the third. "I thought I'd forgotten all the words," he confessed, bending close to Anna's ear.

"You sang beautifully," she said, as the boys quibbled, choosing the next carol.

"I hate to be a killjoy, but it's begun to snow again, and there are chores to be done." Gabe stood up and the boys ceased their chatter, casting longing glances at the tree as they left the room. "Will you tend to the candles?" he asked Rosemary.

"We'll light them again tonight," Anna told Morgan. They watched as Rosemary used a small snuffer to smother each flame and then left the parlor with Jenny in tow.

Morgan stretched his legs out before him, aware of the warmth of Anna's presence at his side. "They've left us alone. Do you think it was on purpose?"

"Maybe so. Mother probably feels we're well chaperoned with her so near by."

"And do you need a chaperon, Anna? A woman who's been out on her own, away from home for the past year."

"Ah, but that's the hitch," she said quietly. "I'm not away from home now. And while I'm here, I'm their responsibility. At least that's the way they feel about it."

"They don't trust me." It was a statement of fact, with no doubt attached.

"They don't really know you," Anna said soothingly.

"Can we talk about my reason for being here?" he asked. "I need to get things out in the open, Anna. I don't have much time."

"Time?" Her head turned toward him. "When do you have to leave?"

"When I left home I promised Jamie I'd be back Christmas morning. My plan was to be on my way tomorrow evening, when the train to Dallas comes through Edgewood." He cast his gaze on the tree, its glory subdued with the candles unlit. "You're not still angry with me, are you?"

Anna shook her head. "No, of course not. I was more upset than angry anyway."

"In Dallas? When I told you I had a proposition to offer you?"

She nodded. "You know what I assumed. Perhaps if you hadn't kissed me—"

"I couldn't help myself, Anna. And that makes me sound like a raw boy, with no self-control. But as you probably figured out in the hotel, I seem to have lost my good intentions by the wayside when it comes to keeping my hands off you." He looked down at her, and she turned away. Her cheek was rosy and her breathing uneven.

"My son needs a mother, Anna, and I need a wife. Now, that's plain speaking, and I know I haven't dressed up my proposal in fancy words or pretty speeches, but I'm asking you to come back to Dallas with me and fill both those places in my home."

"Does Jamie know you're asking me?"

"He sent me," Morgan said, chuckling as he remembered Jamie's last admonishment. *Promise you'll bring her back, Papa.* "He won't welcome me back without you, I fear."

"And for that reason you came all the way to Edgewood? Because a child sent you to bring him back a mother?" Her words were calm, even and somehow portentous.

Morgan hesitated. What had he said to bring this promising conversation to such a halt? "That's part of the reason," he told her warily.

"And the rest?" She turned to look into his eyes and her own were expectant.

"I need a wife, Anna. I've watched you and spoken to you

on occasion over the past months. More so since I've been considering offering you this proposal. My servants speak highly of you. I've seen you care for my son, and I believe you love him. You are beautifully mannered and your temperament is what I would choose for Jamie's mother. I sensed when I hired you that you were of a calm nature and would deal well with him.'' He waited. Surely she would understand.

Her slow nod affirmed that thought and he caught his breath, anticipating her response. ''And so, on that basis, because I don't slurp my soup, and I don't raise my voice to your son. Oh—and your servants think I will serve you well—you have decided that I will do nicely as your wife.'' Again she spoke quietly, holding up three fingers as she enumerated the qualities he had mentioned.

He was silent. Perhaps he'd gone about this all wrong. He'd made more progress with kisses than he had with offering his suit.

''I think we've reached an impasse, Mr. Brady. If you leave now, you'll have time to reach town before dark. I would invite you to supper, but that would cause you to tarry too long.'' She rose and moved toward the kitchen, and he followed close behind.

''What have I done?'' he asked urgently. ''I'm offering you an honest proposal, Anna. I can give you a good life, and if it pleases you, we can have a family, and—''

She snatched his hat from the hook by the door. His coat hung beneath it and she gave it to him. He took it reluctantly and she offered his hat.

''I already have a family, Mr. Brady. And I have a good life here. I'm sorry you have come so far to fail in your mission. Please tell Jamie that I will miss him.''

She refused to meet his gaze, and he suspected that tears filled her eyes.

''Please, Anna. Tell me what I said that offended you. I wouldn't have given you pain for the world.'' He placed his hat on the table and clasped her arm, but she pulled from his grip and he allowed it.

"May I speak with you tomorrow?" he asked. "Will you at least reconsider?"

"No," she said, denying his request with a slow shake of her head. "No. Please leave."

He slid into his coat, slammed his hat on his head and walked past her to the door. The knob turned readily and he jerked the door open, then paced through to the porch. Behind him he heard the sound of the latch closing. Before him the snow lay in swirling patterns on the ground. It looked as if it might stick this time.

Anna was right. He'd given it his best shot, and failed. He needed to be on his way.

Chapter Six

"Was that wise?" Rosemary asked from the doorway.

Anna turned from the window, her tears flowing. "I don't know, Mama. I thought I could marry him, even knowing that he doesn't love me. But then, I just couldn't do it." She wiped her cheeks and forced a smile. "I've wept more in the past few days than in my entire life, I think."

"As long as your tears are not those of regret. Mr. Brady seemed to me to be a fine gentleman. But then, you know him far better than I, having lived in the same house for so long." Rosemary busied herself at the kitchen dresser, her hands rearranging utensils that had been in perfect order to begin with.

"Mama," Anna said softly. "If you have an opinion, I'm willing to listen." She walked to her mother's side, needing to be close. "Did you hear his proposal?"

Rosemary shook her head. "No, I suspected he wanted to be alone with you. I also suspected you would accept."

"He made it sound like a business deal, Mama. He wants a mother for Jamie, and a woman to bear his children. He says he *needs* a wife. He thinks I have nice manners, and his servants speak well of me." Anna drew in a deep breath, her words rushing forth as if a dam had burst within her. "Not one word of love in the whole proposal. Just his admiration for my calm nature.'' Her voice rose in anger. ''My *calm nature,* Mama!'' She stomped across the kitchen, then whirled to face her mother.

Rosemary's lips compressed, and her eyes glittered with laughter. ''I wish he could see you now, sweet.''

''Well, he's not likely to see me again, in any way, shape or form,'' Anna muttered. ''I've sent him on his way.''

''And you're wishing you were riding with him.''

Anna turned from her mother's discerning eye, her own vision blurring as she gazed from the window. ''I'll get over it.''

''I'm sure you will,'' Rosemary agreed. ''But will you find another man who would suit you as well as Morgan Brady?''

''Suit me? You really think he would have made me a good husband?''

''Did you enjoy his company? Does he excite you, Anna? Can you imagine being in his bed for the rest of your life?''

''Mama!'' Anna whirled to face Rosemary. ''How can I imagine that? I've never been near his bed.''

''He's held you in his arms and kissed you. You told me you love him, Anna. Sleeping in his bed is the next step. But you have to want to be there. And if I recall our conversation correctly, you told me that when he held you, you would have done anything he wanted of you.''

Anna's hands flew to cover her cheeks. ''He didn't ask me into his bed. And I know now that I misunderstood him that night in Dallas. If only I'd been thinking clearly I would have avoided this whole mess.''

''It's not too late, dear. He's not very far down that road.''

Anna waved her hand at the window. ''It's snowing.''

Rosemary smiled. ''You won't melt, no matter how sweet you are.''

''I suspect Morgan doesn't think I'm made of sugar right now,'' Anna whispered, her gaze peering through the glass to where the snow fell in huge, floating flakes.

"I don't, either. I think you're a sensible woman who won't let a decent man ride away without trying to mend her fences. Your father loves me, you know. But he didn't always feel that way."

"Angelena told me something of the sort."

"Sometimes it happens that way, my dear," Rosemary said. "Now, go."

"I'll take the buggy," Anna said quickly, reaching for her cloak.

"Ride my mare instead. You'll make better time." She reached for Anna, hugging her for a moment, then handed her her cloak. "He's a good man. Give him a chance. He'll come to love you, Anna. I know he will. Sometimes men just need a little time."

Anna smiled widely, her heartbeat rapid as she fastened the closures on her cloak, then pulled the hood in place. "I hope you're right," she said, reaching to open the door. "Think good thoughts, Mama."

For the first time in his life Morgan had turned his back on a project. His thoughts jumbled, he sorted through the events of the past hours as his horse moved slowly down the road. Everything focused on the woman who had so firmly turned him down.

Anna. She was perfect for him, above reproach, an ideal mother for Jamie, and he'd developed some strong feelings over the past days, feelings he should have acted on more boldly than he had. And he feared that lack would cause him regret for years to come.

He'd have done well to shut his mouth and let his kisses speak for him. All of his planning, and then spouting the rehearsed proposal he'd determined would win her over had been in vain. She'd torn the whole thing to shreds with her quick wit and perceptive mind. If he'd grabbed her and kissed her, pressed her for an answer, he could have caught her off guard, persuaded her to his cause.

His mouth quirked as he thought of Anna in his arms. He'd only begun his pursuit of her. And she was worth the pursuing. She was worth a good bit of groveling if it came to that. But leaving Edgewood empty-handed went against his grain, and facing Jamie without the mother he had chosen was not to be countenanced.

His horse whinnied loudly as the bit halted his progress, and his hind feet skidded in the slush. Morgan bent low over the animal's neck, his hand delivering a reassuring message to the gelding's neck, then he laid the reins to one side, turning in his tracks. The trail he'd left was fast filling in with the falling snow, but there was no need to worry. Trees grew on either side of the road, providing landmarks, and he was only a mile or so from the ranch.

He'd make her listen. He'd kiss her senseless, then offer his proposal in words of few syllables. "Will you marry me?" He said it aloud, repeated it more firmly, then nodded.

"I care for you deeply, Anna." There, that sounded good. A vision of her face rose before him, eyes the color of pussy willows in the spring, her hair falling in a glorious profusion of waves. He felt a quickening in his loins.

"I need you, Anna." His whisper was fervent.

"I want you in my bed, sweetheart." That was more to the point, he decided.

Damn, the woman would drive him crazy.

It was like a fairyland. The snow clung to the tree branches, drifted against the sides of the road and provided a white path for her to follow. Faint depressions gave testimony that another had gone before her, Morgan, no doubt, and she resisted the urge to hasten her pace, fearful of the mare making a misstep. The evening train would not come through Edgewood for hours. Morgan couldn't go anywhere until then.

Ahead, riding through the falling snow, a figure approached on horseback. She leaned forward in her saddle, straining to recognize the rider, then drew her mare to a halt. It was too much to hope for, that Morgan would have turned around, headed back to the ranch. But the tall man riding in her direction wore his hat cocked familiarly over his forehead and his shoulders were broad beneath the dark coat he wore. But then so were those of most of the men of her acquaintance here in Edgewood.

Though none of them had piercing dark eyes that could see beneath all of her layers of pretense the way this man did, she decided as Morgan faced her. The determination written on his features should have warned her. The steely strength of his hand as he reached for her reins might have prepared her, had she been expecting his return. Even the words he spoke would not have surprised her if she'd had her wits together.

''We're going to find a place to be alone, Anna. We're going to talk, and get things sorted out between us.''

She could only nod, releasing her reins into his care, watching as he turned in the middle of the road, to lead her in the direction of town.

''I don't want to hear a word out of you,'' he said firmly, glaring at her from beneath the brim of his hat.

She hadn't spoken, she wanted to say, but then thought better of it. The snow enclosed them in a cocoon of silence and muffled the sound of the horse's hooves. The softly falling flakes formed patterns against her cloak which surrounded her like a tent, covering all but her shoes. She gripped the pommel, holding herself erect in the saddle, wondering at her acquiescence, she of the sharp tongue and smart retort.

And then he turned his head, motioning to a turnoff ahead. ''What's down there?''

''Just a deserted farmhouse. The folks who lived there sold off their land, but the house was too run-down, and they just cut their losses and left.''

"Sounds like an ideal spot," he muttered, tugging her mare to follow in his wake.

A spot for what? She held her tongue, a sense of excitement growing deep inside her. This was a new Morgan Brady, one she had not glimpsed before. This silent, arrogant, stubborn stranger was a far cry from the gentleman caller she had sent on his way only an hour ago. Perhaps a woman with any sense would be apprehensive, but then Anna had been sensible all of her life, and where had that gotten her?

"How will you get inside?" she asked. "What if the place is filled with critters?"

He cast her a glance of reproof. "I'm sure I'll be able to figure out how to break a window if need be. And critters are the very least of my worries. I used to kill mice for a penny apiece when I was a child. Made a tidy sum before my mother got a cat to do the job."

The thought of Morgan Brady killing mice made her smile, even as she cringed at the bloodthirsty image his words brought to mind. "I didn't know you were so money-minded at such an early age," she ventured.

"You don't know much about me at all, Anna Tanner."

And wasn't that the truth, given the events of the past few days. Only one thing was for sure, and she voiced it aloud. "I know that up until a short while ago, I thought you were a gentleman."

His eyes flashed with a dangerous light, and his mouth thinned. "And you've changed your mind?"

"I can't imagine you'd have much trouble figuring out my reasons. Hauling me around this way certainly isn't going to raise you in my esteem."

"That's not my purpose, Anna. I've done all the things a gentleman is supposed to do. I've been polite and well-mannered. For the most part," he amended hastily. "But the point is that I've not been able to make any headway as far as you're concerned.'' He rode his horse close to the back of the house and slid from the saddle.

''Get down.'' He held his arms up to her, demanding obedience, and she hesitated. He would never hurt her, she'd have staked her life on that. ''Come on, Anna. I don't want to haul you out of that saddle, but I will if I have to.''

Her bare hands clutched his shoulders and she leaned toward him. His hands were firm at her waist and he lifted her easily from the saddle. She slid his length, gaining new knowledge of his strength as he held her against him. One long arm slid around her and he turned her toward the porch steps.

''Watch where you walk,'' he told her. ''This wood looks rotten in places.''

She obeyed, then stood shivering on the porch as he tried lifting the kitchen window. ''Why don't you just open the door?'' she suggested. At his dubious look, she shrugged. ''From the condition of this place, I doubt there's even a key to be found.''

Morgan turned the knob and the door opened, the bottom dragging against the kitchen floor. He shoved it far enough to enter, then gripped her hand, leading the way into the dim interior. A scampering in the corner made her shiver and he stomped his foot. A rustle behind the big, iron cookstove announced the presence of another of the critters she had predicted would be in residence.

''Mice,'' he announced. ''Rats would have made more noise than that.''

''I'm sure that's a comfort,'' Anna told him, huddling within the folds of her cloak. She motioned to the wood box behind the stove. ''Why don't you put a couple of chunks of wood in that thing? Some heat would not go amiss.''

''Let's look a little farther,'' he suggested, shutting the door, then leading her from the kitchen into a larger room. A fireplace sat against the far wall, its opening littered with ashes and the remains of a fire, long since extinguished. A dilapidated couch sat at one side and Anna gave it a disparaging glance.

"Is this where we do our talking?" she asked.

"Let me get a fire started in here," Morgan told her, retracing his steps to the kitchen. He returned with a double armful of firewood and set to with a will. In moments he had swept aside the litter beneath the chimney and replaced it with the beginnings of a glowing fire. He hauled the couch before the hearth, then adjusted the damper. With an elaborate brushing of his hands and an exaggerated bow, he motioned for Anna to sit with him.

"My family will begin looking for me before long," she warned him. "I hope you are aware of the anger you may have to face when my father finds us here."

"That's the least of my worries," Morgan said briskly. He reached for her hands and rubbed them between his. "Are you still cold?"

"No." The man was brave, she'd give him that. Gabe Tanner had a temper beyond belief. It had mellowed somewhat during his years with Rosemary, but if he thought for one minute that his daughter was in danger, Morgan Brady was as good as dead. "My brother is very protective of me," she said quietly.

"I should hope so," Morgan said judiciously. "I kept a close eye on my sister until her marriage. Then I turned that duty over to her husband."

"I didn't even know you had a sister," Anna said.

"I told you there were things you needed to learn about me," he reminded her.

"Well, by all means," she said dryly, "do fill me in."

"I wasn't always as well-to-do as I am now, Anna," he said quietly.

"I figured that out earlier," she told him. "When you mentioned killing mice for your mother." His smile was bittersweet, she thought, and then he began, his words slow as he told her of his childhood.

"There were just my mother, my sister and me, once my father left," he said. "He went off to make his fortune, and we didn't hear anything about him until his death. Those years were hard ones. My mother worked at cleaning houses mostly. Whatever she could get to keep body and soul together. I shined shoes in front of the bank, and sold newspapers. My sister stayed sometimes with a neighbor, other times I took her with me."

"Where is your mother now?" Anna asked quietly, as he paused for a moment. He stared into the fire, and his jaw clenched at her query.

"She's in the churchyard." He looked up then and his eyes were bleak. "I bought a monument for her when I heard about my father's death. It seems he was quite successful in New York, and by some strange quirk, decided that the family he'd left behind should share in his wealth."

"He left money for you?"

"Enough to send me to college and my sister to finishing school. She met a man through a friend there, and married him soon after I graduated."

"And then you went into banking?"

Morgan nodded. "I invested well, and within a few years I took over the bank." He clenched his jaw, then spoke. "I think I need to tell you about Jamie's mother now."

"There's no need," Anna said hastily. "Cook told me she died right after Jamie was born."

"There's more to it than that. She came from a well-to-do family, and she liked my looks."

Anna resisted the urge to smile. She could understand the woman's feelings perfectly.

"We were married, and I had my house built right away," Morgan continued. "We spent a lot of time socializing. Things were going well for me, and I worked a lot of late hours, but she didn't mind going out without me when I couldn't make it. Then when she found she was going to have a child, things began going wrong. She wasn't happy about being in the family way. She resented being alone in the evenings, and I still had to work long hours.''

''And when Jamie was born? Was it better then?'' Anna asked. How any woman could not want to bear Morgan's child was beyond her.

''She never recovered after the delivery. Jamie had to have a wet nurse, and then when his mother died, I let the woman stay on for three years. It was hard on my staff. The nurse went home at night, and returned midmorning. Her own family had needs, too. And then it was too much, and she left us to stay at home.''

His smile was warm as he scanned Anna's features. ''That's when you answered my advertisement, and came to us.''

Anna thought of the months past, when she'd grown to love the man before her, and her heart would no longer allow her to remain silent. ''When did you decide—about me, I mean? What made you ask me?''

He hesitated. ''I'd been watching you for weeks, growing to appreciate you more every day. But Jamie was the catalyst, Anna. He told me he'd been wishing on the Christmas star, asking for you to be his mother.''

''Can you marry a woman you don't love?''

Morgan nodded. ''I've already done that, Anna. I did it six years ago.''

''I wish we were at Gabe and Rosemary's place.'' Angelena paced the parlor, her agitation a source of amusement to Wes. He'd watched her for the past half hour, walking to one window, then the other, gazing out into the fading daylight, then returning to add another decoration to the tree he'd set into place.

''You told me just the other day that we were going to begin our own Christmas traditions, beginning with decorating the tree today, then wrapping presents tomorrow and church later.''

''I know. But that was before Anna came home, with that rascal fast on her heels. I want to know what's going on, Wes. If he's just toying with her, he'll break her heart.'' She turned to face her husband. ''She loves him, you know.''

''Who says so?'' Wes scoffed openly.

''Well, she told me she loves him, and if the man would ask her right out to marry him, she'd snatch him up. I know she would.'' She cast him a sidelong glance. ''Besides, there's something to be said for a city man.''

He moved quickly and she grinned as he grabbed her, pulling her to him. ''I knew that would get you, Wesley.''

''And you know what it'll get you, don't you, pretty lady?'' He bent to take her lips and she sighed, wrapping her arms around his neck. ''You'll be in trouble before you know it.''

''I don't mind being in trouble,'' she whispered. ''I just wish I weren't so worried about Anna.''

Wes drew in a deep breath. ''You're not gonna be happy till we make the trip to the ranch, are you?''

She traced his lip with her forefinger. ''You're worried too, I just know it. The only difference is that you won't admit it.''

''All right. I'll hitch up the buggy. You wrap up Joy Marie and fix a basket with whatever we need to spend the night.'' He caught her errant finger between his lips and she allowed it.

''They won't mind, will they?'' Her voice was wistful, and he grinned, releasing the captive fingertip.

''What do you think? Mother will be thrilled at the thought of having Joy Marie there. And Gabe can always use a hand. We'll come back after church tomorrow night and have our Christmas here.''

She lifted on tiptoe and delivered an enthusiastic kiss. "I love you, Wes Tanner."

"I'm counting on that," he told her, gathering her close for his own benefit. Damn, the woman could twist him around her little finger. And he enjoyed every minute of it.

"You didn't love Jamie's mother?"

Morgan shook his head. "No. She came from wealth and she was a good hostess. We wanted the same things. At least I thought we did. I wanted a child. More than one, for that matter. I didn't know then that it would be a point of contention."

He glanced at the fire, as if he were uneasy with the discussion of his feelings for Jamie's mother. His sigh was deep. "Are you getting warm yet?" he asked, stretching his feet out before him. He'd long since removed his coat and placed his boots near the fire to dry.

Anna nodded. "I'm fine, thanks."

"Then take off that cloak and relax, will you?" He turned to her, unfastening the front of her outer garment, his hands clumsy at the task.

"I've talked enough, Anna. I've told you probably more than you want to know about my past. Now I want to know why you won't marry me. I made my position pretty clear, I think," he began. "I'm willing to compromise if there is anything you don't like about my house or my habits. I can't believe that Jamie is the issue. I'm not asking you to assume any household duties. I have servants to tend to all of that. I'll give you a generous personal allowance."

"That's quite an offer, Mr. Brady," she said quietly. Her eyes remained fixed on the fireplace, as if the glowing coals and flickering flames were fascinating.

"Damn it, Anna. Will you look at me?" His voice rang out, more than tinged with anger, and she sent a glance in his direction.

"What would you like me to say?" She waited expectantly.

"How do you feel about me?" he asked. "What more do I need to offer you?"

"Ah, now then," she murmured. "Those two questions are very telling. You want to know how I feel about you. But you've never said what your own feelings are. Only that you married a woman once that you didn't love. I have no idea if you care for me, Morgan. All you seem to be interested in are the things your wealth can give me. I don't know what your feelings are, do I?"

"My feelings?" His voice rose in volume. *"My feelings?"* His movement was swift, his hands demanding as he seized her, lifting her to lie across his lap. "This may give you some idea of what I'm feeling for you, Anna." His mouth found hers, his lips warm and urgent as he captured her mouth in a kiss that set free the desire he'd struggled to hold in check. His hand was free to touch her as he would, and his fingers were tender as they traced the line of her brow.

"I'm going to kiss you here," he said, his voice musing. And then his hand moved downward, fingers warm against the soft skin they touched, as if he were learning each small increment of her face.

"Here," he whispered, attending the slope of her jaw, "I'll fill my lungs with the scent you use." His finger moved to her throat. "Here and here," he said, "I'll taste the sweetness of your skin." Beneath her ear that exploring digit moved, causing her to shiver and inhale sharply.

His head bent and he lifted her upward, his mouth closing on the tender flesh of her throat. Her heartbeat was rapid and he smiled against the spot where her pulse moved beneath his lips. "I need to loosen your buttons."

It was not a request, simply a warning of what was to come, and he waited for a moment, watching as her eyes opened. Her lashes lifted slowly, revealing gray eyes dark as thunderclouds, with barely a line where the pupils began. ''My buttons?'' The words were but a breath of air.

''Just a few, for now,'' he said reassuringly, his fingers already busy at the task.

''Morgan, are you trying to seduce me?''

His hands stilled their movement. ''Is it working?'' His grin was sudden and she responded quickly, her palms covering his hands.

His grin turned wistful. ''I knew you were being too obedient.''

''I'm a virgin.''

''I know you are, sweetheart.'' He allowed her to halt his foray, and bent to kiss her again. His lips were soft and gentle against hers, and then his hands opened her collar to his touch. One long finger traced the horizontal measure of her collarbone, then edged the lower side. On its return it slid another button from its moorings. His words were husky, spoken almost as a vow. ''When you leave here, Anna, you'll still be a virgin.''

She hesitated, then murmured a word beneath her breath.

Lifting his head, he closed his eyes, considering the strength of his willpower, as his fingers lingered on the skin he had uncovered. ''Did you tell me to stop?'' he asked gruffly, then, opening his eyes, sent his gaze to mesh with hers.

She shook her head, the movement ever so slight.

''What did you say then?'' he whispered, the insidious finger nudging another button from its place, then another, exposing the fine lace edging on her chemise.

''Promise?'' she asked. ''I asked if that was that a promise.''

His breath caught in his throat as he recognized the trust implicit in her plea. If he nodded now, she would give him her trust, give herself into his keeping. And that responsibility weighed heavily. No matter that his body urged him to complete the act of loving. He would not bring dishonor on the woman he was determined to make his bride.

"I promise."

Her smile was slow, her lips damp, and her eyes were huge pools, threatening to swallow him whole. "Will you kiss me again?" she asked. "Or will that interfere with keeping your promise?"

"I'll kiss you as much as you like," he told her, bending to her, his mouth loving her, coaxing her response, until she parted her lips, offering him whatever he would take. He was gentle, his hand brushing the curves of her breasts, his fingers tender as he loosened the ribbons of her chemise.

"I'll have *your* promise now," he said quietly, raising his head, catching a glimpse of hunger in her eyes, of desire that brought color to her cheeks.

"Mine? What would you ask of me?" Her words ran together breathlessly.

"Tell me you'll marry me." The words were tender, his voice husky with emotion.

She blinked rapidly to stave off the tears that threatened. No matter that he felt only passion and desire. Her love would be enough, and as Rosemary had said, he might learn to love her. Her lips trembled as she spoke the words that would decide her future, the words that were a gamble she was willing to take.

"I love you, Morgan. I'll marry you."

"Tomorrow?"

She nodded. "Tomorrow."

He lifted her closer into his embrace, his kisses reverent now, asking nothing but the pressure of her lips, the sweetness of her breath as she spoke the words again. "I love you," she whispered, her smile radiant.

She was his. His heart vibrated with the thought. She had given her vow, and she was his. He cradled her in his arms, lifting her legs from the floor to rest against the couch, holding her as he would a priceless treasure. They spoke softly, the glow of the fire revealing her to his gaze, and he held her closely. His words told her of the future they would share, and she murmured soft responses. Her sigh was deep as his kiss told her of his desire, but the night was late, and she wearied before his eyes. He bent again to press his lips against her forehead and then relaxed his hold, watching as her eyelids closed in slumber.

Chapter Seven

"Hangin' a lantern on the front of the porch isn't gonna do a hell of a lot of good," Wes said. "Especially when I doubt that son of a sea cook is plannin' on bringin' Anna back here tonight anyway."

"Your mother wants a lantern hung, and that's what we're going to do." Gabe may have privately agreed with his son, but Rosemary's needs were uppermost as far as he was concerned. As to Anna's safety, he hadn't a doubt that Morgan Brady would look after his woman as well as her family could.

The only problem was that the man was in a strange town, although if Gabe's suspicions were on target, the banker from Dallas knew exactly where his Pullman car was sitting. And if he and Anna weren't there right now, Gabe would be mighty surprised.

No matter. He and his son weren't going anywhere until dawn.

"Come on back in the house." Gabe slapped a hand on Wes's shoulder. "Anna's a big girl, and she's the one who chose to go after the man. Give her a little credit, will you?"

"Lena told me Anna's in love with Brady. You have any idea what he can talk her into? Her feeling that way about him?"

Gabe's grin was crooked and his eyes lit with humor. ''Yeah, I sure do. And so do you, son. Seems like we've both had experience at that game.''

Wes glared into the darkness. ''That was different, and you know it. We both married the woman.''

''Seems to me the man's doin' his best to accomplish that very thing. Rosemary said he offered an honorable proposal, right there in our parlor.''

''Well, if she wanted to marry him, she would have accepted, wouldn't she?''

Gabe shrugged, as if women were a mystery he'd only begun to solve. ''She must have had her reasons for keepin' him danglin', I suspect. Rosemary let her go after him. Probably sent her on her way, if I know my wife.''

He looked up at the sky. The snow had stopped and the ground held several inches. ''Shouldn't be too hard to track them once it's daylight. We'll start out early.''

''Wind probably drifted snow over the road by now,'' Wes said glumly.

''Come on, no sense havin' a fit over it now. It's too damn cold to stand out here and fume. The women are waitin' in the house.''

''And that's some comfort, I'll admit,'' Wes told him, his grin halfhearted.

The candles on the Christmas tree were lit and the women shared the couch, overseeing the proceedings. Joy Marie sat on the floor at their feet, between Jenny's outstretched legs, watching the tree with wide eyes. Surrounding her, the boys sprawled as close to the magnificent tree as they could manage. The last notes of a carol hung in the air as the men watched from the hallway, and they shared a smile of mutual understanding.

This was family at its best. The only one missing was Anna, but it looked like that might become a permanent situation, and they'd as well adjust to it. For tonight, worry was futile, and probably unnecessary. Tomorrow would bring a resolution to Anna's situation, and if Wesley had his way, Morgan Brady would do the honorable thing and Anna would behave herself and make her vows.

"I told you we'd leave at dawn, and the damn sun's not up yet," Gabe muttered as he tightened the cinch on his saddle. Lowering the stirrup, he tugged on the saddle horn, adjusted the blanket a final time, then swung into place atop his horse.

Wes watched him impatiently, already outside the barn door, his hat pulled low over his forehead. "You can see in the dark and you know it. The sun'll be up in fifteen minutes. And look, Mother's watchin' from the window, probably got a hot biscuit for us to eat while we ride."

"Hope she stuffed a piece of sausage in mine," Gabe said, directing his mount toward the back porch.

Rosemary stepped out the door, a shawl covering her shoulders, two towel-wrapped packages in her hands. "Here's breakfast. Seems like the pair of you could have waited to eat with the family before you set out. Whatever's happened isn't going to change in the next half hour."

"Nothing better have happened," Wes said, reaching down from his saddle to accept the offering. His voice softened as he touched Rosemary's hands. "Thanks, Mother. You still make the best biscuits in the world. But don't tell Lena I said that."

Gabe swung from his saddle and stepped up on the porch, his arms circling Rosemary's waist. His whisper in her ear was low. "I'll keep Wes's temper down to a slow boil." His kiss was brief but warm, and Rosemary pressed against him for a moment.

"Don't get in an uproar, no matter what happens," she warned, then placed his breakfast in his hands before stepping back into the house.

The horses pranced, blowing steam from their nostrils impatient to be moving, and the men set off down the lane, eating as they rode, holding their animals to a trot. Once on the road to town, they began scanning the road ahead of them. The horizon was lightening, with pale bands of spreading daylight, and they watched as the sun made its way into the morning sky.

"Where do you think they are?" Wes asked. "He wouldn't take her to the hotel. Hell, Anna wouldn't go with him to his room."

"Well, if they're not between here and town, they'll be in his Pullman car, on the siding."

"Where the whole town can stand and watch when she comes draggin' out in broad daylight?" Wes asked harshly.

"Wait and see," Gabe advised. "Just keep an eye on the road. You can see pockets in the snow where they rode."

"It could have been anybody," Wes grumbled. "Probably more than one rider was through here yesterday."

"Maybe," Gabe agreed, "but I have a notion we need to keep our eyes open."

To their left, a trail of smoke drifted across the sky, and Wes pointed his gloved hand in that direction. "Somebody finally buy the old Hackerd place? Looks like there's smoke comin' from the chimney." And then he sat up straighter in his saddle. "Damn! I'll bet you two bits that's where they are. Anna knows that place is there. They might have thought to get out of the snow, and then Brady wouldn't let her leave."

"Don't get your temper up," Gabe warned him. "I doubt he'd have kept her against her will. And anyway, we don't know yet what's goin' on, Wes."

"Well, we're sure as hell gonna find out." Wes urged his mount into an easy canter and turned from the road to the narrow track that held faint imprints in the snow. "There's enough proof here for me."

From the dilapidated shed behind the house a horse's whinny greeted the men, and their own mounts answered the call. "What do you say now?" Wes asked, riding to the back door, and sliding from his saddle.

"Take it easy," Gabe was fast on his heels and only a step behind as Wes opened the door, forcing it back until it shattered, the wood splintering, and then stomped past the destruction he'd created, into the deserted kitchen.

Anna awoke once in the night, aware of the man beside her, his arms holding her fast. Her cloak covered them, and she snuggled beneath its warmth.

"Anna?" Morgan's voice was rough with sleep. "Are you warm enough? I put more wood on the fire when I went out to take care of the horses."

"Yes, I'm fine," she murmured. Fine for now, anyway. Until morning, when she would face the recriminations of her family.

"Sleep, Anna," he told her, his arms shifting, but not releasing the grip he held. "Everything will be all right. I'll take care of you."

And of that she was certain. Morgan Brady was a man of his word, an honorable man. The man she had promised to marry.

It seemed she had only closed her eyes, that she only just snuggled against Morgan's chest, her nose warmed against his throat, when the house exploded with sound. A door creaked, then scraped loudly, just before Wes's voice shouted her name.

"Anna! Are you in here?" His boots shook the house as he thumped across the kitchen.

She lifted her head, barely awake as Morgan rolled from the couch and stood to his feet. Anna's eyes widened in the dim light as Wes stood in the doorway, the hot coals in the fireplace turning his face crimson with their reflection. His fists hung loosely at his sides, his eyes glowed with unmistakable anger, and he took one step into the room.

"You miserable son of a—"

Morgan stepped toward him, one hand raised. ''Hold it, Tanner.''

''Damned if I will,'' Wes growled, hurling himself across the room, plowing Morgan to the floor. But not for long. They rolled across the room, and then staggered to their feet, fists flying.

''That's enough, Wes.'' Gabe stepped across the threshold, his gaze snagging Anna, scanning her from head to foot as she stood before the couch, her mouth open, both hands covering her cheeks.

''You all right?'' he asked her.

She nodded and burst into tears. ''Stop them, Papa. Please.'' Her cry was forlorn, and Gabe heeded its message.

His hands gripped shoulders, his body forced its way between the two men, and in spite of their muttered threats and the peril offered by their angry fists, he managed to separate them.

''Look what you're doing to Anna,'' he shouted. And they did. In tandem, two pairs of eyes turned in her direction and both men stepped toward her.

''Anna.'' Morgan spoke her name, holding out his arms.

''You've done enough already,'' Wes snarled, shoving him aside and enclosing Anna in his embrace. He held her for a moment, then grasped her shoulders and held her away from him, peering at her tearstained face. ''Did he hurt you?''

''No, of course not,'' she said quickly, her sobs ceasing as rapidly as they had begun. She wiped her eyes, rubbing her hands on her cheeks to erase the tears.

''He's going to marry you,'' Wes said firmly.

Anna lifted her hand to touch the bruises already forming across his cheek and around his eye. ''I know,'' she murmured. ''He told me.''

''Now will you release her?'' Morgan snarled from behind her. Anna turned from her brother to face the man who had held her throughout the night. And muffled a cry of horror.

His features were in worse shape than Wes's, his eye puffed, blood seeping from a cut just beneath his cheekbone, his jaw swollen. ''Oh, Morgan!'' she cried, her fingertips tracing the damage, catching her breath as he winced from her touch.

Morgan shot a look of triumph in Wes's direction. ''I'll let you repair the damage, sweetheart,'' he murmured to Anna.

''I think you both need a dose of Rosemary's witch hazel and something for the swelling. Maybe a chunk of ice from the watering trough would help.'' Gabe stood, hands on hips, and surveyed the damage. ''Let's head back to the ranch. Angelena and Rosemary will be pacing the floor.''

They were, as Gabe had predicted, both women admitting to their worry as they mended the cuts and bruises. Rosemary supervised the operation, recommending treatment, sending Gabe to the yard for ice, then crushing it inside a towel to form ice bags for the cringing warriors.

''Damn, that hurts worse than it did before,'' Wes complained as Angelena held the towel in place.

''Always does,'' Rosemary told him placidly. ''Goes with the territory, son. Anyone dumb enough to be involved in a fistfight deserves whatever they get.''

''He had it coming,'' Wes mumbled as Angelena bent to press his face against her shoulder.

''He's going to look mighty handsome standing in front of the preacher,'' Gabe surmised, drinking his third cup of coffee at the end of the table.

''They both will,'' Anna stated firmly. ''I think Wes needs to stand up with Morgan.''

Wes jerked away from Angelena's hands, his mouth open, anger flashing from the one eye still usable. ''That sounds like a wonderful idea,'' Angelena said quickly. ''After all, they're going to be brothers.''

Wes subsided, then exchanged a sheepish grin with the man across the table. Morgan stretched out a hand, knuckles swollen and reddened, and Wes stared at the peace offering for just a moment, then muttered a low curse word under his breath and accepted the gesture.

"How soon can we put this thing together?" Morgan asked Rosemary, recognizing her as the acknowledged leader of the household. Gabe might be the man of the house, but Rosemary was the heart, a fact Anna had confided during the hours of the night, and he found himself agreeing wholeheartedly with her opinion.

"Baths all around," Rosemary said quickly. "That'll take a couple of hours. I'll check out the boys' good clothes."

"I've got my new dress," Jenny said brightly. "It's all ironed and everything."

"How about you, Anna?" Morgan asked. "Would you like a new dress to wear? There must be something appropriate in that store I was in."

"Pip's place?" she asked. "That's good of you to ask, but I have something I can wear."

"A new dress would be nice," Angelena said wistfully. "Brides should be beautiful, Anna. Why not go see what Pip has to offer?"

"You didn't wear anything new when we got married," Wes reminded his wife. "And you were more than beautiful."

She wrinkled her nose at him. "You seemed to think so, as I remember."

Morgan spoke up again. "Anna and I will get ready first and head into town. We'll find her something appropriate to wear and she can change at the hotel." He pulled his watch from his pocket and opened the lid. "We'll meet you—" He looked down at Anna expectantly. "Where, sweetheart?"

"At the church," she told him, her smile lighting up her face, until it was obvious to all that she was not under duress in this undertaking. "We'll meet them at the church."

"I need to be in town when the afternoon train comes in," Morgan said quietly.

"Are you expecting something to arrive?" Anna asked.

Morgan nodded. ''In a manner of speaking. Yes.''

''Well, we'll be there in plenty of time for that,'' Anna told him. ''At least we will if I hurry now.''

''Will you stay for the Christmas Eve service?'' Rosemary asked.

''Only if the train from Shreveport to Dallas doesn't come through before then,'' Morgan told her. ''I'll send a message for them to stop here and attach my car.''

The package from Dallas indeed arrived on the afternoon train, and Anna was the recipient of the best surprise she'd had yet. Jamie stepped from the coach, his short legs stretching to reach the platform, Harley close behind. With a whoop of joy, the child flung himself into Anna's arms, and Morgan could only look on as Jamie squealed in delight.

''Oh, Papa! You really did it, didn't you? You got me Miss Anna for Christmas.''

''I'm trying hard, son,'' Morgan told him, bending for his own share of Jamie's hugs. ''We're going to the church in a few minutes and Miss Anna and I will be married. Then later there will be a Christmas Eve service. You'll get a chance to meet all of Miss Anna's family. Will you like that?''

The child looked from one to the other of his two favorite people, and then his attention fixed on Morgan. ''Papa, what happened to your eye? And your mouth? You look like you had an accident.'' One small hand reached to touch Morgan's cheek. ''Did you ask Miss Anna to kiss it and make it better?''

Morgan paused for but a moment, then turned his head to kiss Jamie's palm. ''I'm fine, son. I had a bit of an accident, but perhaps Miss Anna would like to…'' He paused and glanced at Anna, his good eye gleaming with mischief.

''Not right now,'' she said quickly. ''We have to hurry on to the church. Your new family is waiting to see you, Jamie.''

He tilted his head and sought her gaze. ''Will they like me, Miss Anna?'' he asked, concern coloring his words.

''Oh, Jamie,'' Anna said, tears not far from the surface. ''How could anyone not like you? You are a dear, dear boy. Of course my family will like you. They'll love you. I know it.''

''As long as you love me, Miss Anna. That's all that matters,'' he said vehemently, clutching her hand in his, his fingers surrounding hers to the best of his ability.

The service was short, but filled with emotion as Angelena stood beside Anna, wiping her eyes as the newlyweds spoke their vows. Wes, next to Morgan was grim, his jaw set, his one good eye narrowed, as if he must see that this wedding was conducted with all due ceremony. Jamie stood in the center of the group, looking solemn, yet joyful, one hand clutching Morgan's, the other buried in the fabric of Anna's new dress.

Behind them, an assortment of townsfolk gathered. Once the news of an imminent wedding spread from the doors of Pip's general store to the streets of Edgewood, the excitement could not be contained, and so Anna's wedding was not the private event she had expected. Instead, she and Morgan left the church amid a flurry of well wishers, with smiles and nodding heads giving their approval.

The hotel dining room awaited the family after the ceremony, and Morgan hosted a feast that sent the hotel kitchen into a flurry of activity. The children were delighted, and Jamie was gathered into the center of a whispering, merry group, his own laughter bringing a smile to Morgan's face. All too soon, dusk fell, and with it the chiming of church bells that announced the Christmas Eve service.

''Are we *all* going to church?'' Jamie asked, gazing at the family that surrounded him. ''Can we all sit together?''

''We certainly can,'' Rosemary assured him, leading him from the dining room and out the front door of the hotel. Jenny skipped beside him, telling him of the songs they would sing and the telling of the Christmas story they would hear. And bringing up the rear, Anna and Morgan walked apace, her hand circumspectly placed on his arm. He bent to her and smiled.

"Do you feel like a wife yet?" Amusement colored his words, and she shook her head.

He leaned closer. "You will, sweetheart. Soon," he promised.

The church was beautiful, a tall Christmas tree at the front, splendid with more than a hundred candles flickering, and blown glass ornaments reflecting their flames. Families lined the pews, the Tanners filling two almost to overflowing. The organ pumped music that thrilled the hearts of those who listened, and the congregation joined their voices in tribute to the babe in the manger.

And in their midst, Jamie Brady sat in regal splendor between his father and Anna, his eyes gleaming with delight, his attention scattered as his gaze flickered from person to person. And then, as if it drew him like a magnet, he watched the tree.

Children took turns standing before the congregation, reciting their verses, twisting their hands in anguish if they forgot a word, grinning in delight as they completed their part in the program. Jenny was resplendent in her new dress, her voice piping loud and clear as she spoke the three verses she'd practiced for weeks.

"Over the hills of Bethlehem, the stars shone clear and bright—"

She had memorized them well, and her eyes sparkled as she recited without hesitation. She bowed her head, curtsied at the congregation, then stepped down sedately to sit between Wes and Anna, whispering loudly as she asked their opinions of her performance.

Morgan watched silently, filled with elation at the circumstances he had brought into being. Sending the telegram to

Dallas yesterday had been the thing to do. Bringing Jamie here had been a stroke of genius on his part.

The boy had come near to spending Christmas Eve alone, awaiting word from his father. Now, Morgan vowed silently, he would never spend the holiday in such a way. They were a family now, Anna, Jamie and himself, and if God was good, perhaps next Christmas would find another child on the way. He reached for Anna's hand and she looked up at him, her smile beaming.

''Everyone has been looking at us,'' he whispered, bending to her.

''Do you blame them?'' she asked. ''Between you and Wesley, you're quite a pair.''

The sound of a train whistle brought Morgan's head upright, and he sent a silent signal to his bride. She nodded. ''This is the last of it,'' she said quietly, as the congregation stood as one, the organ pealing out the vibrant strains of ''Joy to the World.'' As the first words were sung, they slipped from the pew, Jamie between them, and walked down the aisle, Anna nodding and smiling to the familiar faces they passed.

At the railway station the final adjustments were being made to the Pullman car, and Morgan walked to speak to the conductor. Their baggage already in place inside the elegant car, everything was in order for their departure, and Anna looked back at the small town she had called home all the years of her life.

Around the corner of the depot, just out of sight, she heard the unmistakable sound of Jenny's voice. ''They can't go without a hug, Mama.''

And then the family was there, the boys standing back, Daniel sober and tight-lipped as he sought her gaze. Anna walked to the three of them, her arms outstretched, and they were gathered to her, her kisses falling indiscriminately over their cheeks and foreheads. ''I love you all,'' she murmured. And then pressed her face against Daniel's, just for a moment holding him close.

Jenny clamored at her skirts. "Me, too, Anna. Me, too."

Anna bent to hug her. "Yes, love. I won't forget you." She lifted her head to see Rosemary before her, and beyond her Angelena and Wes. All of them so dear. All of them so much a part of her life. They shared her hugs, promised to visit her in Dallas, then turned her over to Gabe.

He held her close, speaking over her head to the man who waited by the Pullman car. "Take care of her, Brady."

"I plan on it," Morgan said quietly. "You have my word." And apparently that was good enough for Gabe. He turned Anna around and placing one hand on her shoulder, he offered the other to his new son-in-law. The two men shook hands solemnly, and then, as if a dam had burst, Morgan was surrounded by the rest of the family. His cheek was kissed soundly by the womenfolk, Jenny being lifted high to hug his neck.

The boys offered their own smaller hands to be swallowed up by his, and finally Wes approached. They eyed each other warily, then grinned, their matching bruises apparently a source of amusement.

Morgan turned as the engineer blew the whistle and the conductor sounded the final boarding. He lifted Jamie up the steps. Then his hand was on Anna's elbow as she stepped up and into the car, Harley waiting within to offer a hand. Morgan followed, and then the three of them turned as one to wave as the train began its noisy departure.

"Wait! Wait!" It was Rosemary, waving, running beside the conductor, holding her skirts up with one hand.

The man stepped inside the car and within seconds the train had come to a halt. "What is it, ma'am?" he asked leaping to the platform. "Is there an emergency?"

"I'll say so," Rosemary blurted. "Have them unhook your car, Morgan. You and Anna need to come back to the house for Christmas. That child needs to spend some time with his new family.'' She pointed at Jamie with her index finger, and he nodded in response.

''Oh, yes, that would be fine,'' he told her, jumping from the step into her arms.

Rosemary caught him quickly, planting a kiss on his forehead. ''Do you know that you're my very first grandson?'' she asked him.

''I am? I'm a grandson? Did you hear that, Papa?'' he asked, turning to grin widely at Morgan.

''Yes, I heard.'' Morgan spoke to the conductor, slipping a coin into the man's hand, then called a command into the Pullman car. ''Harley, come on out. You're staying the night with Anna's parents.''

The butler hesitated in the doorway. ''Shall I stay here instead, sir? Keep an eye on things?''

Morgan shook his head. ''No, my wife and I will stay in the Pullman and come out to the ranch early in the morning. You'll go along and look after Jamie.''

As they spoke, the train backed up, easing the Pullman car to a siding, and then two men began working at removing it from the rest of the train. Harley went inside to gather his belongings, and carrying two small valises, he joined the family on the platform.

''Go with Harley, son. He has your things. Miss Rosemary will look after you, too. We'll see you in the morning.''

''I'll keep an eye on him, sir,'' Daniel said quietly. ''He can sleep with me.''

''Thank you,'' Morgan said.

''Smile, sweetheart,'' he whispered in Anna's ear, and she did, her tears happy now as Morgan led her to the Pullman car once more. She turned to watch as her mother led the family from the platform, the three boys surrounding Jamie, chattering a mile a minute.

They climbed the steps and Morgan drew Anna from the

door, closing it firmly and locking it. He leaned against the wooden panel and watched as she made her way the length of the sitting area of the car. Lamps hung from the walls, lighting the plush interior, and she stopped to admire their fittings, the globes made of hand-cut glass. Couches and chairs provided comfortable seating, but sitting in the midst of this splendor was not what Morgan had in mind.

He took her hand, leading her to the doorway just ahead. A heavy drape hung over it, and he pushed it aside, revealing a room lit only by a single lamp. A large bed took up much of the space, their baggage sitting at its foot. ''Are you all right?'' he asked, his eyes focused on the rise and fall of her breast. She was apprehensive, and he knew it. She might be past the age most women were when they married, but his Anna was as innocent as the day she was born, at least in all the ways that truly counted.

He lifted her face, his palms framing the beauty he had traveled to claim. ''Don't be afraid of me,'' he said quietly. ''I'd never hurt you, sweetheart.''

''I know that, Morgan. It's just that I didn't have time to talk to Rosemary, and I think I need to know a few things.''

He grinned, unable to hide his delight with this woman-child of his. ''I'll tell you all about it, honey. We'll do this step by step, and you're going to love every minute of it.'' He brushed back a wisp of her hair and eyed the artful arrangement Angelena had formed on top of Anna's head. ''Would you do me a favor and take out your pins while I'm out there turning out the lamps? I'll be right back.''

Taking down her hair was the least of her worries, Anna decided, doing her best to get out of her dress. Morgan had talked her into it, and she'd fallen in love with the simple white gown, except for the fact that numerous buttons held it in place. She turned to him as he came back through the curtained doorway.

''I need these buttons undone,'' she said, breathless from her endeavors.

''I'd counted on that,'' he told her, turning her before him, his fingers nimble as he worked at the task. His hands were warm against her skin, his breath hot as he bent to brush her hair aside, placing his lips against her nape.

A surge of pleasure had her bending her head, and he obliged, nuzzling her throat, openmouthed kisses marking her shoulders as the dress slid from place. It caught on her hips and he eased it off. ''Step out of it.'' His words were strained and she obeyed, willing to do as he asked. Her petticoat ties were next and his arms circled her, his fingers adept as he released the yards of material to fall around her feet. He lifted her chemise and she raised her arms, allowing its removal, left to stand before him in drawers and stockings.

''Turn around, sweetheart,'' he said. ''Let me look at you.'' The note of pleading in his voice touched her heart and she could deny him nothing.

''Take off the rest, Anna.'' His eyes narrowed, his look resting on her breasts. She felt them swell, the flesh tightening in response, and she was enveloped by the heat that rose upward to stain her cheeks and throat. No one had ever viewed her so, and in the past even her own image in the mirror had been enough to make her slide into her clothing quickly. Morgan, on the other hand, had no such problem with her nudity.

He'd asked, and she would do as his words dictated. Loosening her drawers, she let them go the way of her other clothing, stepping from the voluminous circle that surrounded her. Only white stockings were left, and for a moment his gaze was fixed on them. Then, kneeling before her, he did the unthinkable. His fingers slid her new garters down her calf, smiling up at her as he admired the pink rosebuds that trimmed them. Her stockings were a small matter, his hands adept as he lifted each foot in turn to strip the fragile silk from place.

He held them up to the light, their gossamer threads catching the glow.

''Pretty aren't they? I imagined all evening how they would look on you.'' He glanced down at her legs, and his lips curved in a smile she thought was dangerous to her heart, causing it to clamor in her chest. ''Your legs are beautiful, Anna. So firm and curved.'' His palm cupped her calf and his fingers slid the length of it to circle her ankle.

Her breath caught and she felt the tingle of desire, traveling from her foot, up the length of her leg to settle somewhere in the pit of her belly. ''Morgan.'' She whispered his name, watching as he tossed aside the stocking he held.

Her mouth opened and then she bit her lip. She'd never owned such fine things, and her concern drove her to caution him. ''Be careful,'' she whispered. ''Don't snag them.'

He laughed aloud. ''I'll buy you a hundred pair, sweetheart. A thousand, maybe.''

Her smile was spontaneous, and he rose quickly, lifting her hand to bless its palm, his kiss sending the same shimmering warmth the length of her arm. Then she was caught up in his embrace, lifted high against his chest as he carried her to the bed and put her down. For a moment she stood before him while he tossed back the coverlet, and then he arranged her on the sheet.

His hands lingered on her hair, spreading it above her head, over the pillow and across her breasts. She reveled in the attention he lavished, his gaze so ardent, his hands so tender, she could not be other than beguiled by his pleasure in her face and form.

''You're a beauty, Anna. I don't know how you managed to hide those curves so well, but it's probably a good thing you did. I'd have been in a constant state of arousal if I'd had any idea what you really looked like beneath all those dark dresses you've worn for the past year.''

He stood back, looking pensive, then leaned forward to lift

a curl, admiring it before he placed it just so on the rise of her breast. "Now that I think about it," he mused, "it was for the best. I learned to know you first, and found much to admire."

Sitting on the edge of the bed, he lifted his foot, resting it on the other knee, then turned his head to face her.

"I like you, Anna, and I'm pleased that came first. The liking, I mean. How much better to like the person you are, and then, as an added bonus, discover the wealth of your beauty that only enhances the woman within."

She'd known he was eloquent, had heard his masterful descriptions of the projects he was involved in, had listened as he praised his servants for performing well, had even been the recipient of his words of adulation when he'd recognized her work with Jamie. Now that same skill had gifted her with phrases that would be impressed on her memory, to be taken out and examined, and stored again for all time.

His fingers were nimble, removing his shoes and stockings, his gaze never veering from her. Buttons were undone before he rose, and his hands moved quickly, removing his clothing, leaving only his drawers to cover him as he found his place beside her. She could not take her eyes from him, from the muscular chest with dark hair covering its center and spreading wide to include the small male nipples that were similar to her own, yet so different. He was well-formed, and she, who had been in the vicinity of tall, handsome men all of her life, knew that Morgan Brady was truly of that breed.

His legs were long, his thighs hard, his calves roped with firm muscles. The flesh covering his body was not pale, but olive-skinned, and she wondered what ancestor had bequeathed him his dark beauty. Her hands formed fists as she restrained them from reaching and touching, and as if he knew her thoughts, he clasped one within his own, unfurling her fingers, and placing them flat against his chest.

"I'd like to feel your hands on my skin, Anna. It would give me pleasure."

For this night she had waited what seemed an eternity. For this moment she had turned aside the attentions of other men. And she knew, without a doubt, that for this giving of herself she had chosen wisely. And so the fear was set aside, the apprehension vanquished, both smothered by anticipation and joy as she did his bidding.

That her actions would give this man the pleasure he spoke of was a thought both appealing and satisfying. And in moments she discovered his words to be truth, his involuntary groan and the quiver of masculine flesh affirming his claim. His muscles were taut beneath her fingertips, the hair she gripped clung to her skin, curling and crisp. Spreading her palms over his abdomen, she measured his width, then moved them to his sides. She could have counted his ribs beneath the sheath of muscles, but moved on, lowering her grip to the narrow span of his hips, her fingers clenching.

"Anna!" His voice held a note of desperation as he turned more fully, leaning over her. "I think you'd better stop for now, sweetheart." He bent low and his mouth pressed a kiss against the rise of her breast. Then his hand moved to cradle the firm flesh, forming it and molding his palm to fit snugly beneath, fingers edging ever nearer the crest. His index finger brushed back and forth, touching with gentle care. He murmured her name as she cried aloud. His thumb joined the dance and she jolted, splashed with waves of sensation beyond her wildest dreams.

His touch was knowing, exploring her body as if it were a treasure he'd waited years to discover. There was no hurry, his careful movements were not designed to rush her along this path they took, and he listened carefully for each sign, each whispered word she spoke.

As he had called her name with that shard of desperate yearning so evident, so her own plea magnified his name

''Morgan, ah, Morgan!'' She arched beneath his touch, her body curving, her legs drawing upward.

With a growl of satisfaction, and words she barely comprehended, he rose above her, making room with his hands on her thighs, lifting and moving her to his liking. He knelt, his gaze hot and narrowed, his hands smoothing over the skin of shoulder, breast and hip, and then bent lower, his mouth following. Nibbling, and suckling, tongue and lips left a trail of yearning behind as he pressed openmouthed, wet kisses against her warm flesh.

His palms lifted her bottom, and she was open to his manhood. Somehow he'd stripped from his drawers, and there was no longer a barrier between male and female, only the patience and tender care of a gentle lover to save her from pain.

And he was gentle, watching her carefully as he began the process of turning his bride into his wife. She winced and he held his breath. ''Anna?'' He bent low to kiss her, and as she lifted her body, reaching upward to receive his lips against her own, she eased his path and he groaned aloud.

It was fullness as she had not imagined, her whole being taken by the sensation of joining with this man. He was *there,* inside of her, and she felt her muscles clutch at him, heard his moan of pleasure as her innocence was breached. For a moment it stung, and her breath caught. Immediately he was still, his arms taut as he trembled above her.

''I won't move, sweetheart, until you tell me.'' His voice was raw, the tendons on his throat told of passion barely held in restraint, and yet he waited.

''Please, Morgan. Please move. I need you to—'' Her whimper turned to a moan as she captured him between her knees, then lifted her legs to hold him in place. ''Morgan!'' The cry was high and thready, and he answered her plea.

She was cast into a whirlwind of pleasure, of aching need, and finally the glorious blaze of release that filled her with breathless delight. Her head swam, and she sank limply onto the mattress, her gasping, pleading cries turning to sobs of joy.

"Stay with me, sweetheart," he whispered hoarsely, his movements changing, his body driving against her, urging her beyond herself, into another place where pleasure awaited once more.

Surely she could not. And yet, he coaxed her, his hands hard against her skin, lifting her, his fingers drawing new excitement into being. Her cries were for mercy, for completion, for whatever wonder he would bestow upon her seeking, striving body. He rose high above her, his head back, his jaw thrust forward. His shout was wordless, a primitive sound that thrust her beyond the barrier, and she was catapulted into wonder and passion and a fulfillment that promised to bind her soul forever to his.

Chapter Eight

"When we go home to Dallas, will you share my bedroom with me, Anna?" Morgan held her against himself as the sun rose, wondering that they'd gotten any sleep at all.

"I'd expected to," she said quietly. "I didn't know there was an option."

"Then I won't give you one," he told her, rising on his elbow to look into her face. "Many husbands and wives sleep apart. But we'll share my bed." He bent to kiss her and she reached for him, twining her arms behind his neck.

"Try and chase me away," she threatened, "and you'll be a sorry man."

His laughter rang out, joyous and uninhibited. Anna had that effect on him, and he nuzzled her throat, his pleasure spilling over as he rolled with his bride across the wide bed. "We'll never get to the ranch, you know," he told her. "I think we'll just spend the day right here."

"Oh, no! I forgot. Jamie will be looking for us." She sat upright, and he allowed it, his gaze filled with the mass of waving hair that spilled over her shoulders.

His voice was strained as he buried his hands in the vibrant cloud. "I can't believe you're truly mine, Anna. You've made me happier than I deserve." He sat up beside her. "I have some things for you, back in Dallas, sweetheart. I had Harley bring you a dress to wear today, though. Will you try it on for me?''

''A dress? You bought me a dress?''

''I had the housekeeper go shopping while I was gone, Anna. I'm afraid she filled closets with beautiful things for you. Perhaps I should have waited, let you choose your own clothing, but I wanted to surprise you. Please don't be angry with me.'' His voice was low, and his arms tightened around her waist. ''I wasn't sure if you would come back with me or not, but my hopes were high. And after promising Jamie...''

Anna turned to him, her head finding a resting place against his chest. ''I don't know what to say, Morgan. I've never had a lot of clothes. But I'm sure it will be fine. I really don't need them you know. I'll be happy just to have you as my husband.''

He lifted her face with one hand, his eyes moist as he looked into hers. ''I wasn't altogether truthful with you, sweetheart. I came after you for my sake, more than Jamie's. When I awoke and found you gone, I thought my life would be forever desolate. I'd missed my chance to have you in my home, and I was desperate. I know I've made a botch of things, Anna, saying all the wrong things and going about this in the wrong way, but my intentions were always honorable. I want you to believe that.''

''Oh, I do. You know I do, Morgan. I know you care for me.'' She tilted her face, inviting his kiss, and he obliged her sweetly, and with more than a touch of passion.

''I can't tell you how anxious I am to introduce you to my bed back in Dallas,'' he whispered, his words fervent. And then he smiled ruefully. ''I'd better not talk about that now, had I? Or we'll never get to the ranch.'' He reached for his clothes, gathering them up from the floor. ''Shall we wash up and get dressed? I'll walk to the livery stable and get a rig. I know it's Christmas, but I'll make it worthwhile to Bates Comstock.''

He watched as Anna washed and then he opened the doors of a wide wardrobe, drawing a dress from inside, offering it for Anna's consideration. ''Do you like it?'' he asked, holding it over his arm. Deep red in color, it bore ecru lace at collar and cuffs, with layers of fabric making up the skirt.

Morgan's fingers undid onyx buttons as he spoke and Anna's fingers stroked the fine fabric. ''It's lovely, Morgan.'' She touched the buttons, allowing her fingertips to admire the smooth, black finish. ''I feel as though I'm in a dream,'' she whispered. ''In all of my life, I've never had so elegant a dress. I feel guilty that you've spent so much to outfit me.''

''Anna.'' His hands were on her bare shoulders, fingers brushing against her skin, his breath warm as he bent to whisper in her ear. ''Don't you know why I've done my best to make this a happy day for you? I know I haven't told you what's in my heart. I meant to last night, but the words didn't come readily to me. But now that my plans have come to pass, I must try to make you aware of how deeply I care for you. I don't give my love easily, I fear, but when I love, it is forever. I married once without love. This time was different.''

His face was somber, his eyes searching hers. ''You said you loved me, last night. Did you mean it? Do you truly care so much? It's not just for Jamie that you married me?''

She shook her head. ''Oh, no! I told you. I love you, Morgan. I meant that. I want a marriage like my parents have, one that will last for my whole life.''

He kissed her forehead. ''And you shall have it, wife of mine. I give you my word on that. I've given you my love. All that I have is yours.''

She felt her heart quicken, and her hands rested against his chest. ''Will you say the words outright, Morgan? Will you give me the pleasure of hearing those words?''

''As often as you please, sweetheart.'' He kissed her, softly, gently and lifted his head. ''I love you, Anna. You are my heart.'' His mouth sought hers again, and he repeated his vow. ''I love you as I have loved no other in my life.''

The kitchen table was full to overflowing. Persuading the children to eat breakfast was an almost futile exercise, Anna decided after fifteen minutes of excited chatter. Jenny shared a muffin with Jamie and they'd exchanged giggles as they drank their milk. Gabe laughed and shook his head.

''We might as well finish this meal later, Rosemary. There's no hope for it. Your children are not going to settle down to eat until they open their presents.''

''*My* children?'' she said, one brow tilted as she mocked him. ''I know you too well, Gabe Tanner. You're the one having a hard time waiting.'' She waved her hand, and before she could speak, the boys slid from their seats, Jenny fast at their heels. With a clatter of shoes on bare floors, they were down the hallway and into the parlor. And there they came to a halt, Jamie at the forefront, his eyes wide with anticipation.

''Oh, Papa,'' he whispered, looking back over his shoulder to seek Morgan's presence. ''Did you ever see such a beautiful tree?''

Morgan shook his head. ''No, son. I can't say that I have.'' His own in Dallas would be more richly decorated, he knew, with a multitude of crystal balls and spiraling cascades of silver raining down the branches. But this tree, in this house, surrounded by this family, had captivated father and son alike. There was no other like it. No other family held him with such fascination as the Tanner clan.

They exuded love and generosity of spirit. Their arms welcomed Jamie to their midst, including him in the process, and even Wes had shaken his hand this morning. They'd peered at each other from blackened eyes and grinned like idiots, he recalled, even as Angelena and Anna were tucked into place beside their husbands.

Now he sat on the sofa, Anna at his side, watching as the family opened gifts, one at a time, each being given its fair share of attention. The process was long but not tedious, and he watched carefully as each recipient gave thanks for the simple treasures.

Even Harley was remembered, wearing a red knitted scarf over his proper black ensemble. He'd been bemused by all the fuss, and Morgan watched with good humor as Jenny climbed on the venerable butler's knee and coaxed him into her web. There was no defense against the child. His own experience was proof of that.

At last, a small box was placed in Anna's hands and she opened it slowly. "It's from me, Miss Anna," Jamie sang, jumping from one foot to the other as he watched her impatiently. "Cook helped me pick it out."

Anna peeked inside the box, drawing forth a slender chain with a heart of gold catching the lights from the Christmas tree. Her eyes filled with tears as she handed it to Morgan. "Will you help me?"

He opened the clasp and placed it around her neck, fastening it slowly, his fingers not so adept with such a fragile closure. "Now will you open a gift from me, Anna?" he asked, removing a velvet box from his pocket.

She took it, her hands trembling, and lifted the lid carefully. A ring sparkled from within the box, comprised of several stones surrounding a larger, brighter gem in the center. "Oh, Morgan, it's lovely. But you've already given me a ring," she reminded him, holding up her left hand, where a plain golden band encircled her finger.

"I'd like to add this one to it, Anna. I had Harley fetch it from the bank vault. It's very special to me, for you see, it belonged to my mother." He looked down at the simple setting for a moment. "Under other circumstances, it might have been your betrothal ring. It's not very extravagant, Anna. We can afford something much more elegant if you like."

''Oh, no. It's lovely, Morgan.'' Anna offered her hand and he lifted it, then slid the ring into place next to her wedding band. Bending his head, he kissed the finger that wore his token, then held her hand between his palms. ''Right now, I have another task to perform that will give me great pleasure.'' He turned to Jamie and lifted him onto his lap.

''I want to introduce you to your mother, Jamie.''

''But I know Miss Anna, Papa. I've known her for ever so long a time.'' Jamie laughed up at his father and then shook his head, as if he were scolding him. ''Miss Anna is the answer to my Christmas wish, Papa. I knew you'd get her for me.''

''She is no longer Miss Anna, son. From now on you will call her Mother.''

''Oh, Morgan...'' Anna began, fearful of forcing the boy into such an intimate gesture.

''May I, Miss Anna? May I really call you my mother?'' Jamie squealed with delight, scooting from his father's lap to throw his arms around Anna's neck. ''Mother. How does that sound?'' he asked and then frowned. ''No, I don't think so. I think I'd like it better if you were Mama.'' He leaned back to peer into her eyes. ''Would that be all right?''

Anna's heart seemed fit to burst, so swollen with joy, so full of love for the child she held. ''I'd like to be your Mama, Jamie. You may call me whatever you wish.''

''And I'll be your grandpa,'' Gabe said, crouching before Anna, his hand touching Jamie's shoulder. ''Will you like that?'' His gaze touched Morgan's, and they exchanged a long look.

''I'm sure he will,'' Morgan said quietly. ''I know I appreciate the gesture.''

''It's no gesture,'' Gabe said firmly. ''That's just the way things are in this family. Your boy is a part of the Tanner bunch now, Morgan. And so are you, son.''

''Papa,'' Jamie tugged at Morgan's hand. ''I got more than

just a new mama, didn't I?'' His grin was wide as he looked at the family surrounding him. ''Tonight, will I be able to see the star from here? I didn't look last night. I was too sleepy when we got here, and I don't even remember going to bed.''

''I'm sure you'll be able to find it in the sky,'' Morgan told him. ''I'll help you look.''

''Will you watch with me, too, Mama? So when I say my prayers, I can say thank you for my wish coming true? Can we all three watch out the window?''

Morgan slid closer to Anna's side, his arms encompassing the woman and boy alike. ''We'll both be with you, son. I'll add my prayer to yours.'' His eyes tangled with Anna's, and he bent to press a kiss against her forehead. ''No one is more thankful than I, Jamie.''

''This is what kept me in pursuit, Anna. The thought of having you here, in my bed, as my wife.'' They were back in Dallas, after two days spent at the ranch, and she had yearned for this moment. He held her closely in his arms in the center of the big bed with a possessive embrace and she gloried in it, feeling his heartbeat vibrate against her cheek. She was well loved, sated with passion, her body pressed beneath his. He shifted to curl behind her and together they looked out the window, where the brilliant star hovered at the horizon.

''Christmas is over, I know, but it's never too late for the wishing star. Do you have a wish, Anna?'' he whispered.

''I can't think of anything I lack. I'm full to the brim with everything I could ever desire,'' she told him. ''And so I'll wish only that I might always be as happy as I am tonight.''

''Would a child of our own please you? Not right now, but perhaps in the next year or so?''

''It takes nine months, Morgan,'' she said softly. ''If we work on it diligently, we should be able to celebrate next Christmas with two children. I think Jamie would like that.''

He chuckled in her ear and his arm tightened around her. ‘‘I am of all things, a diligent man, Anna. Most diligent.’’

‘‘Will she be happy?’’ Rosemary Tanner looked from her bedroom window, her gaze fastened on the star she’d watched nightly for almost a month. ‘‘Shall I make a wish on her behalf, Gabe?’’ Her voice was wistful. ‘‘I used to wish on the Christmas star when I was a child.’’

‘‘And did your wishes come true?’’ he asked.

She turned to smile at him. ‘‘You know they did, Gabriel. All of them.’’ He lifted his hand and she obeyed his unspoken request, moving toward the bed where he waited.

‘‘Morgan’s a good man, Rosemary. He’ll treat her well. I think he loves her. But you go ahead, honey,’’ he told her, waving toward the window. ‘‘Wishing on a star never hurts, I always say. After all, wishes have been known to come true.’’

Dear Reader,

The idea for the heroine Abbie Doyle's adjustment to Southern California's warm December weather in "Christmas Wishes" came directly from my own experience. Like Abbie, my family moved from a true winter climate to sunny Southern California. I was stunned! How could it be this hot—only two weeks before Christmas?

My snowbound relatives in Virginia were truly envious when we telephoned on Christmas Day and reported we were dressed in shorts, with our doors and windows open.

Christmas is one of my favorite holidays. Because of my husband's career in the U.S. Air Force, I've tried extra hard to provide strong traditions for our children. As a result, a dozen boxes of Christmas decorations—some of which we've had the entire twenty-eight years of our marriage—go with us every time we move.

Another of our Christmas traditions is baking homemade goodies for the young troops who work for my husband. Every year my daughters and I spend a full day baking all sorts of treats to provide a little taste of home for those who can't be with their families.

I hope that like Abbie and Jack in "Christmas Wishes", you will find love and family warmth this Christmas season.

Happy holidays!

Judith Stacy

Christmas Wishes

Judith Stacy

To David, Judy and Stacy—
you make all my wishes come true.

Chapter One

San Bernardino, California
December, 1895

How could it be this blasted hot—in December?

Abbie Doyle glanced at the windows of her little office. Both were thrown open wide and had been all morning, but nothing resembling a breeze floated in.

December, and it was hot. It just wasn't natural. It wasn't normal.

Abbie sighed.

Nothing about her new home was normal. At least, not to her way of thinking.

Determinedly, she turned back to her cluttered desk trying to make some sense of the chaos. She pressed her wrist to her forehead, fearing she might perspire. A lady never perspired, her employer, Mrs. Merchant had informed her.

Abbie jerked her chin. That haughty old heifer was a fine one to talk—she didn't move around enough to work up a sweat.

Grumbling to herself, Abbie sorted through the piles of papers, folders and books that littered her desk. Last evening Mrs. Merchant had left her *yet another* list of items requiring

Abbie's attention. She'd risen early to get started but found herself savoring Mrs. Merchant's absence this morning instead.

As the widow of one of San Bernardino's wealthiest businessmen, Mrs. Merchant lived in a three-story mansion, a beautiful home painted green and trimmed in yellow and white, with a wrap porch, and topped with an onion dome. She'd given Abbie a room on the third floor with the other servants, and an office in the back corner of the house.

Not even a month had passed since Abbie had moved from her parents' farm in Pennsylvania to accept The Merchant Company's offer of employment. It had been an opportunity Abbie couldn't resist. At age twenty-two she was raring to see new things. Leave the farm. Learn the ways of gracious ladies living in the city.

With a certificate in bookkeeping, and a referral from a friend of a friend, Abbie had secured a position with The Merchant Company, said goodbye to family, friends and Pennsylvania, and come west to California.

And her dream had turned into a nightmare.

Abbie plopped into her desk chair and gazed glumly at her cramped little office. Green wallpaper, heavy drapes on the large windows, Oriental carpet on the floor, walnut desk, credenza and cabinet all overrunning with things requiring Abbie's immediate attention.

This was the life she'd asked for, even if it wasn't turning out as she'd planned.

When she'd presented herself to the office manager at The Merchant Company, Mrs. Merchant happened to be there at the time and had bridled at the prospect of a young woman working for the company. This was not, Mrs. Merchant had informed everyone, surely within a three-block radius, what her dear departed husband would have wanted.

So instead of being assigned the job of bookkeeper, for

which Abbie was trained, Mrs. Merchant had reluctantly taken her on to act as her social secretary.

As if she were doing Abbie a favor.

Mrs. Merchant was the cream of the city's upper class, which meant Abbie's duties now demanded menu planning, organizing teas and social functions, handling correspondence, as well as anything else Mrs. Merchant assigned her. All to the woman's exacting standards.

But the problem was that Abbie had been raised on a farm. She'd been trained as a bookkeeper. She didn't know the first thing about entertaining high society.

She'd fantasized about it, of course. Herself dressed in a beautiful gown, escorted by a handsome man in a fine tuxedo, descending a grand staircase somewhere into a room filled with gracious women and well-mannered gentlemen. The vision had filled many long hours on the farm. But Abbie never expected she'd be thrust into that life completely unprepared, with no training whatsoever.

Another flash of heat wafted through Abbie and she dabbed at her forehead with the handkerchief in her skirt pocket. It was hot. So dreadfully hot. How could it be this hot in December?

With a heavy sigh, she walked to the window and took in the lovely view of blooming flowers, lush green grass and swaying palm trees. In the distance, mountains rose to the heavens, capped with cloaks of white snow.

Snow. While it frequently blanketed the tops of the mountains, snow came to the valley only every few decades, or so everyone had told her—after they'd laughed at her question, of course.

Abbie straightened her shoulders and turned away from the window. Somehow, she would have to make a life for herself here in California. So far she'd failed to live up to Mrs. Merchant's standards. Already she'd made several mistakes and Mrs. Merchant was displeased. So displeased, in fact, that she'd told Abbie she'd be dismissed if she bungled anything else.

Abbie didn't have enough money to get back home to Pennsylvania, and if she was fired from her position as social secretary to the most well-known woman in the city, who else would hire her?

"Damn..."

The word tumbled from Abbie's lips in a most unladylike fashion. She gasped and whirled, then relaxed seeing that she was still alone in the room. A lady did not curse, Mrs. Merchant had decreed.

Mrs. Merchant was always decreeing *something.*

With a resolute sigh, Abbie headed back to her desk. She was trying so hard to fit in, to learn, to be a part of this grand life here in the city. And she was determined to succeed at this job, too. Somehow.

Even though the thought of a working woman was frowned upon by most of society, some people had turned their eye toward the future and embraced the idea. Luckily, Abbie had found a few friends here in the city who supported her. The others were busy trying to marry her off.

Irritated, Abbie tossed files and papers across her desk. Two would-be suitors had been presented to her at church by some well-intentioned acquaintances. Another had conveniently showed up at the home of a friend with whom she was having dinner. Abbie had declined the attention of each and every one of them.

Gracious, a man in her life. The very last thing she needed. Her goal right now was to keep her job. Nothing else—absolutely nothing else—mattered to Abbie.

Deep within the house, a clock chimed the hour, jarring Abbie from her thoughts. She hadn't realized so much of the morning had passed. Mrs. Merchant would return soon.

Abbie pawed through the clutter on her desk searching for

her latest list of instructions. It wouldn't do for Mrs. Merchant to return and learn that she hadn't even begun today's work.

A lady was always in control of her day, Mrs. Merchant had told her. A concise plan led to a day of leisure.

"Day of leisure, my foot," Abbie grumbled. "Of course it's leisurely when someone else is doing all the work and she's sitting on her lazy—"

"Miss Doyle?"

Abbie gasped and jerked upright. A stack of papers slid from the corner of the desk. She scooped them up, hugged them to her chest, then whirled toward the door.

The figure filling the doorway was Mrs. Walsh, the housekeeper, looking down her long nose at Abbie. Tall—terribly tall for a woman—Mrs. Walsh always dressed in black and drew her gray hair back in a severe bun. She ran the house with an iron fist, disapproving of everything, suspicious of everyone.

Mrs. Walsh's eyebrows drew together and her lips curled down. "You have a *gentleman* caller."

"A gentleman…?"

With great show, Mrs. Walsh removed a small tablet from her skirt pocket, checked the time on the mantel clock, then jotted down a note.

Abbie cringed. Mrs. Walsh kept records of everything the household staff did. She passed it on to Mrs. Merchant—everybody said so.

Mrs. Walsh tucked the tablet in her skirt pocket and folded her hands in front of her.

"Mr. Jack Graham is here to see you," she said, then spun around and disappeared.

Abbie's knees quivered. Darn that Mrs. Walsh. She'd tell Mrs. Merchant a gentleman had come to call on her during business hours. Mrs. Merchant wouldn't be pleased. And Abbie knew her position with Mrs. Merchant wouldn't bear up under much more of the woman's displeasure.

A gentleman caller? She wasn't expecting anyone. In fact, she didn't even know a gentleman who might call on her. Unless—

Anger tightened Abbie's stomach. She plopped the stack of papers down on her desk. No gentleman would come to call unless he'd been arranged for by one of her well-intentioned friends from church.

How presumptuous of the man, Abbie fumed. How egotistical. To think she was so desperate for a husband that he could barge into her place of employment and introduce himself. That she, in turn, would be so pleased at the prospect of having a husband, she'd go to pieces, all happy and giddy that he'd chosen to turn a little attention her way.

"Oh!" Abbie tugged on the sleeve of her dark-green shirtwaist, her anger boiling. Maybe that was the way city women handled such matters, but it didn't sit right with Abbie.

The stack of papers on the corner of her desk started to slip again. Abbie reached for them.

"Miss Doyle?"

A deep, mellow voice froze Abbie in place. She looked up to see the man who must be Mr. Jack Graham standing in the doorway, only vaguely aware of the papers cascading onto the floor.

Gracious, he was handsome. Quite tall—even taller than Mrs. Walsh. He had light-brown hair with strands of blond in it, and deep-brown eyes. His shoulders were wide and straight, barely contained in the brown suit he wore. The white turned-down collar of his shirt contrasted with the tan the sun had brought to his face.

Abbie's knees quivered again and might have given out completely if she hadn't realized that Mr. Graham was gawking at her. Ogling her. Staring as if he hadn't seen a woman in a year.

He was sizing her up, Abbie decided. Determining whether he'd been given a bum steer by the church ladies who'd sent him to call on her. And that sent anger racing up Abbie's spine all over again.

Jack stepped farther into the room. "I was asked to come here today to—"

"Oh, I know why you're here, Mr. Graham."

He paused a moment. "Good. Then we should get down to business."

"Business? Is that what you think this is?" Abbie rounded her desk and marched over to him. "Let me assure you, Mr. Graham, there is not now, nor will there ever be, any sort of *business* that will take place between you and me."

Jack frowned slightly. "I was told this was an emergency."

"Emergency?" Abbie's spine stiffened. "Do I look like I'm someone's idea of an emergency?"

He tilted his head. "I beg your pardon?"

"Do I look as if I'm in desperate need of a man in my life?" she demanded, spreading her arms wide.

Abbie knew she wasn't a beautiful woman. She'd seen herself in the mirror. But she wasn't ugly, either. She had thick brown hair, eyes that had been compared to the blue summer sky, and a figure that had never given a dressmaker a moment's concern.

So she certainly wasn't desperate. Hardly an emergency. Angry, Abbie stood with her arms flung out, glaring at Jack Graham, daring him to differ with her.

Instead, he looked at her. Slowly, his brown eyes started at the tips of her high buttoned shoes, rose over her dark-green skirt to her waist, lingered for a moment on her bosom, then jumped to her brown hair coiled in a knot atop her head.

He looked away, and pulled in a deep breath, shuffling his feet.

"Well, no..." A wave of pink rushed into his tan cheeks. He swallowed hard, still not looking at her. "You don't look...desperate."

Abbie's insides jolted. She lowered her arms as her breath

came a little slower. She was having trouble holding on to her anger.

Abbie straightened her shoulders. "I'll—I'll have to ask you to leave, Mr. Graham."

That brought his gaze to meet hers again. "Well, all right, if you're sure..."

"If course I'm sure!" Abbie exclaimed. "I don't know who you think you are parading yourself in here as if—"

"Ah, Mr. Graham, you're here."

Mrs. Madeline Merchant chugged into the room, gloved hand extended, and planted herself in front of Jack Graham. He bowed slightly, seemingly relieved the older woman had arrived.

She clamped her hand around his forearm. "Oh, I'm so glad you came over right away. So glad, indeed."

Jack threw a glance at Abbie. "You said it was an emergency."

"Emergency, indeed," Mrs. Merchant declared. "Now, did Miss Doyle explain everything to you?"

A little smile jerked the corner of Jack's mouth as he looked at Abbie again. "Miss Doyle made herself perfectly clear."

Abbie's eyes widened. She gulped twice. Gracious, she'd perspire for sure now.

Mrs. Merchant turned to Abbie. "Very good. I'm glad you read my instructions this morning."

Without wanting to, Abbie's gaze jumped to the jumble of papers on her desk.

"So," Mrs. Merchant said to Jack, "I trust everything will be handled?"

Jack smiled. "Miss Doyle has everything under control."

"Excellent. I'll leave it all in your capable hands," Mrs. Merchant declared. "Good day, Mr. Graham. Miss Doyle, come to the music room. We have things to go over."

Abbie stood rooted to the floor as Jack Graham and Mrs. Merchant walked out of her office. Heavens, what had she done? She'd insulted a man sent for by Mrs. Merchant. A man who was supposed to handle some emergency for her. A man who'd assured Mrs. Merchant that Abbie had everything under control.

But she didn't have *anything* under control. She didn't even know what Mrs. Merchant wanted Jack Graham to do.

Abbie pressed her lips together. Good gracious, she'd done it again. She'd bungled a task Mrs. Merchant had assigned her.

She had to find out why Jack had been summoned this morning, or she'd lose her job for sure.

Darting to her desk, Abbie riffled through everything, frantically searching for Mrs. Merchant's list, tossing papers over her shoulder. It had to be here. The list just had to be here somewhere.

A little mewl escaped Abbie's lips as she got to the bottom of the stacks. No list. Not today's, anyway.

Abbie's future flashed before her eyes. Mrs. Merchant firing her. No place to live. No job. No way to get back to Pennsylvania. What would become of her, left to wander the streets homeless?

It was a small consolation that at least she wouldn't freeze to death in this awful Southern California heat.

Abbie rushed out of her office and peered down the long hallway that led to the foyer just in time to see Jack accept his derby from Duncan, the butler. She had to talk to Mr. Graham. He was her only hope. Mrs. Merchant had sent for him. They knew each other. Surely he had some idea of why he'd been called here on an emergency.

Abbie crept down the hallway. She slipped behind a potted palm and watched as he left the house and the stoop-shouldered butler ambled out of sight.

She glanced around. No sign of Mrs. Merchant or Mrs. Walsh. Abbie dashed across the marble foyer, yanked open the door and rushed outside.

Blinking against the bright morning sunlight, Abbie spotted Jack halfway down the walk. She hiked up her skirt with one hand and waved with the other as she hurried down the steps.

"Mr. Graham? Mr. Graham?" she called, running toward him.

He spun around and leveled his gaze at her. Abbie froze in her tracks. Gracious, the way he looked at her. A chill tingled up her spine and her fingers turned cold. But how could that be, in this heat?

He watched her, studied her, making Abbie achingly aware of the loose strands of hair fluttering against her neck, the press of her collar against her throat. Only moments ago she'd been willing to beg him for the information that would save her job. Now, she wanted to slap his face.

Abbie marched up to Jack and stretched herself up to her greatest height. Though it brought her nose only to his shoulder, she looked him straight in the eye.

"Mr. Graham, I'm quite sure that you—"

He kissed her. Caught her arms, pulled her to her toes, and kissed her. On the mouth. With his lips open.

Abbie hung in his embrace, too stunned to move. Then, just as quickly, he released her and strode away. Dazed, Abbie swayed and caught herself. She pressed her palm to her chest as her breath came in great long heaves, and Jack Graham disappeared around the corner.

How dare he? How dare he do such a thing? Kiss her in public, on the mouth, with such passion. Abbie's knees shook but she wasn't sure if it was from anger or from—

Of course it was anger, she told herself.

Trembling, Abbie tugged down on her sleeves and touched her hand to her temple.

Of all the nerve…

Jack Graham had kissed her.

And she still had to go after him.

Chapter Two

After an endless morning of sitting with Mrs. Merchant and going over details of the upcoming Christmas celebration, Abbie finally headed back to her own office. Christmas for the upper class was a great deal of work, Abbie decided, as she put aside the latest list of things requiring her attention.

Right now, she had something more important to do. She had to find Jack Graham.

She located his address easily enough in the register Mrs. Merchant had given her, pinned her hat on, and left the house.

By Pennsylvania farm standards, San Bernardino was huge. Wide boulevards, fine homes, shops, elegant hotels and an opera house, much of which had come into being thanks to the citrus industry that surrounded the city. Orange groves spanned the foothills and valleys, spreading out for miles, bringing wealth and power to those who owned them.

After running so many errands for Mrs. Merchant, Abbie knew her way around. The sun shone bright in the clear blue sky, a little breeze doing what it could to cool the heat as she walked toward the heart of the city. Tall, thin palm trees swayed gently as she passed green yards and well-kept homes.

Jack Graham's business was close by, Abbie realized, turning the corner. Apparently he ran it out of his home, which wasn't unusual.

Abbie's feet dragged to a stop as she stood across the street from his home. From the look of the place—a large two-story home painted blue and white—Mr. Graham was prosperous. Whatever *emergencies* he routinely handled, paid well.

But how was she going to talk business with him when she couldn't forget about the kiss he'd given her?

Abbie touched her fingers to her lips. A strange warmth spread through her. A most unladylike warmth.

A soft moan slipped through her lips, as she silently admonished herself for yet another error. A woman must be a lady at all times, Mrs. Merchant had told her. And that, of all Abbie's shortcomings, was proving the most difficult.

On the farm with her brothers and sisters, Abbie had learned proper manners—her mother and father had seen to it. But she'd also learned how to speak her mind, stand up for herself, and conduct herself with a large dose of common sense.

Little of which, according to Mrs. Merchant, had anything to do with being a lady.

And nothing, Abbie was sure, with the way Jack Graham had kissed her.

With a shake of her shoulders, Abbie focused on the task at hand. Enough thoughts about kissing. About the warmth that had radiated from Mr. Graham. The strength in his hands, the softness of his lips, his tongue—

''Heavens…''

Abbie adjusted her wide-brimmed hat. Jack Graham was wrong to kiss her—and she was wrong to be so intrigued by it. None of that mattered now. Keeping her job did.

Abbie crossed the street, climbed the wide porch and banged the big brass knocker. A moment later running feet and a wail of giggles drifted out, then the door opened.

Abbie wasn't sure whom she'd expected here at Jack's

house, from where he ran his business. A butler? A valet? A business associate?

Certainly not the attractive young blond woman standing in front of her.

Certainly not the three little blond-haired girls chattering and circling the woman's skirts.

"Girls, please..." The woman gave Abbie a weary but good-natured smile. "Good afternoon, can I help you?"

"I'm not sure I'm in the right place," Abbie said, glancing at the slip of paper she'd written the address on. "I'm Abbie Doyle. I work for Mrs. Merchant and I'm looking for Jack Graham."

"Mama, can we—"

"Just a moment, Lizzy," she said to the oldest girl. "Please come inside, Miss Doyle. I'm Beth, Jack's—"

"Mama?" the child asked again.

"Wait, dear," Beth said. She stepped back from the door drawing the crowd of little girls with her, but Abbie didn't come inside.

"I have the right place?" Abbie asked, glancing at the children. "Jack Graham lives here?"

"Yes, certainly," Beth replied, herding the girls to the side of the foyer. "Come in."

"Mama, can we go out to play?" Lizzy asked, bringing another round of gleeful chatter from the other two girls. "Papa said we could."

Abbie looked at the three little girls. Stairsteps, aged six, five and four, Abbie guessed, all with bows in their long golden hair, wearing sparkling white pinafores over their dresses, dark stockings and high buttoned shoes.

Beautiful children. All of them. With an equally beautiful mother, Abbie decided as she turned to Beth again.

A different kind of chill passed through Abbie, this one pooling in the pit of her stomach.

Jack Graham had kissed her.

And he was married.

"Yeah, let's play outside!" the youngest girl shouted, clapping her hands.

"Janie—" Beth began.

"Yippee!" the middle child exclaimed, hopping up and down.

"Can we take our dolls, Mama?" Lizzy asked. "The new ones? The ones Papa—"

"Girls," Beth admonished gently, "we have company."

Janie tugged on her mother's skirt. "But Mama—"

Beth, unable to keep from smiling despite the chattering girls, took Janie's hand and waved Abbie into the house. "Jack's in his office. It's just down the hall— Oh, there he is now. Jack, Miss Doyle is here to see you."

Jack stopped as he stepped from a room down the hallway, his gaze bouncing from the children, to Beth, to Abbie. But Abbie had seen him a second before he'd spotted her before he'd stopped so suddenly at the sight of her standing in his foyer.

Was he wondering if she'd told the lovely young Beth that he'd kissed her? Abbie thought. Was he afraid she'd blurted out what he'd done?

Her stomach tingled as she locked gazes with Jack Graham. Troubled. He certainly looked troubled. As well he should be.

"I'll leave you two to your business," Beth said, smiling. "Come along, girls."

The three children swarmed around Beth as they disappeared down the hallway.

A moment passed in the foyer, suddenly silent in the wake of the girls' leaving, while Jack stayed rooted at one end and Abbie at the other.

"Would you like to come into my office?" Jack asked finally, pointing.

No, she wanted to leave. She wanted to turn and run and not stop until she got to Pennsylvania. Until the memory of

Jack's kiss disappeared. Until the memory of his wife and three little daughters went with it.

A heaviness settled in Abbie's chest. Disappointment, she suddenly realized. Disappointment at finding the lovely wife and three adorable children.

Jack gave her a lopsided smile and gestured toward his office, and the disappointment in Abbie's chest turned into something stronger.

She pulled herself up straighter. ''Yes, Mr. Graham, I'd like to have a word with you.''

Abbie marched past him into his office, a large room with shelves of books, two desks, leather chairs, and a heavy Oriental carpet on the floor. A decidedly masculine room.

She whirled around to face him.

''You, Mr. Graham, are a low-down, no-good skunk,'' she told him.

His little lopsided grin melted as his mouth sagged open slightly and his eyes widened.

''You are the most common, disreputable scoundrel I've ever known,'' Abbie informed him. ''And believe me, I've known a few.''

Jack's brow rose slightly. ''You came all the way over here to tell me that?''

''No! I came here to discuss business with you,'' Abbie told him. ''But instead I find you have the gall—the *gall*—to kiss me while all along you were *married*.''

''Oh...'' Jack reeled back slightly. He touched his forehead, as if everything were clear to him now.

''And you with those three little girls, too. You ought to be ashamed of yourself,'' Abbie said. ''Why, how you can treat your wife like that I'll never understand, you—''

''Beth is my sister.''

Abbie's jaw snapped shut, his words hitting her like a cold bucket of water. ''She's your...?''

''Sister,'' Jack said. ''Beth is my sister.''

"Oh, dear." Color plumed in Abbie's cheeks. "Oh, dear. Well, when I saw her here at your house, and all those little girls, I thought— Well, I assumed— That is, I figured—"

Abbie gulped hard, her gaze wandering to the ceiling, the floor, anywhere but on Jack's face. "I'm terribly sorry, Mr. Graham. I owe you an apology."

"No harm done."

Flustered, Abbie fiddled with her handbag. "I shouldn't have jumped to conclusions like that. I shouldn't have thought the worst of you without knowing the facts."

"Really, it's all right."

"No, it's not," she insisted. "Jumping in without benefit of the facts is my worst trait. Well, not my *worst,* maybe. I have quite a few. Everyone says so. But it's certainly in the top five."

"The top five?"

"Oh, yes, easily," Abbie said. "But there's no reason you should pay for my faults. So I do, in fact, owe you a tremendous apology."

"So, does this mean it's all right for me to kiss you again?"

Abbie's gaze came up quickly to find Jack standing in front of her, watching her, as a slow heat enveloped her. A heat he gave off and she soaked up. And suddenly, Abbie wanted very much for Jack Graham to kiss her again.

The realization stunned her. He seemed to be equally stunned by his question, because he backed up a step breaking the spell between them.

"Miss Doyle, I, um..." he muttered, pulling at the back of his neck. "I—"

"Can you come outside with us, Papa?" a tiny voice asked.

Abbie whirled and saw one of the children—the middle one—standing in the doorway. Her brown eyes were bright as she clutched a rag doll in her hand.

"Please, Papa? Please?" she begged.

Abbie's gaze impaled Jack but he ducked around her.

"I'll be out in a while, Natalie," he said, kneeling in front of the child.

She wrinkled her brow in what was supposed to look like a stern frown. "You promise, Papa?"

He smiled broadly. "I promise."

Natalie leaped into his arms. Jack held her against his chest until she wriggled away and scooted out of sight.

He got to his feet slowly and turned to Abbie, opening his mouth to speak. She beat him to it.

"You snake. You filthy, stinking, lying snake!" Abbie ground out the words, spewing her anger. "Believe me, Mr. Graham. I know a whole lot more names for a man like you, but I'm trying hard to conduct myself as a lady so I don't dare say them!"

"My wife died."

A stunned moment passed while the words hung in the heated room. Pink darkened Abbie's cheeks while Jack's went white.

"Two years ago," he said, softly. "Natalie is my daughter. We live here with my sister and her husband. The other two children are theirs. Beth helps me with Natalie."

A wave of pain washed over Abbie with such intensity that her shoulders slumped. She looked at Jack, their gazes locked, his words bombarding them both.

"I'm very sorry for your loss," Abbie whispered, and had never meant anything more in her entire life.

She turned away, her stomach knotted. His wife, so young, allowed so short a life. That beautiful little girl without her mother. This man without his wife.

The mantel clock ticked off the minutes. A carriage passed the house, harness jangling, hoofs clip-clopping, amplifying the silence in the room.

"You—you said you'd come here on business?" Jack asked.

Abbie nodded, glad to focus on something, anxious to get this ordeal over with before she made a bigger fool of herself.

"I came here, Mr. Graham, to ask you to go to Mrs. Merchant and find out what she wanted you to do for her."

Jack frowned. "Why would I do that?"

She gestured around the room. "You run some sort of business, don't you?"

"Construction," he said. "I own a construction firm."

Abbie nodded, glad for this one clue. "Obviously Mrs. Merchant wants you to build something for her. The rest will be easy. All you have to do is go to her and ask—"

"Impossible."

"No, it's not," Abbie said. "It's very simple, really. Just—"

"No," Jack told her, his scowl deepening. "I will not go to Mrs. Merchant and discuss any sort of business with her."

Abbie gulped, her future crumbling before her eyes. Losing her job. Returning to Pennsylvania—somehow—defeated.

Maybe it was for the best, she thought suddenly. Maybe it was just as well that she lost her job and went home. No more dealing with Mrs. Merchant. No more fearing Mrs. Walsh's prying eyes. No more taxing attempts to behave as a lady. It would be so easy, so refreshing to leave, return to what was familiar. Wouldn't it?

No. In a flash Abbie couldn't reconcile herself to the possibility. She didn't want to go home. In her heart, she knew she wanted to stay here, to make her new life work.

And to do that, she needed Jack Graham's cooperation. Which didn't seem forthcoming.

"But, Mr. Graham, if you'd just let me explain."

"I don't need any explanation," he said.

"You don't understand."

"I understand perfectly," he told her. "And nothing—absolutely nothing—is going to change my mind."

Chapter Three

"You're being awfully pigheaded about this," Abbie told him.

Jack raised an eyebrow. "Is name-calling also in your top five faults?"

"I was merely making an observation," Abbie said. "Now, really, Mr. Graham, I don't understand why you won't do this, why you won't talk to Mrs. Merchant. It can only benefit you and your business."

"How long have you known Mrs. Merchant?" Jack asked.

"A month."

"And what is your opinion of her?"

Abbie shifted uncomfortably, sensing the direction of this line of questions. She raised her chin. "Mrs. Merchant is a perfectly delightful woman. A joy to work for. An inspiration to the community."

Jack uttered a bitter laugh. "Lying certainly isn't in your top five. You're not good at it."

"Mr. Graham, you must—"

"No."

"Well, why not?" she demanded.

"Because Mrs. Merchant is a contrary old woman who makes everyone's life miserable. Believe me, I know. I've done work for her before. No matter that I build to her specifications, she doesn't like it. She changes her mind. She wants it done over. She wants something different.''

''Oh, well, really, Mr. Graham, you must expect a few problems in the business world,'' Abbie said. ''Please, if you'd just go talk to her, maybe—''

''I already know what she wants,'' Jack said. ''She wants something done to the house in time for her annual Christmas ball. Something that requires an impossible timetable.''

Abbie pushed her chin up. ''You're blaming me for this, aren't you?''

''You?'' He frowned at her.

''Yes, me. Because of the way I acted when you arrived in my office. I offended you and now you're trying to teach me some sort of lesson, aren't you?''

Jack waved away her words with his big hands. ''This has nothing to do with you, Miss Doyle.''

''It has everything to do with me,'' she insisted.

''I would have refused Mrs. Merchant's offer no matter what.''

Abbie fumed a moment and pushed aside her anger in order to think more clearly. She had to find some way to get Jack Graham to accept this job.

''Since it's a rush job I'm sure you could charge her double, maybe triple,'' Abbie said. ''Mrs. Merchant has tons of money. She wouldn't care.''

Jack shook his head. ''Money wouldn't matter.''

''She would refer your business to all her friends.''

''I have plenty of work already.''

''I'll see to it you're invited to her Christmas ball,'' Abbie offered.

''I'm already invited.''

She was about out of reasonable incentives. Of course, she could always pour out her heart to him, explain that she'd lose her job. She could always beg.

Abbie couldn't bring herself to do it. She tried another tack.

"It's Christmas," she said. "There must be something you want. Some Christmas wish?"

"Nothing. There's nothing I want."

Jack turned away sharply, scrubbing his hand over his face. Had his deceased wife come to his mind? Abbie wondered. Was she his Christmas wish? The one thing he wanted but couldn't have?

"If you'll just think this over a bit," Abbie said softly, "things will look differently to you. Maybe sleep on it?"

He sucked in a big breath, his chest expanding, his gaze raking her from head to toe, and Abbie got the idea he wasn't thinking of his dead wife at all right now.

Jack shook his head. "Nothing is going to change my mind."

So, that was that. She'd seen that determined look on the faces of men before. Her father, her brothers, uncles, cousins. For a brief moment, Abbie reconsidered the option of begging or whining. Maybe working up a few tears—ladylike tears, of course.

But something wouldn't allow her to do that.

"Very well," Abbie said, drawing in a deep breath. "Although I think you're being perfectly unreasonable, Mr. Graham, not to mention shortsighted and, as I said earlier, pigheaded, I will explain your wishes to Mrs. Merchant."

Head high, Abbie crossed the office, determined to go out with her dignity intact. A lady was known by her walk, Mrs. Merchant had said. Feet moderately turned out, equal steps, firm and light. This was exactly how she'd look descending the front steps of Mrs. Merchant's house after she'd been fired, Abbie thought, Mrs. Walsh peering after her, the rest of the staff pressing their faces to the windows.

And how would she look arriving at her parents' farm? If she could get there.

Abbie paused at the doorway and looked back at Jack, tempted to try one more time. But he brushed past her.

''I'll see you out, Miss Doyle,'' he said.

From the front porch, Abbie saw the three little girls playing in the side yard. A blanket was spread out in the shade with dolls and tiny teacups scattered about. Beth, Jack's sister, left the giggling girls.

''Finished already?'' she asked. ''I was about to bring in some refreshment.''

Abbie nodded toward the blanket. ''Looks like we just missed the tea party.''

''We had a guest,'' Beth said. ''Sweet old Mrs. Hatcher from down the street. The girls love her. In fact, when she asked what they wanted for Christmas—''

''Did Natalie answer?'' Jack asked quickly. ''Did she tell her what she wanted?''

''Not a peep,'' Beth shook her head sorrowfully, then turned to Abbie. ''Natalie won't tell anyone what she wants for Christmas.''

''She doesn't think she has to tell anyone,'' Jack explained. ''Being five years old, she believes that whatever she wishes for will simply appear under the tree on Christmas morning.''

''How adorable,'' Abbie said, looking past him to the little girls playing in the yard.

''Yes, except that I don't want her to be disappointed on Christmas morning,'' Jack said.

Beth laughed softly. ''Jack makes such a fuss over Natalie. He's spoiled her—and my girls—terribly.''

Abbie smiled, thinking of Jack, all frowns and scowls in his office just now. She'd never imagined this side of him.

''Nothing wrong with little girls being spoiled,'' Jack insisted. He gazed across the yard at the children and shook his head. ''I'd give anything to know what she wants for Christmas.''

Abbie whirled toward him. *''Anything?''*

"Of course," he said. "I want her to have—"

Jack stopped suddenly seeing the look on Abbie's face. "Just a minute, now. I didn't mean I'd be willing to—"

"But Natalie *is* your only child?" Abbie said. "Your precious little girl. The light of your life."

"Yes, but—"

"You don't want her disappointed on Christmas morning," Abbie told him. "You said so yourself."

"And I suppose you think you can get Natalie to tell you want she wants for Christmas, Miss Doyle?" he challenged.

"Of course."

Jack shook his head. "You don't know my daughter."

"And you don't know me," Abbie told him. "I have nine brothers and sisters, only two of them older than me. Young cousins, nieces and nephews. I deal with little children all the time."

"Really?" Beth asked hopefully. "Do you think you could get Natalie to tell you?"

"I'm certain of it."

Jack shook his head. "I don't know...."

"Children are entirely different around people other than their parents," Beth said. "It just might work."

Jack scowled at Abbie. "And in return you'll want...?"

"You already know what I want," Abbie said.

Jack turned away mumbling a curse. He looked at Abbie, then at Natalie, and at Abbie again. "You're sure? You'll guarantee you can find out."

"Absolutely," Abbie swore.

Jack stewed for a moment, obviously unhappy, reluctant to agree.

"You really have nothing to lose," Abbie said. "Aside from having to deal with Mrs. Merchant, you'll make lots of money, enhance your company's reputation, plus have a wonderful Christmas for your daughter."

Jack grumbled a few more minutes. "All right, I'll do it."

He pointed his finger at Abbie. ''But you'd better find out what Natalie wants. I won't have my daughter disappointed.''

A big lump rose in Abbie's throat. She gulped it down, hoping Jack didn't notice. ''Don't worry. I'll handle everything.''

Mrs. Merchant prattled on and on but Jack hardly listened. It didn't matter. Only about a quarter of what she said actually applied to the work she wanted him to do.

Standing in her dining room, nodding, Jack's thoughts drifted down the hallway. To Abbie's office. To the work Abbie should be doing right now. To Abbie.

He didn't know why she kept creeping into his mind. He didn't like her. Too many faults—she'd said so herself. Outspoken, pushy—

Pretty, self-assured, warm lips, full bosom—

''So, you understand, Mr. Graham?''

''Hm?'' Jack's attention snapped back to Mrs. Merchant. ''Yes, of course. I understand completely.''

''Good. Now, also I'd like...''

The woman's words faded, as his mind filled with images of Abbie again. She was more than pretty, he decided. Beautiful. Yes, definitely beautiful. But not untouchable, as so many attractive women were. Abbie was honest and open. Full of spirit.

Spirit, certainly. Lots of it. Other images of Abbie played out in Jack's mind, visions of where that spirit might lead, how it might be enjoyed, shared.

A hot rush surged through Jack, pooling and blooming, startling him with its ferocity, its unexpectedness. Especially standing here in Mrs. Merchant's parlor, listening to her incessant chatter. Jack was quite sure no man had been aroused in Mrs. Merchant's presence in decades.

It hadn't been quite that long for him. But long enough.

Since before his wife fell ill. And afterward, the weeks had turned into months, then somehow became years.

Jack rubbed his eyes and shook his head, pushed the thoughts aside, and focused on Mrs. Merchant. She droned on, unaware, while he forced himself to concentrate on her words. When she finally got to the end of her spiel, he just stared at her.

"You want me to do *what?*"

Jack was in the house. Abbie heard his voice drifting through the hall, winding its way to her little office. He was the reason for the giggling she'd heard from the young maids. Without a doubt the cause of Mrs. Walsh's scowls.

Abbie looked over her cluttered desk, dreading the work still left this afternoon, never more anxious to leave it undone than at this moment. Jack hadn't been happy about accepting this job from Mrs. Merchant. Maybe Abbie should go to him now, be there to soften things between him and Mrs. Merchant? Intervene on his behalf? Smell him?

Such unladylike thoughts, Abbie admonished herself. Although Mrs. Merchant had never specifically said a lady shouldn't sniff a man—regardless of how good he smelled—surely it wasn't the thing to do.

Jack had already seen her at her worst, witnessed her most unladylike behavior—on several occasions. He was a man of consequence in the city, a man of wealth, good breeding and a fine family. A gentleman. He expected women to conduct themselves as ladies.

Abbie's heart sank, wishing she'd presented herself in a better light, especially at his home this morning. His fine, upper-class home.

But she had accomplished what she'd gone there for. Too bad *that* wasn't a valued asset in a lady.

Her gaze roamed to the half-dozen volumes of etiquette instruction Mrs. Walsh had given her. Looking down her long, disapproving nose, she'd given the books to Abbie, pointing out her many shortcomings in doing so. She'd sneered equally when she'd caught Abbie reading them.

But it was all there, all the information Abbie needed to conduct herself as a lady. She'd read from a few of them, when she'd had time. She knew what to do.

Abbie's mood brightened. Yes, she knew what to do, and she would prove it when she walked in on the conference Jack was having with Mrs. Merchant at this very moment.

Abbie dropped into her desk chair, remembering. A lady should enter a room wearing a smile, the book had instructed, with a light step and a graceful bearing.

A smile touched her lips as she imagined the stunned look on Jack's face, so surprised at her ladylike behavior.

The envisioned scene glowed in Abbie's head as she turned, knocking a stack of papers to the floor.

"Damn..."

Abbie retrieved the papers, then leaned back in her chair trying to pin the last one with the toe of her shoe and drag it from under the desk. She slouched lower, stretching out her leg, but without any luck. Pushing aside her chair, Abbie hiked her skirt up to her thighs, dropped to her hands and knees, and crawled under the desk.

The pleasant little fantasy played in her mind again. Her walking into the room, how Jack would be positively enthralled as she sank gently into a chair in true ladylike fashion, maintaining an upright position, her feet tucked out of sight, never crossed. How, as the etiquette book dictated, she would avoid stooping or sitting stiffly. Of course, the book had also stated she should carry a handkerchief—an elegant handkerchief, actually. Abbie paused, stretching her arm farther under the desk until her cheek touched the carpet. She didn't have an elegant handkerchief. All hers were fully functional, as any reasonable person's would be.

No matter, she decided, inching forward on her knees. If

she managed everything else, surely Jack wouldn't be appalled that she carried no handkerchief.

Abbie thought hard, remembering what else was required of a lady when entering a room. No breathing heavily, or coming in sweaty or shivery. The main thing was to look composed, dignified and—

"Miss Doyle?"

Abbie jerked upward and banged her head on the underside of the desk.

"Damn it!" She scooted back holding her head, and looked up to see Jack towering over her.

"Damn..." The word slipped out again, bringing a rush of color to her cheeks. Abbie sat frozen, staring at Jack, who by the look on his face, was equally horrified.

Gracious, she'd just been mentally practicing how to present herself as a lady, and here he'd found her crouched on the floor with her behind in the air and her dress hiked up.

She was humiliated. Positively mortified. Why couldn't that bump on the head have killed her?

Apparently Jack was thinking the same thing—or worse, she concluded, by the way he looked at her. His cheeks were flushed and his breathing had quickened.

Holding her head with one hand and pointing with the other, Abbie said, "I was trying to get that piece of paper."

Jack sank to his knees beside her, as if his legs wouldn't hold him up any longer. He took an unnecessarily long time to peer under the desk, then stretched out his long arm and retrieved the paper.

"There," he said, sitting up on his knees, presenting it to her. He looked at her head rather than her face. "You're sure you're all right?"

No, she wasn't all right at all. Her heart pounded and her palms had begun to sweat. Jack was close—only inches from her. He was warm, too, and he smelled delightful. Like no other person she'd smelled in her whole life.

And in that instant, she didn't care if it was ladylike or not to enjoy Jack's scent.

The smile faded from his face as he drew closer. He gazed at her hair, her cheeks, her eyes, then at her lips.

A little moan rattled in Jack's throat. He leaned forward and kissed her.

Chapter Four

Maybe she should write her own etiquette book describing the manner in which a lady might recover her dignity after being discovered sprawled on the floor in an unladylike position.

Abbie considered the possibility as she climbed the steps to Jack Graham's home, the evening breeze tugging at her hat.

Certainly the etiquette books she'd read hadn't addressed that particular situation. The solution Abbie had stumbled upon this afternoon in her office was quite unexpected. And positively delightful.

Have the gentleman take you in his arms and kiss you, she decided her book should read. Wrap his arms around you, hold you close, breath warmly against your face, then kiss you until you see little stars.

Abbie smiled at the memory of the warmth that had spread through her this afternoon, the heat that had wafted from Jack. Her stomach tingled. She touched her fingers to her lips, sure she could still taste him.

She glanced around, wondering if the neighbors or carriages passing by could see her, recognize some sign in her, know what she'd done.

That fear, of course, led to the next logical thought: what would happen next?

Abbie contemplated the problem as she knocked on the front door. She recalled no passage in her etiquette books that addressed how a lady should respond after being kissed by a gentleman. This afternoon, on the floor with Jack in her office, she'd simply kissed him back. That seemed to inspire him. He'd kissed her even harder.

But what about now? Tonight? Beth had invited her to supper. Should the incident be ignored? Discussed?

Repeated?

''Goodness...'' Abbie clanged the knocker again. Where were her thoughts these days? Not to mention her good sense.

After a moment she heard giggling and running feet. The door opened and three little blond heads appeared. Three bright faces smiled up at her.

''Good evening, girls,'' Abbie said.

''Good evening, ma'am,'' they chimed in unison.

''Come inside, please, ma'am,'' the oldest said, swinging the door open wider.

''You're Lizzy, aren't you? And you're Natalie, and your name is Janie,'' Abbie said, stepping inside and pointing to each girl in turn.

They smiled, pleased that Abbie had remembered their names.

''We're sisters,'' Natalie said, and all three girls linked arms.

As good as sisters, Abbie thought. Though Lizzy and Janie, the oldest and youngest, were actual sisters, Natalie probably didn't know the difference. None of them did. And if they did, it wouldn't have mattered.

''Abbie, you're here,'' Beth called, coming down the hallway. She smiled and waved her inside. ''Oh, you look lovely. What a wonderful dress.''

Abbie touched the skirt of the soft pink dress she'd selected for the evening. Because of Mrs. Merchant's standards, she couldn't allow her social secretary representing her wearing Pennsylvania farm clothes, so soon after her arrival she'd sent Abbie to her dressmaker for a new, more appropriate wardrobe. The cost of which she deducted from Abbie's pay every week.

Still, Abbie was glad she had the dress. She felt more comfortable wearing it. More acceptable. More like the lady she strived to become.

Beth walked with her into the front parlor, a large room filled with satin-covered settees, crystal lamps, gilded mirrors and marble sculptures. It might have been an intimidating room were it not decorated in soft blues that made it so inviting.

Charles, Beth's tall, good-looking husband, greeted her as introductions were made, then the three of them sat and made polite conversation, while Abbie wondered where Jack was.

"Actually, I find the weather here needs a bit of getting used to," Abbie said.

"But that's what brings so many people here," Charles said.

"I miss the snow," Abbie said, "especially this time of year."

"You'll get used to it," he predicted.

A servant appeared in the doorway a moment later advising Beth that supper was served.

"I thought Jack would be here by now," Beth said, glancing at the mantel clock. She nodded to Abbie as an apology. "I'm sure he'll be along soon. He's probably working late."

The dining room was done in mahogany with a carved table and chairs, a buffet and cabinets displaying fine china. The table, set for four since the children had eaten earlier, held a snowy linen cloth, crystal and a delicate blue-patterned china. Abbie cringed at the extensive silverware fanning out from her place, mentally rehearsing which fork should be used when.

But just as she'd gained her composure, Jack strode through the door, yanking at his tie.

"I don't know what the hell I was thinking. That old battle-ax is going to make me— Oh."

Jack froze, tie yanked down, collar open, gaze on Abbie. She gulped, staring at the dark, crinkly hair that curled out of his shirt collar, desperate at that moment to know what the rest of his chest looked like.

"You're just in time," Beth said, breaking the awkward silence, glancing between the two of them.

"I—I didn't know we were having…company," Jack said, pulling his gaze from Abbie and closing up his collar.

"Sit down," Beth told her brother. "Let's get started."

Supper passed pleasantly enough, given that Abbie worried about which utensil to use, saw Charles and Beth exchanging surreptitious glances, and imagined Jack was staring at her. Regardless of the undercurrents, it was nice to have supper with a real family. Abbie had missed that since leaving Pennsylvania.

Afterward, Abbie went upstairs with Beth to see the girls.

"Natalie still isn't talking," Beth said. "I'm getting worried. Christmas is only a few weeks away."

Abbie pushed the thought aside, trying to forget how much work still waited for her at Mrs. Merchant's house. The Christmas greeting cards, the shopping, the decorations, the staff dinner, the ball. The wealthy worked incredibly hard at having a good time, it seemed.

At the end of the hallway was the nursery where the girls played quietly, dressed in white nightgowns. The big room faced the east to catch the morning sun, but outside it was dark now. Shelves lined the room holding two dollhouses, a theater, surprise boxes, bright-colored rubber balls, blocks, books. A baby carriage and fur-covered rabbit on rockers were in one corner. In another, a little table was set with a miniature tea service. A tin stove stood beside it.

Abbie smiled. A child's wonderland. Jack—somebody—spoiled these girls, all right.

"I'll give you a few minutes alone with them," Beth whispered and went back down the hall.

Lizzy and Janie saw her first and rushed over. Natalie continued playing with her doll.

"Come see what we've got," Lizzy said.

Abbie took a seat in a child-size chair while the girls showed her their toys and talked excitedly. She couldn't stop smiling. The girls had so much to say, so much to share.

"So tell me," Abbie said after a few minutes, "is anyone here expecting a visit from Santa Claus?"

That set off another round of chatter. By this time Natalie had joined in. Abbie eased her onto her lap.

"What do you girls want for Christmas?" Abbie asked.

Janie hopped up and down. "A doll carriage of my very own."

"And I want a doll," Lizzy said. "A beautiful doll in a sailor suit."

"Paints," Janie said. "And drums."

"Drums?" Abbie smiled. "How fun."

"And I want lots of new bows for my hair," Lizzy said.

"What about you, Natalie?" Abbie asked.

The little girl looked up from the book she was holding, raised up and cupped her hand against Abbie's ear.

Abbie smiled. So easy. Just ask the child. Had no one thought of that already?

She turned her head snuggling closer to Natalie's little hand. "Yes?"

"It's a secret," Natalie whispered.

Hm. Well, maybe not so easy after all. She smiled down at Natalie.

"You can tell me," Abbie whispered. "I know lots of secrets."

Natalie pressed her lips together in a smile wise beyond her years. "I already told Santa Claus."

Obviously, a little more finesse was needed. But Abbie didn't want to belabor the point tonight, and moved on.

"Well, then," Abbie said. "How about if I read you a story?"

"Papa usually reads to us," Natalie said.

"Uncle Jack reads good," Janie agreed. "He makes funny voices."

Lizzy selected a book from the shelf and sat on the floor in front of Abbie, combing her doll's hair. Janie squirmed onto Abbie's lap along with Natalie. Abbie gave the two girls a little hug and began reading about the adventures of a frog and mouse on a country farm.

When she finished, Natalie nodded thoughtfully. "You do good voices, too, Miss Abbie."

Those few words of praise meant more to Abbie than anything Mrs. Merchant had ever said to her.

"Thank you," Abbie said. "Now, what's next?"

"Bedtime," Lizzy said, and pointed across the room. "Uncle Jack will tuck us in."

Abbie turned and saw Jack leaning on the door casing, arms folded, feet crossed. His tie was pulled down and his collar open. She didn't know how long he'd been there, watching and listening.

"All right, girls, off we go." Jack scooped Janie and Natalie into his arms, and herded Lizzy into the adjoining room furnished with three beds and three chests where everything was decorated with lace and pink bows.

After two rounds of kisses and hugs, Jack turned out the light and closed the door. He took Abbie's elbow and guided her down the hall and onto the balcony that overlooked the backyard. Fresh floral scents wafted up to them on the breeze. A few lights from the neighbors' houses twinkled in the darkness.

''Did Natalie tell you what she wanted?'' Jack asked.

He was at her elbow as they stood at the railing.

''No, not yet,'' Abbie said. ''But I didn't expect she would right away. She needs a little more time.''

''Time is something I don't have a lot of,'' Jack pointed out.

''I'm sure I can find out Natalie's Christmas wish in plenty of time,'' Abbie said.

A few moments of silence passed between them. They gazed off into the dim light of the yard, both content with the silence.

After a moment Jack asked, ''What's your Christmas wish?''

''Mine? Oh, that's easy—the wish that is, not the granting of it,'' Abbie said. ''I want it to snow.''

Jack considered it for a moment, then nodded. ''That seems reasonable.''

''I thought so, too,'' Abbie said, a little surprised that Jack hadn't made fun of her as everyone else had when she mentioned the weather here. ''But, I understand, it's not likely to happen.''

''Hasn't snowed here in years.'' Jack smiled. ''We're due.''

He eased closer and it suddenly occurred to him how beautiful Abbie looked in the faint light. Fresh. New. Inviting. His heart beat a little faster, looking at her, thinking that anything in the world was possible—and he hadn't thought that in so long.

He touched his finger to her chin and tipped her face up to his. Her eyes sank closed as he settled his mouth over hers.

Jack's knees trembled at the sheer joy of their exchange. He'd kissed her twice today and already she felt familiar to him. Warm and comforting. He slid his arm around her waist and pulled her close, her breasts brushing his chest. She curled her arms around his neck.

For a moment he was lost in their kiss. How good it felt,

the touch of a woman, the softness, the scent. His body responded, making demands, urging him on, causing him to consider possibilities he'd not even thought of in two years.

Jack pulled his lips from Abbie's mouth. She smiled up at him and swayed. He pulled her tighter against him.

They gazed into each other's eyes. Before when he'd kissed her, like this afternoon in her office, he'd just left without a word, not knowing what to say. Even now he couldn't come up with one rational thought, or put three words together to form a sentence.

To his relief, Abbie spoke.

''And what is your Christmas wish?'' she asked softly.

''My wish?'' The question startled him. He thought a moment, then shrugged. ''I don't have a Christmas wish.''

Her eyebrows drew together. ''You have everything you want? Everything?''

Jack loosened his grip on her, still gazing at Abbie but not really seeing her.

It was true, he realized. He didn't wish for anything. He didn't want his life to change—certainly didn't want it turned upside down.

And Abbie Doyle would do just that. Jack backed away from her, putting distance between them. She'd already done it.

He'd kissed her three times in one day. *One day.* He hadn't kissed a woman in two years. Hadn't so much as held a female hand. Hadn't wanted to. Hadn't been interested.

But now, suddenly, it was all he could think of. Abbie. She consumed him. His attraction to her had been immediate. It was unexpected. Overwhelming.

Frightening.

Jack turned away.

''I think you should go.'' He glanced back to see the confusion, the hurt in her face. ''This isn't right. I should never have allowed you here, gotten involved....''

That seemed to make her mad. Her shoulders stiffened and her cheeks flushed—not the lovely flush as when he'd kissed her. Now, it was from anger.

She wanted to demand that he tell her why, Jack judged by her expression. But Abbie pressed her lips together, forbidding herself to speak. She turned sharply and walked away.

Jack hurried down the hallway, away from the lingering scent of Abbie, went into his own bedroom and closed the door. He switched on the lamp on the bureau and walked to the little shelf in the far corner of the room.

He'd put up this shelf himself, the day he and Natalie had moved in. He'd arranged the items on it himself; the staff knew never to touch them.

In the faint light, Jack's gaze settled on the picture in the ornate frame. Rose. His lovely wife, Rose. The photograph had been taken after she'd given birth to Natalie, before she'd fallen ill. The photographer had captured her beauty, but not the things Jack loved about her. Her laugh. The gentle touch of her hand that made all his problems vanish. The sound of her voice welcoming him home at the end of the day.

Beside the photograph was the locket she'd always worn. She'd pointed it out to him in a shop window one day. Jack had gone back and bought it, and surprised her with it. She was never without it. Until the day they buried her.

Jack leaned closer and sniffed the perfume atomizer on the shelf. That scent. Rose's scent. He closed his eyes and swayed against the wall.

He turned away then and scrubbed his palms over his face. Abbie came into his mind. She'd asked what his Christmas wish was.

There was nothing he wished for. Not any longer.

Chapter Five

Back home on her parents' farm when she'd slept this poorly, felt this bad and looked so terrible, she could slip up to her room and take a quick nap. Here in Mrs. Merchant's house, time away from her desk just caused more work to pile up.

Abbie shifted in her chair, squinting her eyes and dutifully writing the personal message Mrs. Merchant had dictated in the next Christmas greeting card. The stack seemed to be growing, rather than shrinking.

But, surely, she simply wasn't thinking clearly. In fact, she wasn't thinking at all. Except about last night.

Abbie still didn't know what had gone wrong, what had caused Jack to make his sudden announcement on the balcony, though it had occupied her thoughts since leaving his house, running most of the way home, then tossing and turning all night.

She'd conducted herself as lady, seated at Beth's fine table, and had picked up the wrong fork only once. At least, only once that she knew of. Still, she'd covered it well, she thought. Conversation at supper had been light and she'd been careful to follow Beth's lead. Both Beth and Charles had seemed interested in her, not put off because she grew up on a farm, though Jack had definitely raised an eyebrow when she'd said it.

Was that it? she wondered. Was Jack put off by her humble background? She wasn't as much of a lady as she wanted to be.

Maybe it was their kiss, Abbie thought. Their kiss on the balcony. None of the etiquette books she'd read so far specifically stated how a lady should kiss a gentleman.

Jack had kissed her three times, but on two of those occasions he'd done it and run. She hadn't really *let* him kiss her but once.

Then he'd told her he didn't want to see her anymore.

Abbie sealed the greeting card and tossed it in the outgoing stack. Maybe it was just as well. Thoughts of Jack occupied too much of her time. After knowing the man for only one day she couldn't stop thinking about him.

Her mother had said it was that way when she fell in love with her father. One look and that was it—they knew they were meant for each other. Her mother had long lamented the fact that Abbie wasn't married, never much interested in the men who courted her. Abbie's father had only laughed, predicting that when Abbie fell, she'd fall hard.

Abbie pressed her hand to her stomach, feeling the tingling there. Her heart beat a little faster. She felt wobbly all over. Jack caused these things, and the ache in her heart and that hollow feeling inside.

Determinedly, she picked up the next greeting card. Jack was too much of a distraction. He'd said he didn't want them to see each other again and surely that was for the best. Right now Abbie should be concentrating on Christmas preparations. And keeping her job. In fact, it suited her all right if she never saw him again.

That decision made, Jack walked into her office.

His work crew had arrived this morning, a half-dozen men

carrying ladders and toolboxes, causing a commotion in the house. But Abbie didn't know that Jack was here, too.

She might not have recognized him. Instead of the dapper suit she'd seen him in before, now he wore boots, denim trousers with black suspenders, and a coarse blue shirt. Yesterday, the businessman. Today, the rugged workman.

Her heart tumbled again, her legs refusing to let her rise.

"You're going to help me," he announced, scowling, marching to her desk.

"Help you?" Annoyed, Abbie gestured to the stack of greeting cards. "I'm terribly busy."

"Then you can just un-busy yourself," he told her, gazing down at her. "Mrs. Merchant's got me renovating her dining room. Tearing out the windows—"

"The dining room?" Abbie came to her feet. "But I need the dining room the night of the Christmas ball. Can you get it finished in time?"

"I can—or I *could have,*" he told her. "Except that Mrs. Merchant informed me that I have to pick out the fabric, the wallpaper and the color of the paint. She claims she's too busy, doesn't have the time."

"You?" Abbie's eyes widened. "What do you know about doing that sort of thing?"

"Nothing! That's why *you're* going to help me!"

Abbie shook her head, backing away. Picking out colors and fabrics that would please Mrs. Merchant? Impossible. What better way to get fired?

"I'm not helping you," Abbie said, waving him away, dismissing the whole issue.

"Yes, you are. You got me into this mess. You're going to get me out of it."

"I have my own problems," Abbie told him. "I'm up to my eyeballs in things that absolutely have to be done, and not nearly enough time to do them."

Jack scanned the cluttered credenza and cabinet on the other side of the room, then scowled at her desk.

''If you'd get yourself organized you wouldn't be having these problems,'' he told her. ''Look at this mess. No wonder you can't get anything done.''

''Out!'' Abbie thrust her finger toward the door. ''Get out!''

God help him, he wanted to kiss her again. She was full of fire and energy, full of life. Jack's body hummed with the desire to have her right here, right now.

And that made him angry. Angry at Abbie, angry at Mrs. Merchant and her damned renovations, angry that he didn't know what his daughter wanted for Christmas...angry at himself.

Jack turned and left.

With the excuse that she had to post the greeting cards, Abbie escaped Mrs. Merchant's house into the hot afternoon. She dispensed with the cards quickly, then headed for Jack's house.

He wasn't home. She was sure of that. She'd heard him yelling at his crew—words she hadn't heard since leaving her brothers behind in Pennsylvania. His mood, it seemed, was no better than hers.

Beth answered the door smiling and invited her inside.

''Is it all right?'' Abbie asked lingering on the doorstep. ''Jack didn't...say anything?''

''Such as?''

''Nothing. Never mind,'' Abbie said, walking inside. The foyer was cool, a welcome relief from the heat. She was glad to know that Jack hadn't said anything to his sister about what happened last night. Though it was the hardest thing she'd ever done, Abbie had kept herself under control long enough to say a proper goodbye to her host and hostess; a lady could do no less.

"I have a little time off," Abbie said, "and I thought I'd spend it with Natalie and the girls, if you don't mind."

"Oh, please do," Beth said, leading the way through the house. "I've tried everything I can think of to get Natalie to tell me what she wants for Christmas. I may have to resort to bribery, but I'm not sure even that will work."

Abbie spent the next hour upstairs in the nursery, the windows thrown open wide, a breeze wafting in, playing with dolls, serving imaginary tea, building towers of blocks and reading stories. Just because Jack had decided the two of them shouldn't see each other anymore didn't mean Abbie could ignore her promise. She'd given her word, something she didn't take lightly.

Besides, spending time with the girls reminded her of her family back home. And home had never seemed so far away.

Surely Jack Graham had to be the most patient man in the world, Abbie thought.

For four days now she'd watched him with his work crew. The dining room they were renovating was down the hallway from her office so she could see the men working.

Construction had never seemed so fascinating to Abbie before. She'd seen her father, her uncle, her brothers working on the farm, constructing barns, fences and all sorts of outbuildings. But she'd never noticed the play of muscles through their shirts, as she did with Jack. Never appreciated the bulge of their forearms exposed by rolled-up sleeves. Never been enthralled by sweat.

Jack worked alongside his men, hammering, sawing. One of his crew was hardly more than a boy and Abbie had seen Jack frequently explain things to him.

Jack had seen her watching him. Occasionally he'd turned around and caught her looking at him. Abbie had moved away quickly, of course, pretending interest in something on her desk. And just as often, she'd looked up, thinking he'd been watching her.

Neither of them said anything. Never once had Jack come back to her office. Abbie hadn't ventured into the dining room.

This morning, she couldn't have gotten there if she'd wanted to—and she did want to. Once she'd heard Jack yelling at his crew. He'd thrown something and cursed. Not exactly in the best of moods.

Abbie was faring no better, but might have been if she had anyone she could yell at. Instead, everyone yelled at her. Technically, no one actually raised their voice. But they may as well have. It hurt just as much.

The morning was only half over and already the cook had come in demanding the menus for the Christmas ball and the staff supper, wanted to know which china service would be used at which event, and exactly how many guests were expected. Mrs. Walsh had insisted on knowing which rooms would be used, where to direct the cleaning staff, how many extra servants to arrange for. Mrs. Merchant's maid had wanted to know what color scheme Abbie had decided on so she could coordinate the mistress's ensembles appropriately. Duncan, who somehow had wound up in charge of the Christmas decorations, needed the date Abbie wanted everything displayed.

Relentlessly, one after the other, they had come into her office asking for things, making demands, reminding her that she was behind in everything, that she wasn't doing her job properly.

But Abbie had no answers for any of them. What she did have was a headache, a sour stomach and tears that threatened to fall.

She had to escape. Just for a few minutes. Surely, she'd choke to death in the confines of her little office.

Hurrying through the halls, Abbie turned the corner and ran smack into Jack. They both froze, staring at each other.

Seeing him, Abbie was nearly overcome with the desire to melt into his arms. To feel them, so strong and powerful, wrapped around her. She wanted to lay her head against that wide chest of his, soak up some strength, be comforted. Everything felt so wrong this morning, and being with Jack felt so right.

''I have to talk to you,'' he said, not kindly at all, as she'd have liked.

What had come over this man? she wondered. So grumpy and grouchy all of a sudden. She'd seen him so patient with his work crew. She'd seen him cuddle three little girls in his arms, snuggle them into their beds, kiss their little foreheads and tuck the covers around them. He read them stories, did funny voices.

A lump rose in Abbie's throat. It appeared that it was she who provoked his foul mood.

Jack strode off down the hallway, leaving Abbie to follow. In her office he turned to her.

''I have wallpaper, paint and fabric samples,'' he said. ''You need to pick out something.''

Abbie's shoulders sagged at the prospect. She couldn't take on another task. Especially this one.

''I can't help you, Jack,'' she said softly. ''I told you that already.''

''You have to.''

''Ask someone else. Ask your sister. She has excellent taste. She'll help you.''

''Hell, yes, I could ask anybody but that won't solve my problem,'' he said. ''I need to know what Mrs. Merchant wants. She said she'd told you.''

''Me?'' Abbie's head snapped up. ''She didn't tell me.''

''She wrote it down, careful instructions, explaining everything,'' Jack said.

Abbie shook her head. ''She's always saying she's done that, but half the time it's just not true.''

''How can you be sure?'' Jack demanded, waving his hand over her desk. ''Her instructions could be here and you'd never know it.''

Abbie looked at the disorganized stacks on her desk and her shoulders slumped.

''This job is important,'' Jack told her. ''In order for that dining room to get finished in time for Christmas I have to know which wallpaper to get, what fabrics, what color paint. Otherwise, Mrs. Merchant is going to have a house full of guests eating Christmas supper in a half-finished dining room.''

''Oh, well, thank you!'' Abbie shouted, tears popping into her eyes. ''I had no idea what was going on! Thank you so much for that very useful piece of information!''

Abbie yanked the handkerchief from her pocket and swiped at the tears rolling down her cheeks. She hated to cry. Hated it. But she just couldn't take any more. Not now, not after what the staff had put her through this morning, and certainly not from Jack.

''I know I'm disorganized,'' Abbie said, sniffling. ''I've been told that since I arrived here. But I don't know how to fix it, how to get organized. I'm supposed to plan a Christmas ball. I don't know how to do that, either. I don't know what the placement of the refreshment room and cloak room should be. Or the number of servants required to attend the guests. Or the desired lighting, the floor preparation, the correct number of musicians. I don't know the number and variety of quadrilles, waltzes and other dances.''

Abbie gulped, not bothering to wipe away her tears now, and straightened her shoulders.

''I don't know,'' she said, clenching her handkerchief in her fist, ''but I'm going to find out. I'm going to figure it out and I'm going to put on the best damn Christmas ball this city has ever seen!''

Abbie ran from the room. She didn't look back. She wanted to, but was afraid she'd see an empty look on Jack's face. See, once more, that he didn't care.

Abbie couldn't bear the thought. Because she was falling in love with him.

Chapter Six

A gray dress for a gray day, Abbie decided, as she closed the button on her sleeve and descended the staircase from her bedroom. Although, actually, the sun was shining, a cloud of gloom hung over Abbie. When the dressmaker had suggested this gray fabric Abbie hadn't much wanted it. But today it seemed appropriate. It matched her mood. She'd never felt so alone in her life.

Heading down the hallway toward her office, Abbie drew in a deep breath, telling herself that today would be better. She would dig in, figure things out and get the Christmas ball arranged.

If nothing else, she'd ask for help. She hadn't done it before because such a request would announce the fact that she didn't know what she was doing. Didn't belong here. Didn't deserve the job. And, consequently, wouldn't have it much longer.

Abbie stepped into her office and stopped short. Jack sat at her desk, his head down reading from a paper in his hand.

And her desk was nearly empty. The clutter and chaos she dug through every day was—gone. Nothing remained, except a couple of folders neatly stacked on the corner. Abbie scanned the room. The credenza and cabinets were bare, too. Where had everything gone?

Jack's head came up and he surged from the chair. They just looked at each other for a long moment, then Jack cleared his voice and waved her over.

"I made new folders and put them down here," he said and pulled open the drawer on the bottom right. "In each—"

"You did this?" Abbie asked.

"I came in early," he said, and dared to glance at her. "You just needed a system in place to organize everything. Whoever had this job before you had a real mess here. No wonder you couldn't figure anything out."

"But—you did this?" She gazed up at him. "For me?"

Jack had never wanted to put his arm around another person so badly in his whole life. Her eyes were puffy and he could see she'd been crying. She looked as if she may tear up again. And he couldn't really blame her. Mrs. Merchant wasn't the most pleasant person to work for. Abbie had a great deal put on her here at the Christmas season.

And Jack had only added to her problems.

He could have hugged her so easily. Wrapped her against his chest and comforted her. Kissed away her tears. His heart, his soul, screamed that he do just that. But the rest of him refused. Jack went on with his explanation.

He described the filing system he'd devised for her, told her where he'd put everything, how to use her calendar to follow up on things that needed attention.

From the desktop, Jack picked up the paper he'd been reading. "Here's a list of what you need for a Christmas ball. Musicians, dances, menu, china, everything. All the things you mentioned yesterday. And it's in order, too, so you'll know when to do what."

Abbie took the paper from his hand and stared at it. Here it was, all right. Everything she needed. All the answers to her many questions.

"Where did you get this?" she asked softly.

"I had Beth write it down."

"But she's so busy. She has her own house to run and the children to care for. I wouldn't dream of bothering her with my problem."

"She's my sister. I can impose whenever I want," Jack said, then regretted his words. Abbie had no family not within thousands of miles, anyway.

"If I've left anything out," Jack said, "just let me know. Beth's more than happy to help."

"But—"

"I have my own work to do now," Jack said, and hurried from the room.

Abbie just stared after him, clutching the paper.

The shady spot his crew had found at the side of the house for their noon meal was a good one, under a fruitless mulberry, in the cool grass. One of the wives had sent a worn, tattered quilt that the men spread out and ate on, or caught a quick nap.

Jack leaned against the trunk of the tree, crunching the last of his apple. He could have gone home to eat, it wasn't that far. But he didn't have the time to spare. Getting this job done on schedule would be tough.

He didn't usually work alongside his crew, just supervised. But for this job, because of Mrs. Merchant's impossible timetable, he'd joined in the work himself.

And it was just as well, Jack thought. His body had been strung tight. His mind was fogged, too. He hardly slept at night. Nothing seemed clear-cut anymore. He didn't know why, what had caused it.

Jack tossed the apple core into his lunch pail and shut the lid. He knew, really. He just didn't want to think about it.

"Let's head back in," Jack said, getting to his feet.

The men rose, closed up their lunch pails, but stopped suddenly, piling up against each other. Jack peered around them and saw Abbie coming around the corner of the house.

Warmth and need surged through Jack. He hadn't seen Abbie since yesterday morning when he'd organized her desk—and been tempted to take her in his arms again. Something about his woman always caused this reaction in him. Damn, why did this always have to happen?

Abbie looked pretty today. Bright and fresh in a pale-green dress, with no sign of yesterday's tears. The men in his crew noticed, too.

"You boys go on in," Jack said.

The men hesitated a moment, eyeing Abbie then Jack, and finally moved on.

Abbie stopped and didn't come any closer, listing to one side, weighed down by a satchel.

"Garden Star or Fern Delight," she said. "I've narrowed it down to two."

"Two what?"

"Wallpaper patterns. I talked to Mrs. Merchant last night and found out, vaguely, what she wants. I thought we could go over them and decide. Together...if you have no objections."

Jack eyed her warily, his mind forming a response, his body insisting on quite another.

"Well, all right," he finally said.

Abbie sheltered her eyes from the sun. "Is out here all right with you? I'm inside so much these days, I miss the outdoors."

He took the heavy satchel from her and they sat on the quilt together. Abbie pulled out the sample book and spread it between them.

They looked at wallpaper samples, paint chips and fabric swatches, but Jack didn't seem to notice them as much as the way little strands of Abbie's hair curled around her face when the wind blew. Or how she frowned when she concentrated. Or pursed her lips. How small her fingers were. How he wanted to lay her back on the quilt and—

"Well, I guess we're finished," Abbie said, closing the satchel.

Jack raked his fingers through his hair and shifted uncomfortably on the quilt.

"I'll run them over to the decorator this afternoon, for a final opinion," Abbie said. "If I lose my job over this, that old fussbudget Mr. Simpson will be just as responsible as me."

Jack frowned, her words finally penetrating his wandering thoughts. "Lose your job? Mrs. Merchant would fire you over this?"

"She's already threatened it several times," Abbie said. "I wasn't exactly her first choice for social secretary. The previous secretary left unexpectedly, I understand. Probably ran screaming from the house tearing at her hair."

"What would you do," Jack asked, "if you got fired?"

Abbie shrugged. "Go home, I suppose."

"Back to Pennsylvania?" Jack frowned. "Don't you like it here?"

She thought for a moment. "Actually, I do like it here. The city is beautiful, of course, but I grew up on a farm. I miss the open spaces. I didn't think I would, but I do."

Jack didn't say anything and Abbie thought she knew why. He'd grown up in the city, probably lived here most of his life. Jack didn't understand the joy of open spaces, the solitude, the closeness with the land. Raising crops, toiling in the soil was a far cry from running a construction company.

"I guess a lot of things are different out here," Jack said. "Very different from where you came from."

Abbie nodded. "Yes, but different is all right with me. That's why I came here, because it's different. I still miss my home, though."

But at the moment, her family, the farm and Pennsylvania seemed of little consequence. What mattered to Abbie was here in the bright sunshine, under the shade tree, with Jack.

Emotions rose in Abbie's chest, making it a little difficult to breathe. Jack was a handsome man. He worked hard, had built himself a good business, he adored his daughter. She felt a connection with him.

But Jack didn't feel the same about her.

Abbie got to her feet. "I'll let you know what the decorator says about our choices. If he approves, I guess you're all set to finish up the dining room."

"How about the ball? How is it going?"

Abbie smiled. A big, wide, smile. Jack rose and smiled back, unable not to.

"Wonderful," Abbie said. "Beth's list was like a treasure chest of gold. I went through the files you organized and found information from last year's ball. I'm happy to report that everything is under control. I'm predicting this year's ball will be nothing short of spectacular. It's going to knock Mrs. Merchant on her great big fanny."

Jack threw back his head and laughed. Abbie slapped her hand across her mouth.

"Oops. Sorry," she said. "I shouldn't have said that. Not very ladylike."

Abbie picked up the satchel but hesitated a moment, chancing one last glance at Jack, reluctant to let go of this time with him. But he didn't say anything, didn't call her back, made no move to walk along with her.

Abbie headed for the house alone.

Abbie could hardly believe the weeks had passed so fast. At the doorway to the dining room, she stood off to one side not wanting to bother the workmen as they closed up their toolboxes and carried their equipment away. The room was bigger now, expanded to take over the pantry next door, and the windows had been enlarged. Faint smells of paint and wallpaper glue hung in the air.

Abbie stepped aside as the last man left the room carrying

a ladder. He nodded pleasantly to Abbie and disappeared down the hallway. The work was done. They wouldn't be back.

And neither would Jack.

Abbie stepped into the room and took her time walking around the walnut table that seated twenty, the buffet, the sideboard, studying the improvements. Jack and his crew had worked nonstop on the renovations, allowing no one inside while the work was in progress. He'd said it was for safety reasons, but Abbie knew it was because he didn't want Mrs. Merchant to see it and change her mind again.

''Like it?''

Abbie whirled and saw Jack standing in the doorway. Her heart ached, seeing him, wanting to go to him, but knowing she couldn't.

''Yes,'' she said, and managed a smile. ''It's beautiful.''

Jack walked into the room, studying it with a critical eye. ''Let's just hope Mrs. Merchant agrees.''

''She has to like it,'' Abbie said. ''The ball is tonight.''

Jack circled the table but stopped a few feet from Abbie. ''Is everything set?''

''All done,'' Abbie said. ''After tonight my holiday duties come to an end. Since tomorrow is Christmas Eve, Mrs. Merchant has given me that day off, as well as Christmas Day.''

''She must be pleased with your work.''

''Either that or she wants to get rid of me,'' Abbie said.

Jack looked around the room one more time, then nodded with satisfaction. ''Seems we both got everything accomplished in time for the holiday.''

A little knot gnawed in Abbie's stomach. She'd gotten everything done for Mrs. Merchant. She'd sent out her own greeting cards, gotten gifts for friends and family and sent them to Pennsylvania. The only thing she hadn't accomplished was the most important thing of all.

She hadn't figured out what Jack's daughter wanted for Christmas.

Chapter Seven

"You're an angel for doing this," Beth said to Abbie as she walked into the house.

"I'm not ready to give up yet," Abbie declared, stepping aside as Beth pushed the door closed. "I know I can get Natalie to tell me her Christmas wish. I just know I can."

Beth bit her lower lip. "Are you sure you can spare the time? The ball is tonight."

"If I don't find out this afternoon, when will I? Tomorrow is Christmas Eve." Abbie glanced at the staircase that led upstairs. "I don't want Lizzy and Janie to feel left out."

Beth waved away her concern. "Don't worry. Charles's mother is coming over. The girls adore her."

"Well, then," Abbie said. "I guess we're all set."

"I'll get Natalie and—"

The front door opened and Jack strode inside. He stopped suddenly seeing Abbie in the hallway. For an instant she thought he looked pleased at seeing her, then dismissed the notion. Surely she'd imagined it.

Jack frowned and turned to his sister. "What's going on?"

"Abbie is taking Natalie for the afternoon," Beth said.

Jack's frown deepened and he cut his eyes to Abbie. "Taking her? Where?"

"Gracious, Jack, she's not selling your daughter to the Gypsies, they're going into town," Beth said. "Abbie is taking her to look at toys in the shop windows. To find out what she wants for Christmas."

"You're—what?"

"I told you I'd find out," Abbie said. "I've tried everything else I know but Natalie won't tell me. This is my last chance."

"Last chance?" Jack waved his hand encompassing the house. "You've been here before?"

Beth rolled her eyes. "Of course she has. Abbie has been here almost every day visiting the girls. You'd have known that if you hadn't been working so much these past weeks."

"But—" Jack just stared at Abbie.

"It's all right if Abbie takes Natalie to town, isn't it?" Beth asked.

He straightened his shoulders and looked back and forth between the two of them. "I don't like the idea of a woman and child on the streets alone. Especially this time of year. There's all sorts of pickpockets and con men out there."

"Oh, honestly, Jack," Beth said. "Abbie is more than capable of taking care of Natalie."

"It's not safe," Jack insisted.

"Then go with them," Beth told him.

Jack and Abbie's gazes collided, and they both looked away just as quickly.

"Go with them," Beth said again. "Natalie is looking forward to the afternoon. She's talked about it all day. And if we don't figure out what her Christmas wish is she'll be terribly disappointed come Christmas morning."

"Well…" Jack shuffled his feet and looked at Abbie.

What was he thinking? she wondered. Searching for a reasonable excuse not to go? Trying to think of a graceful way to get out of being in her company?

"All right," Jack said after a moment. "We'll all go."

Twenty minutes later Jack was in the foyer again dressed

in a dark-blue suit with a white shirt and gray necktie, while Natalie bounced on her toes beside him wearing a green drop-waist dress, nearly losing her matching hat.

"Papa, Papa, Miss Abbie says there's a store in town with *this many* toys in it," Natalie exclaimed and spread her arms wide.

Jack couldn't resist smiling. "Is that so?"

"And we're having lunch at a special place," Natalie said, "where they cut the food in funny shapes."

Jack's smile curdled as he looked at Beth and Abbie. "Not that what-its-name tearoom."

"It will be fun," Beth insisted as she shooed them out the door.

Abbie had intended to walk into town. It wasn't that far. But instead she found Jack's carriage waiting out front. The three of them climbed in and Natalie sat on Jack's lap, chattering the whole way.

Seated across from them, Abbie tried to read Jack's face. She couldn't tell anything from his expressions, except that he was enchanted by his daughter. He listened to every word she said and patiently answered her dozens of questions. He didn't even make a face when she mentioned eating at the tearoom.

They left the carriage on Third Street. Natalie grabbed Abbie's hand and pulled her toward the closest shop window, her eyes bright and her mouth open.

"Look, Miss Abbie!" Natalie caught Jack's hand and pulled him along, too. "Look, Papa! Look at all the toys!"

Jack and Abbie smiled at each other over Natalie's head. Behind the glass was a display of toys. Dolls in bonnets and frilly dresses, baby carriages, horns and drums, dollhouses with tiny furniture. There were clowns and jumping jacks painted bright colors, stick toys and animals mounted on wooden wheels, a merry-go-round and a mechanical train.

Jack knelt down beside Natalie. "Do you see something you like?"

''Oh, yes, Papa,'' she declared. ''I like *everything!*''

Jack rose and exchanged a rueful smile with Abbie.

''Why don't we go inside for a closer look?'' she suggested.

With Christmas Eve only a day away the store was crowded with shoppers. They walked through the aisles together, Natalie fascinated with everything she saw. Abbie noted everything she looked at, waiting for her to name that one special toy she couldn't live without. Near the back of the store she found Jack playing with a mechanical circus train complete with miniature wild animals.

''Look at this, Natalie,'' he called. He picked her up and showed her the train. ''Now here's a great toy.''

Natalie turned up her little nose. ''No thank you, Papa,'' she said and wriggled out of his arms.

Jack looked at Abbie. ''This would be a fun toy to have.''

Abbie grinned. ''Perhaps Santa Claus will bring you one. Have you been a good boy this year?''

He looked at Abbie for a long moment. ''I'm beginning to think I was a lot better than I should have been.''

Abbie flushed. Her heart thundered in her chest. But Jack walked away.

Her initial response was to go after him, demand to know what he'd meant by his comment. But Abbie stopped herself. A lady would never do such a thing.

But would a lady allow herself to be so affected by what he'd said? Abbie doubted it.

After a few minutes they moved on to the next store. The streets and shop windows of the city were decorated with tinsel, candles and figures of Santa Claus. Shoppers hurried along, arms laden with packages.

Abbie's steps lightened as they walked along, Natalie between them. Here amid the hustle and bustle of shoppers, for the first time if felt like Christmas—even though it was hot.

They went from shop to shop looking at Christmas toys

until Jack and Abbie were exhausted. Jack didn't complain when they went to the Wildwood Tearoom.

They settled around a tiny table. The room was quiet, except for low voices and the clink of silver on china. Jack, one of the few men there, looked too big for the room, too masculine for the delicate table settings and ruffled curtains.

"What was your favorite toy you saw today?" Abbie asked.

"The fort," Jack said. He looked up and grinned, realizing she'd asked the question of Natalie. "It had soldiers and horses and everything."

"I liked *all* the toys," Natalie declared.

"But there must have something you liked the most," Abbie said. "Something special? Something you've always wanted?"

"Well..." Natalie's little brow wrinkled.

"Yes?" Abbie exchanged a hopeful glance with Jack and they both leaned closer.

"What do you want, honey?" Jack asked.

"Well..." Natalie pressed her lips together, then said, "I liked everything."

Jack and Abbie shrugged helplessly and turned back to their tea.

Afterward, they visited several more shops. But despite all their prodding and suggesting, Natalie pointed out nothing special she wanted for Christmas. Exhausted, they called it quits. In the carriage, Natalie fell asleep on Jack's lap. When they arrived home the house was quiet, except for laughter drifting in from the backyard. Jack carried Natalie up to her bedroom. Abbie waited in the nursery doorway as Jack took off Natalie's hat and little shoes, and folded the spread over her. He stood by her for a moment, then bent and kissed her forehead.

Natalie's eyes fluttered open. "I love you, Papa."

He stroked her hair and kissed her again. "I love you, too, sweetie."

She snuggled into the pillow and drifted off again.

Jack didn't leave her bedside right away, just stood there watching her sleep. Abbie wanted to do the same, to slip into the room, kiss Natalie's little forehead and stand next to Jack.

This was as close to having a family as she'd come since leaving Pennsylvania. Beth felt like a sister to her. The girls, like her own nieces…or daughters.

On the street and in the tearoom today Abbie had caught a few looks from other shoppers and diners. For all they knew, Jack and she were parents taking their daughter for an outing. Abbie's heart ached with the want.

After a moment, Jack walked into the hallway where Abbie waited.

''I owe you an apology,'' Abbie said.

''For not finding out Natalie's Christmas wish?'' Jack waved away her concern. ''You gave it your best effort.''

''Still, Natalie will be disappointed on Christmas morning.''

''Come Christmas morning she probably won't even remember what she wanted, what with all the gifts and the family and the excitement,'' Jack said. ''No need for you to give it another thought.''

Abbie nodded. She understood completely. Jack was right. He had his family and friends, and no reason to think Christmas morning wouldn't be wonderful for his daughter. How could it not be in their fine home, among all the people who loved him?

Abbie had shared in his family for a little while, but that was over now. No need to visit Natalie and the other girls again. No reason to expect another invitation from Beth.

These were well-to-do people, after all, and Abbie was Mrs. Merchant's hired help.

She wanted to ask Jack if he was coming to the ball tonight, but didn't. Maybe he'd had enough of Mrs. Merchant's house, of Mrs. Merchant…of her.

"I'd better go," Abbie said. "I still have a few things to do before this evening."

"Yes, I guess you do," Jack said.

Abbie backed away. When Jack said nothing further, she left.

Jack turned back to the nursery and slid his hands in his trouser pockets, thinking while he watched his daughter sleep. Footsteps sounded on the stairs. He turned quickly. A little wave of disappointment washed over him when he saw that it was his sister.

"Where's Abbie?" Beth asked. "Didn't you invite her to stay for supper?"

"No," Jack said, looking down at his feet. "I—I didn't want her here."

"Didn't want her here? For heaven's sake, Jack, why not? She's a wonderful girl. The children adore her. She's a terrific—" Beth stopped suddenly. "Oh."

Jack glanced up at her and shrugged helplessly.

"Oh, Jack," Beth touched his cheek. "It's Rose, isn't it."

He managed a small nod.

"You have feelings for Abbie, don't you?" she asked.

Jack turned his head away.

"I know how much you loved Rose. We all loved her. But she was so sick for so long. She's in a better place now," Beth said. "Rose loved you, Jack. She wouldn't have wanted you not to find happiness again."

Jack slumped against the door casing. "But everything was going along just fine. Now I can't stop thinking about her."

"About Rose?"

"Abbie."

Beth grinned. "Abbie?"

He nodded miserably. "Yes, Abbie."

"Maybe that means it's time, Jack," Beth said softly. "Time to move on."

Beth stretched up and kissed his cheek, then left him alone in the hallway.

Jack pulled on the back of his neck, paced, yanked on his chin. His chest hurt.

Abbie floated into his mind, and this time he didn't try to push her away. Along with that visage came the thought that maybe Beth was right. Maybe it was time.

Jack drew in a deep breath and went to his bedroom and the little shelf in the corner. He stood there for a long moment looking at Rose's photograph, her locket, her perfume atomizer.

Minutes dragged while he studied each of those keepsakes. It was time.

From the bottom drawer of his bureau Jack took the lockbox he kept valuables in, found the key under his handkerchiefs and opened the box. He took a final whiff of the perfume and placed the bottle inside. Slowly he rubbed the locket against his cheek, then placed a kiss on the photograph and tucked them into the box as well. They would be safe here, always close, if he ever wanted to see them again.

He closed the lid, turned the key in the lock and put the box away.

Jack drew a deep breath, a cleansing breath, then let it out slowly.

And then he knew. He had a Christmas wish after all.

When Abbie arrived at Mrs. Merchant's house, instead of going inside by the front door, she used the servants' staircase at the side of the house and climbed to the third floor. In the dimly lit hallway she found a package outside her bedroom and carried it into her tiny room. Turning up the gaslight, Abbie's spirits lifted. It was from her family in Pennsylvania.

She tore open the wrapping and found Christmas gifts inside. Homemade jam, a knitted scarf and mittens, cookies and letters from everyone in the family.

Sitting on the bed, Abbie read every word they'd written, over and over. Who was sick, who was well, who'd become engaged, how the weather was…how they all missed her.

Tears came to Abbie's eyes. Her family missed her. She missed them, too. Here it was Christmas and she was all alone. Everyone she loved was on the other side of the country—well, almost everyone she loved.

She envisioned Christmas morning at Jack's house. Crowds of family, gifts ripped open by anxious children, the Christmas feast, laughing and caroling around the piano. Not so different from her family's Christmas in Pennsylvania.

Abbie pushed away her tears. Maybe she'd been fighting an uphill battle all along.

Maybe she should go home.

Chapter Eight

Tonight, come hell or high water, she was going to be a lady. This, after all, would be her last chance.

That thought firmly in mind, Abbie watched the crowd of men and women moving past her through Mrs. Merchant's house. The ball was just getting underway and women arrived wearing beautiful gowns, the likes of which Abbie had never seen, sparkling among the gentlemen's black tuxedos.

By comparison, her own gown was a modest creation. Garnet silk taffeta with oversize cap sleeves and a neckline more daring than she'd ever worn in her life. Still, Abbie felt like a princess, even if she was working tonight, even if in a few days she'd be on her way back to Pennsylvania.

Faint strains of music drifted from the ballroom on the second floor. Mrs. Merchant was there, receiving her guests. It was Abbie's duty to greet them after they dropped off their wraps. There was a cloakroom for the ladies with two maids to assist them, and a hat room for the gentlemen. Abbie smiled, wished everyone a good evening as they passed in front of her, and directed them up the stairs.

So far, everything flowed smoothly, thanks to the list Beth had provided her. The ballroom had been properly prepared. Upstairs in the refreshment room tables laden with tea, lemonade, iced sherbets, cakes and bonbons awaited guests. Supper would be served later in the dining room Jack had renovated.

Jack. He'd been in her thoughts since she'd left him at his house this afternoon. Abbie watched the door each time Duncan opened it, wondering if it would be Jack walking into the house, hoping it wouldn't be him, then afraid it would.

Her heart skipped a beat a moment later when Jack came into the house. How handsome he looked in his white tie and tails. Beth and Charles were with him. Abbie raised on her tiptoes, lost them in the crowd for a few minutes, then caught sight of them again.

They looked so comfortable here. Beth's gown was exquisite. Both Charles and Jack wore tuxedos as comfortably as any casual suit of clothes. And why shouldn't they? This was a normal, everyday occurrence in their lives.

Abbie watched as Beth and Jack put their heads together, talking. Deciding whether to acknowledge her presence here at the ball tonight, perhaps? Here, among their prominent friends? After a moment, Charles urged them forward. Beth smiled warmly and took Abbie's hand.

''You look lovely,'' Beth declared, eyeing Abbie's gown. ''And the house is beautiful. I've never seen it so festive.''

''I was able to look back at notes on how the house was decorated in previous years,'' Abbie said, ''after Jack organized my office for me.''

Beth glanced up at her brother and smiled. ''Jack did that?''

Charles caught her arm. ''Let's go,'' he said, and hustled her up the stairs.

Jack stayed and he and Abbie stared at each other for a moment while guests drifted past them. Finally, he let out the breath he was holding.

''You look…stunning tonight,'' he said.

Abbie's mind went completely blank, unable to recall how

a lady should respond. A simple thank-you? A return compliment? A coy dip of the lashes?

Jack didn't seem to know what to say next, either. They stared at each other for a long moment, Jack's eyebrows drawing closer together all the while.

Finally he leaned toward her. "Can we speak privately?"

Jack led the way down the hall to Abbie's office in the back of the house, away from the guests, away from the laughter, the chatter, the music. He eased the door closed.

Abbie knew what was coming. Her heart thudded in her chest and she turned away from him, wishing she didn't have to hear him explain about the differences in their backgrounds, their positions in society. Wishing she didn't have to tell him she was returning to Pennsylvania.

"Abbie—"

She spun around. "Don't say anything. I know what you want."

How could she know? He didn't even know himself. All he knew for certain was that she looked absolutely beautiful tonight, that he wanted to be alone with her, he wanted to hold her and kiss her, try to explain how everything in his life had been turned on its head and it was all her fault.

Jack came closer, his gaze roaming her from head to toe and finally settling on her face. Her lips, actually. He could almost taste them.

"Abbie, I—" He slid his arms around her and kissed her.

Abbie moaned as he pulled her against him. His mouth covered her tenderly, gently, sapping the strength from her legs. She caught his arms, held him tight, lost in the warmth of their closeness, in the feel of him, the taste of him. She could have stayed that way forever, but the Pennsylvania farm girl in her wouldn't allow it.

Pulling away, she glared up at him. "How dare you kiss me?"

Jack blinked. ''I know. I'm sorry. I wanted to talk to you, but you're just so pretty, I couldn't—''

''Help yourself?'' Abbie raised her chin. ''I'll have you know, Mr. Jack Graham, that I'm no good-time girl.''

''What are you talking about?''

Abbie stepped out of their embrace. ''I realize I'm not a lady—not the real kind. The kind you're used to. But I won't be treated like some harlot you kiss in the back room, who isn't good enough to take to the front parlor.''

''Is *that* what you think?'' Jack stared at her, his jaw set. ''That I'm *ashamed* of you?''

Abbie retreated a step. ''Well, yes. I understand how things work in the world. You're a man of means, with a certain position in the city. And I'm...not.''

Jack glared at her for another moment, then grabbed her hand. ''Come with me.''

He whisked her out of the study, down the hallway, then slowed and tucked her hand around his arm as they climbed the staircase to the second floor. At the entrance to the ballroom Jack paused and nodded toward the guests crowding the room.

''This,'' he whispered, ''is how ashamed I am of you.''

Jack nodded to Mrs. Merchant, then took Abbie in his arms and swung her onto the dance floor.

Abbie wasn't sure her legs would hold her up, as they waltzed among the other couples. To have Jack so close, his strong arms around her, to share this special moment with him, was one thing. But he was dancing with her in front of everyone. The whole of the city's society.

Among the other dancers and the guests crowding the edge of the floor, Abbie saw heads turn their way. Someone pointed. Mrs. Merchant's mouth sagged open, and Beth smiled proudly.

Surely Jack knew this would happen. He'd known, and he'd danced with her anyway. Abbie's heart soared.

"You'll have to forgive me," Jack said, "I'm a little rusty. I haven't danced with anyone in two years."

Abbie smiled up at him. "You're doing fine."

"No, I'm not," Jack said. "I'm doing everything wrong and have been since the first minute I laid eyes on you, Abbie."

The music stopped then, but Jack held on to her.

"You should know, Jack, that I've decided to go home, back to Pennsylvania," Abbie said. "It's for the best. I've thought it over and it's the only reasonable thing to do."

Jack studied her for a long, tense moment, so lost in thought that for a moment Abbie wondered if he'd even heard her.

"I want you to come with me tomorrow," Jack said at last.

"Go with you? Go where? Tomorrow is Christmas Eve," Abbie said.

"There's something I want to show you," Jack said. "I'll pick you up in the morning. Be ready."

Christmas Eve morning arrived gray and overcast. Jack gave off little warmth when Abbie met him in the foyer, under Mrs. Walsh's disapproving eye. The house was quiet, Mrs. Merchant and most of the servants exhausted from last night's ball.

Abbie was tired, too, having slept little, wondering where Jack could possibly be taking her this morning. He helped her on with her dark-blue cape, assisted her into the buggy waiting outside, and drove away without a word.

In the time she'd lived in San Bernardino, Abbie had never ventured out of the city. That's where Jack took her. They traveled east until the businesses disappeared, and kept going past an occasional house, a farm, then finally past the little town of Messina, with its bank, grocery and feed store, and train depot. The road rose into the foothills, into the heart of the orange groves, then wound higher and finally opened into a clearing in the rolling hills. Jack pulled the horses to a stop.

Abbie sat mesmerized, looking over the miles of valley

spread out below them. Acres and acres of dark-green orange groves, scattered houses and towering mountains in the distance.

''Oh, Jack, it's beautiful here,'' Abbie said. ''It looks a lot like home. My home in Pennsylvania. Whoever owns this land must be so proud.''

''Me.'' He looked at her for the first time. ''I own the land. It's mine.''

''You? You're kidding! I had you pegged for a city boy.''

Jack climbed out of the buggy, then lifted Abbie down. He pointed toward the foothills, thick with orange trees.

''No one thought the trees would grow here at this elevation, but I took a chance on this tract of land a few years ago,'' he said. ''I planted the eucalyptus trees for a windbreak, then dug irrigation ditches from City Creek. Three hundred acres, all producing quite well.''

''But, Jack, what about your construction business?'' Abbie asked.

''I started that after my wife died. I thought it better to live in town. Better for Natalie,'' Jack said. ''Come on. This is what I want to show you.''

Jack took Abbie's hand and led her through the high grass to the crest of the next rise. There stood the gray, weathered skeletal frame of a house.

Abbie's heart squeezed in her chest. ''Oh, Jack, this was to be your house with—''

''Rose.'' He gazed at the frame for a long time. ''We'd just started to build when she became ill.''

Abbie looked at the house, the shattered dream. ''Why did you bring me out here?''

''Because I was mad at you.''

''Mad at me?'' Abbie asked, surprised, because he didn't sound mad at all.

''Mad at you for coming into my life, making me feel things again, making me question what I was doing.'' Jack gave her a half grin. ''I was pretty happy until you came along and ruined everything.''

''I guess I have a new fault in my top five.''

Jack's smile faded. He looked at the ground for a moment, then lifted his gaze to Abbie's face. ''I tried hard not to care about you. To pretend you didn't exist, that I didn't like you, or...want you. But I can't pretend anymore.''

''Wait, Jack, don't say anything else,'' Abbie said. ''I meant it last night when I said I wasn't from your same background. I'll never be a grand lady. At one time I thought that was what I wanted, but after being here, seeing that life-style, I know it's just not right for me. Oh, I can live that way on occasion, but it can't be the sum total of everything I do.''

''If all I wanted was a wife who knew which fork to use, I could have been married a long time ago. But that's not what I want, Abbie.'' He slid his hand into hers. ''Would you like to see the house?''

They walked through the field together and climbed onto the wood flooring. A chilly breeze blew as Jack took her from room to room, talking, explaining, sharing his dream with her, until Abbie saw the house not as the decaying frame, but as a live, vibrant home.

''I'm going to build this house,'' Jack said. ''I'm going to move out here, make it my home.''

''Will Natalie be happy here?'' she asked.

''She'll miss her cousins, and Beth, of course,'' Jack said. ''But it's only an hour's ride by carriage, less than that by train.''

Abbie nodded thoughtfully. ''So this is your Christmas wish?''

Jack considered it for a moment. ''No, this isn't my Christmas wish.''

''Then what is?''

He struggled to contain the smile that spread across his face. ''Can't tell you. It wouldn't be proper.''

Abbie's cheeks flushed as an energy leaped from Jack to her. And nothing about it was proper, or ladylike.

"We'd better go," Jack said.

On the ride back to San Bernardino, Jack and Abbie talked nonstop. About nothing, about everything. When they reached the city he didn't take her to Mrs. Merchant's house as she'd expected. Instead, he took her home.

"Why are we here?" Abbie asked, as he pulled the buggy to a stop in front of the house. "It's Christmas Eve. Surely you've got family coming over. Beth must have a thousand things to do. She won't appreciate a guest, Jack."

He laughed. "That's what you think."

When they walked inside, all three of the little girls ran to meet them. Jack knelt to hug Natalie, and Lizzy and Janie took Abbie's hand.

"We're making things for the tree, Papa," Natalie exclaimed.

"Come, see what we've done," Lizzy said, pulling Abbie along the hallway.

Beth came out of the parlor and then broke into a big smile when she saw Abbie. She gave her a hug.

"I'm so glad you're here. Let me get your cloak," Beth said and helped her off with the wrap. "Jack, come help me with this."

Beth hooked her brother's arm and pulled him down the hall. Abbie wasn't close enough to hear the words but apparently Jack was doing a lot of explaining at Beth's insistence. At last, she nodded her approval, gave him a kiss on the cheek and shooed him away.

Jack grinned as he approached Abbie. "She's really glad you're here."

"Come on, Papa, look at the tree," Natalie exclaimed.

In the parlor, Charles stood beside a bare evergreen, surrounded by boxes of decorations.

"Abbie, glad you're here," he said, and waved his arms

around looking lost. "You did such a good job on Mrs. Merchant's tree, we can use your help here."

They spent the afternoon in the parlor, a fire crackling in the hearth to ward off the chilly day, decorating the tree. Beth asked Abbie to help her in the kitchen.

"We keep things simple on Christmas Eve," Beth said. "Just us and the girls. Tomorrow everyone will be here. You'll get to meet the rest of the family then."

"I don't know," Abbie said. "Jack didn't say anything about me coming back tomorrow."

"Oh, you're coming back," Beth assured her, as she placed cups of hot coca and cakes and cookies on trays and they carried them to the parlor.

Beth, Abbie and Lizzy threaded popcorn and berries on strings and everyone draped them on the tree along with silver tinsel garlands. From the storage boxes they took glass ornaments shaped like cones, acorns, stars and balloons and put them on the tree, along with colorful glass balls. Candy canes and wax angels with spun glass wings were tied onto the boughs, and silver candles were set securely in tin holders. Charles added the finishing touch, a silver star at the very top.

"Can we light the candles now, Papa?" Janie begged. "Please?"

The other girls chimed in, too.

"After supper," Charles said.

They ate in the dining room, all of them, even the girls. Afterward, Beth and Charles went ahead into the parlor and lit the candles on the tree. When Abbie and Jack brought the girls in, their faces lit up with sheer delight. They sang carols while Beth played the piano, then it was off to bed for the children.

"We're going to bed early," Lizzy declared, "so Santa Claus will come sooner."

"Good idea," Abbie agreed and gave them each a hug

"Sweet dreams," Jack said as he hugged the girls. He turned to Abbie. "I guess I'd better get you home."

The air was cold and damp, but Jack decided to walk Abbie home rather than take the buggy. Streetlamps burned, windows glowed golden outlining evergreen wreaths, and a group of carolers strolled behind them.

Abbie settled her hand into the crook of Jack's elbow.

"Thank you for such a wonderful Christmas Eve," she said. "It more than made up for not being with my family this year. I'll think of tonight every Christmas, Jack, of you and your family."

"What are you talking about?"

"I told you I was going back home. Remember?"

When they reached Mrs. Merchant's house, Jack guided her to the servant's staircase and climbed up to the third story with her. At the doorway, Abbie stopped.

"Thank you again, Jack. Good night."

"I'm not leaving yet," he said and caught her elbow and pulled her inside with him. "Which room is yours?"

The dim hallway was silent, but wouldn't be for long if anyone discovered Abbie had a gentleman caller upstairs with her.

"Jack, please," she whispered, "you can't—"

"Which room?" he repeated.

Worried they'd be seen, Abbie unlocked her bedroom door and they went inside.

"Jack, I insist—"

"You're not going back to Pennsylvania." Jack closed the door with a thud.

"And I'm not leaving here tonight until I've convinced you to stay."

Chapter Nine

"So, what will it take?" Jack asked, leaning against the door, tossing his hat aside. "What do I have to do to convince you to stay?"

"Jack, stop this," Abbie said, as she turned up the flame in the gaslight. "You don't understand."

"Then explain it to me."

"It's not that simple," she insisted, and yanked off her gloves.

Jack shrugged, and crossed his arms over his chest. "I have plenty of time."

Abbie uttered an exasperated groan and rubbed her upper arms beneath her cape. The room was cold. Flames from the gaslight danced, throwing feeble shadows in the corners.

"You shouldn't be in here," she said.

"You can't expect me to leave until this is settled," Jack said. "You turned my whole life upside down, Abbie. Do you really think I'm going to let you go back to Pennsylvania?"

"Do I have a reason to stay?"

Jack came closer and settled his hands on her shoulders. "I don't want you to go, Abbie. I want you to stay here with me."

Abbie shook her head. ''We've only known each other for a short while.''

''How long does it take to know you're in love?''

She'd known weeks ago. And even though she'd tried to ignore those feelings, they wouldn't go away.

Abbie's insides trembled. ''Are you saying you're in love with me?''

''I'm saying I'm in love with you,'' Jack whispered. He touched his fingers to her cheek and stroked her soft skin. ''I'll shout it out the window, if you'd like. I'll run from room to room through this entire house and tell everyone.''

''Oh, Jack, don't you dare!''

He chuckled and pulled her against him, then brushed his lips against her ear. ''I'll show you how much I love you...one day.''

Jack settled his mouth over hers and tightened her against his chest. A little moan rattled in his throat as he deepened their kiss and Abbie looped her arms around his shoulders.

She pulled away. ''This room—this room has gotten awfully warm, suddenly.''

He popped open the fastener on her cape and tossed it into a chair, then slipped out of his own coat and sent it flying. She unpinned her hat and he sailed it across the room.

Abbie came against him again, their bodies melding together. Their kiss became more frantic. She raised on her toes and twisted her fingers through his hair. Jack slid his hand upward to capture her breast.

She gasped and he moaned, but neither stopped. Quickly, he plucked open the buttons at the front of her dress and slid his fingers inside. His knees nearly gave out at the sheer delight of the feel of her. He yanked off his tie and pulled the buttons loose on his shirt. Abbie splayed her palms against his chest, marveling at his tight muscles beneath his white undershirt.

Panting, Jack kissed a line down her cheek, her jaw, her

throat, to the opening in her dress. He pulled back the fabric and tasted her breast.

Abbie collapsed against him. He held her with one arm and swayed against the wall, barely holding them both upright.

"Abbie..." he whispered, panting. "We—we shouldn't be doing this."

She gazed up at him, her eyes glazed with passion. "We shouldn't?"

"No, we shouldn't"

"You're sure?" she asked.

"Pretty sure."

Abbie stroked his strong jaw. "Is this your Christmas wish?"

"No," Jack said, then smiled. "Although it would be nice."

"It feels nice to me," Abbie whispered.

Jack's heart pounded in his chest. "You're sure?"

She nodded. "I'm sure."

"Oh, Abbie..." Jack sealed his mouth over hers, working their lips together in a deep kiss, as he fumbled with the rest of the buttons and fasteners on her dress. He peeled away the layers of petticoats, stockings, shoes, bustle, corset, camisole and bloomers, then struggled out of his own clothes while she pulled the pins from her hair.

He held her shoulders and gazed at her in the dim light.

"You're beautiful," he said softly, then carried her to bed.

Abbie sank into the feather mattress as Jack stretched out beside her and pulled the cover over them. Her heart pounded with the certainty that what she was doing was right. It was what she wanted. Because she wanted Jack.

He kissed her gently as his hands acquainted himself with her every curve. Abbie moaned as he suckled her breasts, each of them. She touched him, surprised by the power he possessed and the gentleness of his touch.

Their kisses, their caresses grew more frantic until Jack

slipped between her thighs and pressed himself against her. Abbie clung to his neck as he filled her, and lost her breath as he began to move inside her.

Deep within her grew an urgency too great to resist. She moved with him, against him, unable—unwilling—to stop herself. Higher and stronger she climbed. Jack moved faster, driving her onward until she was overwhelmed. Great waves of pleasure broke through her, pushing her hips harder against him.

Jack drove himself into her, moaning her name, with no thought of holding back, making it last. He poured himself into her again and again, until he was spent.

''Well, gracious,'' Abbie whispered breathlessly.

Jack collapsed beside her, using the last of his strength to pull her against his chest. ''I hope that means you liked it.''

''Very much,'' she said, stroking his damp bangs off his forehead. ''And the time before that, and the time before that. I didn't realize it could be done so many times in one night.''

Jack dropped his arm across her, his chest heaving. ''I've mustered extra effort for you.''

''Are you going for some sort of record?''

He grinned. ''I've already passed my personal best. But that was set quite some time ago.''

Abbie snuggled against him. ''I love you, Jack.''

''I love you, Abbie.''

Faint sunlight filtered through the window when Abbie woke next. Morning—Christmas morning, she realized. And realized, too, that Jack was beside her, locking her in his arms, his leg thrown over hers beneath the covers. His steady, even breathing sounded at her ear and his wide chest expanded against her.

She took a moment to look at him, here in the early-morning sunlight. Things had been too frantic last night for her to see him well, know him completely. She glanced at his face, made sure he was still sleeping, then lifted the quilt and peeked under.

Abbie gasped. She didn't know *that* could happen while he slept.

But then his hands started to roam, and she knew he wasn't really sleeping. Abbie rolled on her side to face him.

"Good morning," she said.

"Yes, it is," Jack answered, opening his eyes.

"Merry Christmas."

"Merry—" Jack bolted upright in the bed. "Hell, Abbie, it's Christmas morning. We've got to get home. We've got to be there when the girls open their gifts."

Abbie sat up on the side of the bed pulling the quilt around her, surprised at how cold it was in her room. She'd never been this chilly. But maybe that was because she'd never been so warm before, as she'd been in Jack's arms.

"I'll get ready in a flash," Abbie said. "We'll be on our way before—"

"Well, wait a minute," Jack said, reaching for her. "It won't matter if we're a few minutes late."

Abbie slid off of the bed. "Jack, you know we have to be there. It's Christmas, for goodness sake."

"I'm sure everyone will understand," he said, trying to make his suggestion sound reasonable.

"Natalie won't," Abbie said. She walked to the window. "Besides, how will you— Jack! My goodness, Jack, come look!"

He scrambled out of the bed. "What's wrong?"

"It snowed last night!"

Jack eased up beside her and gazed out the window at the light dusting of snow that covered the grass, the flowers, and the palm trees.

Abbie leaned her head against Jack's chest and he tightened

his arms around her. "I got my wish," she said. "Snow. My Christmas wish. Just like home."

"Enjoy it," Jack said, and kissed her forehead. "But don't get any more ideas about moving back to Pennsylvania. We settled that last night."

"I don't recall telling you I'd decided to stay here," she said.

"You're just going to have your way with me, then leave town?" Jack asked, grinning. "Not on your life."

Abbie leaned her head against his chest, soaking up his strength, looking at the snow outside. "Was this your Christmas wish? Us making love?"

"Nope."

She frowned up at him. "No?"

"No," Jack said. "My Christmas wish was to wake up with the woman I loved. I got my wish."

Abbie bit her bottom lip. "Do you think Natalie will be terribly disappointed that she's not getting her Christmas wish?"

"I guess we'd better go find out."

"Oh, Jack, isn't this snow wonderful?" Abbie exclaimed as they walked down the street. She was bundled in her cape carrying a shopping basket full of gifts, and Jack had his coat buttoned up tight.

"Seems damned cold to me," he grumbled.

Already the sun was starting to peek over the mountains, its warmth sure to melt the thin layer of snow very quickly. Abbie savored the chill in the air, the crunch underfoot.

"Back home we have foot upon foot of snow," Abbie said. "Icicles, snowdrifts, evergreens blanketed with snow. It's beautiful. You should see it, Jack."

"Forget it. We're never moving to Pennsylvania," Jack said. He smiled down at her and pulled her a little closer. "Of course, keeping warm in the winter would make it all worthwhile.''

They reached the house and crept quietly inside, then stopped short seeing Beth standing in the hallway.

Abbie's cheeks flushed and she knew she looked guilty—as guilty as she was. Jack slid his arm around her shoulders.

''Morning,'' he said.

''Good morning to you, too,'' Beth said, coming forward. ''The girls aren't up yet but will be soon. Everyone will start arriving before long. Jack, go upstairs and change. Abbie, come with me.''

Abbie hesitated a moment, sharing a cautious glance with Jack. Beth knew he had on the same suit from yesterday, figured where he'd been all night, and surely knew what he'd been doing.

''Run on, Jack,'' Beth told him. ''If Mother arrives and sees you looking like that, well, goodness knows we won't hear the end of it until next Christmas.''

Reluctantly, Jack stepped away from Abbie, gave her a wink, and headed up the staircase.

''Put on your dark-blue suit,'' Beth called, ''but don't wear that awful green necktie with it. Wear the maroon one. And don't wake the girls. Abbie, give me a hand in the kitchen, will you?''

They stopped at the cloak closet long enough for Abbie to take off her cape, gloves and hat, and set aside her shopping basket, then went into the kitchen. Already the room was warm and smelled of coffee and cinnamon.

Abbie wasn't sure what Beth was about to say to her, but she could imagine. Her concern would be for her brother's happiness, surely. But was there more? Was there something else that troubled Beth?

''Charles is in the parlor setting out the gifts,'' Beth said, taking cups from the cupboard. ''I wanted to talk to you for a minute before—''

''I'm in love with your brother.'' Abbie blurted out the words.

Beth turned to her, startled. ''I know that. Gracious, it's only obvious. I'm glad you two finally figured it out. I wanted to talk to you about something Jack mentioned to me yesterday, Abbie. Your concern that you're somehow not equal to others here in the city.''

''Jack told you that?''

''He did,'' Beth said. ''You have nothing to worry about, Abbie. Most of the people here who have money acquired it though hard work. There aren't a lot of families who've been rich for generations. Oh, there will always be a few like Mrs. Merchant who turn their noses up at others, but who wants people like that for friends, anyway?''

Abbie smiled. ''Thank you for saying that.''

''I want you to feel at home here,'' Beth said. ''Now, let's—''

Squeals and giggles interrupted Beth, and a moment later Jack stepped into the doorway with Janie clinging to his back, Natalie in one arm, and holding Lizzy's hand. The girls wore slippers and robes over their nightgowns.

''Santa came last night!'' Janie exclaimed. ''Uncle Jack said so!''

Beth narrowed her eyes at him and he did his best to look innocent.

''They were already awake,'' Jack said. ''I swear.''

''Can we open gifts now, Mama? Can we?'' Lizzy asked.

''Please? Oh, please?'' Natalie begged.

''Yeah, can we?'' Jack echoed.

''All right,'' Beth said.

''Let's go.''

Charles sat on a footstool beside the Christmas tree passing out gifts. Lizzy, Natalie and Janie squealed with delight as they ripped off the wrapping paper, discovering the treasures inside, hopping up and down, showing off what they'd got. Jack sat on the floor with the girls, helping them untangle bows and open tight boxes.

When they'd finished, Jack scooted close to Natalie as she played with a new doll she'd gotten.

"Do you like your gifts, honey?" he asked.

She hugged the doll to her chest. "Oh, yes, Papa."

"Did you get everything you wanted?"

"Well..." Natalie said, "almost."

Abbie's heart saddened a little, seeing the look on Jack's face. Even after all the gifts he'd gotten his daughter, he hadn't provided her with her one special Christmas wish.

"What didn't you get?" Jack asked.

Natalie looked around, then got up on her knees, cupped her hand and whispered into Jack's ear. A big smile bloomed on his face. He whispered something back, and Natalie nodded.

Abbie couldn't stand not knowing. She slid onto the floor next to Jack.

"Well?" she asked. "What did she say?"

"She didn't get what she wanted, but I told her I was pretty sure I could get it for her next year," Jack said

"What is it?" Abbie asked. "Tell me. What does she want?"

Jack slid his hand into Abbie's. "A baby brother."

Dear Reader,

Although my heritage is Italian and I do keep our special holiday traditions, I also love discovering an old tale that explains the how and why of Christmas traditions as well as allowing me to fashion new ornaments for our tree each year. The holiday season is a time for sharing, and this is one I want to share with you.

When the flurry of cleaning began, to ready the house for Christmas, the spider was banished to the darkest corner of the basement. The parlor doors were kept closed as the mistress of the house decorated the tree. On Christmas Eve, after a sumptuous feast, everyone was invited into the parlor to the the towering, festive tree. Candlelight glowed, people smiled and admired the beautiful tree and array of gaily wrapped gifts. But the poor little spider was very sad. Later that night when all were asleep, the spirit of Christmas came to visit and discovered the lonely little spider. Upon hearing its tale, the spirit invited the spider to come upstairs and into the parlor to see the tree.

The spider went from branch to branch, admiring the blown-glass ornaments, and those of paper and ribbons. Up, up it climbed to the shining star on the top. Asked if it was happy now, the spider replied that this was a wondrous gift. Christmas spirit laughed, and waved one hand so that all the spider's spinnings turned to silver. That is why we use tinsel on our trees.

I fashioned several small webs from thin gold, silver and copper wire (available at craft stores) and used Halloween spider rings with a spritz of gold glitter paint, then trailed a few strands of tinsel from the webs. Children and adults loved the tale, and I hope you enjoyed it, too. May your holidays be filled with an abundance of love, and lots of goodies to eat.

Theresa Michaels

More Than a Miracle

Theresa Michaels

To Michael, Krysta and Tommy—
never stop believing.

Chapter One

The Colorado mountain wind howled around the rafters of the cabin almost lost among the towering pines on this first night of December 1884.

Seated in a rocking chair before the river stone fireplace, Maureen O'Rourke looked up from her knitting. Snowflakes swirled against the panes of the only glazed window that glowed with the light of candles and the newly fed fire.

She listened for a few moments, then shrugged off the vague disquiet that distracted her. It was foolish to think she could hear any sound over the rising wind.

This would be her second winter in the cabin. Since last fall when she discovered the cabin abandoned, she kept expecting someone to come riding up and tell her and the children they would have to leave.

But no one had come to chase them away.

Her gaze swept over this area of the cabin. She still found it difficult to believe that someone had left behind dishes and cooking pots, the very chair she sat upon, an old cedar blanket chest and a pine table and benches.

The mellowed logs of the walls showed care in the building. And cleverness, too. The large fireplace backed a smaller one so that two chimneys warmed the sleeping loft above and the smaller private one below. Her own feather tick rested on a sweet summer-grass-stuffed mattress supported by the rope springs of the pine bedstead.

This cabin had been a home, carefully and lovingly built and tended. Then abandoned.

At first the thought had bothered her, but now all she felt was a warmth, as if this was all meant to be.

Her family back in County Donegal would say she had been favored by the *Odaoine sidhe,* the fairy people of Irish legend and lore.

Maureen hoped it was not true. The wee folk were a most fickle lot, giving good and bad luck upon whims of their own.

With a sigh she turned her attention to the scarf she needed to finish. She had found the woolen shawl in the blanket chest, the only piece of feminine apparel stored there. The yarn she unraveled was the softest she had ever touched. More important, there was enough to make new mittens and scarves for both children. She would add these to the items she had bartered for their Christmas presents.

And she was determined that this would be a good Christmas with plenty to eat and enjoyment for all of them.

She couldn't stop a quick glance to the corner where the tree would stand. Strings of dried berries hung on a nearby peg waiting to be draped over the branches.

Not for her and the children the practice of cutting out woodcuts from a catalogue of some practical item or toy.

She remembered all too well as a child finding a bit of string holding such pictures to the branches of the tree or tucked into a much mended stocking.

As she grew older, she understood how much her parents loved her and wished they could give her the French doll displayed on a shelf in the mercantile, or the shiny new ice skates, or later yet, the sealskin cape just like Miss Alice Potter wore and the kidskin gloves.

She found it far kinder to ask for necessary items well

within her parents means to provide. Her dreams and her longings were hers to share or keep secret.

Far better for all to hold the soft and warmly knitted stockings that her mother had made with love and she could accept with the same feeling, than express a wish for silk stockings and find only a bit of paper.

Maureen thought about that and how from that time she had developed a practical streak that helped her to meet whatever trials life set in front of her to overcome.

Let others wish for the impossible.

She was perfectly content.

This year she could provide a real Christmas feast. Her own good aim with a rifle had brought them a wild turkey. The vegetable garden she'd nursed through the summer had provided them with enough to eat and more for trading.

For the first time she had a whole sugar loaf and could generously grate some over the cookies she would bake. They had corn for popping to string on the tree and some for eating, too.

If there were times when she felt lonely, it was a very small price to pay to see the children warm, fed and happy.

She picked up her knitting, forcing herself to concentrate on the stitches while she worked to banish the thoughts of the past.

Truly, she told herself, such thoughts had no place in the new life she planned and worked toward. The creak of the rocking chair and her humming lulled her deeper into her contentment.

Gabriel Channing knew leaving the trading post and the meager town springing up around it had been a mistake.

The kind of mistake that could get a man killed.

The increasing bite of the wind, the thickening flurry of snow and the pack animals fighting the lead line all pointed to an error in judgment.

The only trial he had not encountered were heavy drifts that would cause the horses to flounder. But he was not sure how much longer his luck would hold.

He needed to find shelter immediately.

His own carelessness added to the bitter frustration of his empty year-long search. Men called him a fool to continue hunting, but everything he had meant little without the one person necessary for his life to have meaning.

So he took risks, like riding out when the mother of storms was beginning, always hoping and praying that this time, this trip, would see an end. *A happy end,* he added to himself.

Gabe bent his head low against a sudden strong gust of wind that whipped snow against his face. He knew how tired the horses were; knew that if he did not push on they would all freeze.

Several times he thought he spotted a likely place to build a brush shelter, but something inside him told him to go on.

It wasn't too much longer that the slow realization that he had left the sheltering woods penetrated his thoughts. He pulled up at the edge of a meadow. He knew he had left the flatland behind and had been climbing steadily through the afternoon into the foothills.

He sheltered his eyes with a leather-gloved hand. He thought he knew this place. If he was right, there was shelter not far ahead.

With a new sense of purpose, he urged his horse forward and tugged the lead line to bring his pack animals closer.

"Just a little farther," he coaxed. "I'll have us safe and warm as if we were home."

The restless stampings of his mountain-bred mustang sent him moving across the meadow at a fast trot. Once across, the wall of pines blocked the worst of the wind and snow.

For a long while he plodded on, wondering if the cold had befuddled his senses. He could swear the cabin was closer, but once more they were climbing a ridge where the trees thinned and the full force of the storm battered him and his horses. His feet were close to numb despite the double layer of socks and thick boots. He couldn't feel his nose.

But he had come this far on a hunch and had to play it out.

He felt blessed relief as the trees thickened to screen him from the fury of the wind and snow.

The faint smell of smoke brought him up short. He forced numb fingers to unbutton his heavy sheepskin-lined coat. He tucked his right hand under his armpit to warm it. He shivered as his body warmth disappeared, but as he touched the well-worn butt of his holstered gun, he knew it wasn't foolish to risk exposure to the cold for his safety.

A man alone never knew what kind of company he would find pulling up to a campfire or a lonely cabin. Having his hand warmed, and his gun free of the thong that held it holstered made him ready for whatever kind of reception he might find.

Minutes before, for the third and final time, Maureen set aside her knitting. The vague disquiet sent her on another restless prowl around the cabin until she stood in front of the window. There was little to see but the thick fall of snow and the darkness beyond.

She questioned her own senses. A feeling that she needed to be aware of something happening was growing inside her, but she was sure the warning was not one of danger to her or the children.

The temptation to light the lantern and take a look around outside rose to an almost overwhelming need.

She stepped back from the window, closed her eyes briefly and tried to concentrate. She knew the animals were safe in the barn. If timber wolves were around, they would not be silent, but a mountain cat would be.

Her knowledge that the team of horses, milk cow and chickens were safe went beyond the stout walls of their shelter to knowing truth she had had as a child. It had never failed her. Her family claimed the magic of the Green Isle was bred in her bones and would always protect her and those she loved.

Perhaps there was some truth to that, for her sense never failed to warn her when some great change was about to happen or when danger was near.

There was no help for it. She opened her eyes. The urge to look around outside remained, even stronger than moments ago.

From the pegs near the door, she took down a heavy wool jacket she had traded her best cloak for, and used her shawl to cover her head and shoulders. Her gloves were serviceable wool and she quickly put them on once the lantern was lit.

She closed the door behind her and stood for a few minutes beneath the overhanging roof.

As she stepped to the edge of the porch, the wind whipped her skirt and petticoats against her legs. It took but a moment to see that the snow was thick and wet, the kind that stuck to the ground and would close the mountain pass to the trading post.

The thought of being isolated with the children did not worry her. She had a smokehouse filled with meat, and her storeroom, while not filled to overflowing, held enough dry foodstuffs and canned goods to see the three of them through the winter.

The air was sharp and biting, the wind more so as she shrugged off her thoughts and stepped down. Sheltering the lantern against her, she kept close to the side of the cabin and made her way to the barn. The footing was not too slippery, but if the temperature dropped the path would become icy and dangerous.

The bar holding the barn doors closed was firmly in place. She pressed her ear against the cold wood planks to listen for any disturbance from the animals.

There was nothing to hear over the rising wind. No chickens

squawking, no panicked whinnies from the horses, no lowing from the milk cow.

All as silent and serene as the woods that surrounded the cabin.

Maureen tightened her grasp on the icy metal handle of the lantern. Something had sent her out here. She looked around once more, then stared into the woods as far as she could see.

The thick trunks and sweeping branches of the towering pines collected snow. Some of the branches would snap beneath the weight by morning, while others would sag low enough to form shadowed snow caves to delight the children.

There was nothing here to alarm her.

The very urgency that had sent her out into the winter cold disappeared far more suddenly than it had come upon her.

Her eyes began tearing. The wet cold seeped through the soles of her boots. With her fingers growing numb and deep shivers coming from where the wind penetrated cloth, she hurried to retrace her steps to the cabin.

More annoyed than worried she turned the corner and found herself too surprised to cry out.

Several animals loomed close to the porch, their packs hilled with snow.

The sight of the horses, heads hanging low as if they had come a far piece, freed her to move. She kept the lantern at her side so not to frighten them into running off.

Her thought of them being strays disappeared as the animals shifted and revealed a rider hunched over one horse's neck.

She lifted the lantern and held the blurred impression of craggy features as the man turned his face toward the light.

Now she understood why she had been summoned outside. The poor man was in need of rescuing. ''Lord, save us all from these greenhorns who come west without knowing what they are about.''

''Greenhorn?'' The word came back at her in a hoarse whisper. ''Lady, I've come home.''

Chapter Two

Gabe stared at the swaying light. He knew what he whispered was wrong, but the cold stinging him like tiny cutting knives demanded he concern himself with getting warm.

He forced himself to sit up in the saddle, easing his hand away from the gun.

"It's too cold to be disputing ownership of the place with you. Do you need help to dismount?"

Even as she spoke, she had to wonder why there was no fear, no sense to be cautious with this lone man. After all, she was a woman alone with two children who depended upon her to keep them safe. She had to be wary.

Since he appeared held in the grip of the cold, she repeated her offer to help, then added, "Come inside and warm yourself. I'll see to your horses."

She thought about explaining her possession of the abandoned cabin for over a year. But as it didn't seem he was going to put them out now, she would deal with that problem when the time came.

Gabe found himself obeying the firm, no-nonsense yet very feminine voice. The cold had seeped down into his bones. Dismounting cost him more effort than he believed possible.

Maureen moved closer to him, one hand reaching out to touch his snow-covered sleeve.

"You poor old man. You must be near frozen. Come inside now. Come on," she coaxed as if talking to one of the children. "But mind you, don't be making noise. With Christmas coming the little darlings have the devil of a time sleeping."

Gabe found himself shocked to silence. Old? Old man, she called him. But he found himself handing over the reins and lead rope just as if he were one of these children she talked about. He struggled to see the face of the woman beneath the shawl. She was shorter than his own near six feet, and unless he was snow crazed, there was a definite Irish lilt to the voice now crooning to his horses as she led them away.

Led them away? His horses?

He cast a longing glance at the glowing window, knowing it must be warm inside the cabin. With a rough shake of his head, he rid himself of the momentary confusion that held sway over him.

No one, but no one cared for his horses but him. His father had taught him that, and it was a good rule for a man to live by.

He shivered with cold, but forced himself to follow after the woman.

Old man, indeed!

He was not sure what was wrong with him. He hoped it was no more than the surprise of seeing a woman step out from the darkness as if she had been waiting for him.

That thought was enough to chill a man.

And if he got any colder, he'd be no better than a side of beef in the ice house.

He hurried to where she struggled with the bar across the barn doors. The wet snow had swollen the wood and it taxed his spent strength to lift the bar free.

The minute he set it down, she wasted no time herding him and the animals inside and closing the door behind them.

Maureen did not glance at the man as she set the lantern on a protruding nail. She quickly slipped the latch on a roomy box stall and moved her horse into its teammate's stall across the aisle. If the stubborn man thought her incapable of caring for horses, it was nothing to her. But then, old men were prone to be set in their ways. Likely that was his problem. She spared a few moments to whisper to her horses and quiet their nervous whinnies at the presence of strange horses.

Gabe listened to her lovely voice crooning nonsense to the animals. He was fighting the needlelike pricks the warmth of the barn brought to his body. The cow turned its head in the wooden stanchion to look at him with large brown eyes then turned back to chew her cud. Even the chickens in their scattered nests blinked open beady eyes and paid no more attention to the invasion of strange animals.

What had he stepped into?

Her efficient moves had already stripped his saddle horse. She rubbed the animal down with coarse sacking and the fool horse nudged her gently as if asking for more. But she turned him into the empty box stall.

He stripped off his gloves and flexed his cold fingers before attempting to loosen the rope of one pack horse.

"Please, let me help you," she offered, coming to stand by his side. "I know how cold effects old bones. There is nothing to be ashamed of in asking for a little help. Besides," she added, "my hands are warmer since I've been inside my cabin and you've been riding in the storm. You should have gone straight inside when I told you to and left all of this to me."

Gabe caught a glimpse of sparkling green eyes and a short uptilted nose before she ducked her head to work the pack's wet knots.

But a man, even one in need of a warm, dry place, could take only so much slander about his age and abilities.

"Ma'am," he said in as firm, but soft voice as he could

then manage, "I'm not old and decrepit. I'm thirty years old and I can't remember the last time a woman scolded me."

"More's the pity," she muttered, gently nudging him out of her way. The knots were proving to be as stubborn as the man who'd tied them.

"But don't take on so," she added without a thought of hiding her amusement. "If a good woman scolded you more often, you would have found shelter for yourself and these poor darlings long before the storm began."

He was speechless as his normal slow-to-rile temper heated his blood.

He glared at her shorter, thickly padded figure, then gently pushed her aside to finish undoing the tie-down rope. He tossed aside the canvas and unloaded the three feed bags and sacks of corn and grain that he carried for his horses. Grain-fed horses tended to give a man speed when he needed it, and although the Indian troubles were behind Colorado, there were plenty of outlaws still riding the mountain trails.

Maureen eyed the corn and grain and never one to keep quiet with a compliment, spoke out. "You take good care of your animals."

"You sound surprised. And you'd be right about having the sense to seek shelter. If I had a woman of my own," he added. "Maybe you've gotten in the habit of scolding children and forget what it's like to speak to a grown man."

"You're right." A charming, light laugh followed. "We haven't had much company since the cold weather."

"I didn't offend you?" he asked, ready to begin on the other pack animal.

"No. Why would I be offended when you spoke the truth?"

Maureen looked up at him. He chose that moment to thumb back his hat. Black hair tumbled across his forehead. But his eyes captured and demanded all her attention.

Stormy blue-gray eyes framed by arched black brows and thick lashes. The color of his eyes seemed familiar. It had to be that, for she was sure that she had never seen this man before tonight.

What she thought were craggy features, were ruggedly handsome. A face of masculine strength from the straight nose, the stern set of his mouth to the almost square cut of his jaw. The high cheekbones, reddened from the cold, reminded her that she had been staring far too long.

He hadn't said a word, just watched her with a great deal of calm, but she turned away, frowning over the very puzzling sense that she should know who he was.

What was wrong with her? She had no fear of this stranger. Not one little jolt of caution rose inside her. But how could that be when he claimed ownership of the very place she called home?

Perhaps the cold had dulled her senses. She bent to pick up the feed bags, but his larger, long-fingered hand reached them before her own.

''I'll take care of the rest,'' he murmured. ''You've been more than kind and helpful to a stranger. I gather you're alone with children here, and caution you not to be so welcoming to every man who rides up looking for shelter.''

''Warning me against yourself?''

''No. I'd offer no harm to a woman. But there are those who'd take advantage of a generous nature and perhaps show less respect than they should. I seek to caution you and no more.''

''Then thanks for your caution. But I'm not helpless, you know.'' And from the deep side pocket of the man's jacket she wore, she lifted out a fairly new Colt Peacemaker.

Gabe showed no surprise as he carefully pushed the barrel aside.

''I'm sure you're a good shot, too.''

''At close range most folks would be.''

For some reason he felt foolish, and it wasn't a feeling he was comfortable wearing.

"Would it be too much to ask for some hot coffee before I bed down here?"

"Here? You intend to stay in the barn?"

"You don't deny there's no man around. You wouldn't be comfortable having a stranger in the cabin with you. The barn's dry and that hay will make a fine bed."

He was right. She knew he was, and the protest that silently formed died in her throat.

Without another word, she left him to see to his animals and returned to the cabin.

It was only as she opened the door that she realized she never asked him his name. More she wouldn't ask, for it wasn't a Westerner's way to question folks about their doings. Especially not strange men who rode out of the night with a well-tended rifle and a tied-down gun.

Maybe he was one of those very outlaws that he warned her against?

Useless to speculate.

She placed another load of wood on the fire. Coffee he asked for and coffee he'd get. Tea was precious and he would likely scorn an offering if she made one.

While she waited for the water to boil, she cut a few thick slices of the corn bread left from supper and spread them with butter. Glancing at the plate it didn't seem enough to offer a hungry man. Not that he said he was hungry, but he had to be. He carried food for his horses and likely had food in the other packs, but he would have had no time to build a fire and cook something for himself.

Bacon wouldn't take long to cook. From that thought she was slicing, and then adding the three eggs set aside for her and the children's breakfast.

She added coffee grinds and a bit of cold water to settle them in the pot. It was then she realized how foolish she would be to carry hot food and coffee out into the cold.

"The man's befuddled what wits I have," she muttered as she quickly dressed against going back outside.

Flinging open the door she found him standing there, his hand raised to knock.

"I was coming to—"

"I thought to save you—"

They both spoke and stopped at the same moment and looked at each other, until Maureen, the first to recover, stepped aside for him to enter.

"I was coming to get you to eat here," she said, closing the door. In the revealing light she saw that he was a man who spent a great deal of time outdoors. The tiny lines that fanned from the corners of his eyes told of squinting up at the sun or long distances. There was a trace of tanned skin, but she noted the weariness that mantled him.

"Sit down. You'll be more comfortable and warmer here."

"And I came to save you another trip in the snow."

The cabin was almost hot compared to the warmth of the barn. He sniffed and smiled. "Coffee and bacon smell mighty fine to a hungry man, ma'am."

Maureen turned aside to hang up her shawl and jacket. Without looking at him, she took the hat and coat he offered and hung them alongside her own. She heard him step away and a quick look over her shoulder showed him near the fireplace, his large hands stretched out to the warming blaze.

"We didn't even exchange names. I'm Maureen. Maureen O'Rourke."

She turned fully and realized that he didn't seem to hear her. With a nervous motion she smoothed down her skirt.

"After you've eaten, we'll talk about the cabin."

That got his attention. He turned toward her. His gaze took in the neatly coiled reddish-brown hair, the faded blue calico gown and the deceptive slender body beneath it. She was younger than he believed, taller, too, with a direct gaze most men would find disconcerting.

Gabe didn't. His eyes narrowed as he continued to stare at the woman he'd been hunting for over a year. He noted the two pairs of smaller boots and the coats that hung above them. He was sure now he had the right woman. One who didn't have the sense to be afraid of him.

"What's wrong?" she asked softly.

"Nothing. For the first time everything's right."

Chapter Three

Maureen was not sure how to respond to his remark.

He didn't give her a chance. "I see you've got berries strung for your Christmas tree. There's a good place to get spruce trees on the other side of the creek."

"I've seen them. But the children and I couldn't drag one of those home."

She stood where she was while he gazed around the room. If what he said was true and this was his cabin, then all of what she found here belonged to him. He couldn't think to put them out now. Or could he? After all, what did she know about him? Not even his name, she reminded herself.

"You've kept the place nice."

"Mister, say your piece and stop playing with me like a cat with a field mouse."

She noted his tension at the same moment she became aware of her own. It didn't please her to see the way his stormy blue-gray eyes narrowed with a hard stare for her.

"You said your name's O'Rourke."

Flat statement, no question, but she answered anyway. "That's right." Her hands curled over the material of skirt and petticoats ready to run if he made a move toward her.

His smile was anything but pleasant. The lifting of his stern-cut lips reminded her of the cat with all the time in the world to play with its cornered mouse.

But Maureen was not a mouse. She shifted slightly so she was closer to the gun she had left in her jacket's pocket. The wrong move might be this stranger's last.

He ran one hand through his coal-black hair that settled over his shirt's collar. "I can't believe that this storm turned out to be my luck."

"Don't be counting on that, mister."

"Oh, but I do. I've been hunting you for over a year. Been up one side of Colorado and down the other."

"Hunting…me?" Surely that breathless whisper was not hers? But she knew it was, just as she knew that she must not show any fear.

"You heard me right."

"But why? I don't know you. You haven't even had the decency to tell me you name."

"Your pardon, ma'am," he snapped with a mockery of a bow. "The name's Gabriel Channing."

The flat intonation told her his name was supposed to mean something to her. It did not. She was anxious, but not exactly afraid of him. That did frighten her.

He stood in the middle of the room, his very size a threat. From his well-worn boots to the long, powerful rider's legs encased in black twill pants to the perfectly fitted pale gray bib-front shirt that stretched across his broad shoulders, to the tied-down gun that looked almost a part of him, Gabriel Channing was a man to be reckoned with. That he wasn't a poor, down-on-his-luck cowhand was evidenced by his quiet, commanding air and the fact that his shirt had never seen a store shelf. The material was too fine for ready-made goods.

But his statement that he had been hunting her was too much for her to deal with right now.

"Sit down and eat before your food gets cold."

''Didn't you hear me, lady? I said I've been hunting you. Haven't you the sense of a sage hen to know what—''

''I've more sense than a hen.'' She stood tall, her chin lifting and the light of battle in her green eyes.

''I offered a stranger food and shelter. They are still yours. But I need time to think about your claim of owning this cabin, and even more time to figure out why you're hunting me. If I had any sense, I'd shoot you where you stand. There's not a jury in Colorado or anywhere west that would blame me for protecting myself and the children.''

She looked at his clenched hands, staring until she saw him relax them.

''That's better.'' She did not look up at his face. ''Please sit down and tell me why you have been looking for me.'' She motioned with her left hand toward the table, then added, ''You're not the law, are you?''

''No. And I've got to tell you, lady, that you're slicker than a clay hill after a rainstorm. If I wasn't standing here and seeing this for myself, I wouldn't believe how calm you are. If you knew who I was—''

''Which should be obvious, even to you, that I have no idea who you are.''

''Do you ever let a man finish what he's got to say?''

''When it's something worth hearing,'' she returned. A spark lit her temper, but she refused to show anger. Once more she motioned him to the table. ''I need some coffee before I hear what you're burning to tell me.''

''Burning about sums it up. Never met such a thickheaded woman,'' he muttered. She had him confused, or maybe, just maybe, he reacted slowly because he was not fully thawed from his ride in the storm.

But part of his trouble was the woman herself. No pleading, no crying or hand wringing, or some other darn fool female way of coping. He knew those women's weapons too well.

Maybe she was having trouble believing him, just as he

could not believe she did not know who he was. But he was armed with the truth, and his wrath was a thing to be feared as many a man in the territory could attest to, if any were around for her to ask.

He warned himself to be calm as he slid the bench aside and sat down. He'd not made his accusations yet, and when he did, he'd like to see her try squirming out of the justice that was his due.

He watched her pour two cups of coffee and found himself admiring the shape of her hands. Delicately boned, but there was strength there, too. They were not the soft hands of an idle woman, nor coarse and rough like many a woman who did for herself and others.

He came to with a start just as she seated herself across the table from him. Not one little feather ruffled as far as he could tell. He'd bet she played a great hand of poker.

"Go on and eat. It's likely cold by now."

"You ever been a schoolmarm?"

"No." Her glare spoke volumes. "You see, you've made a mistake about me. I'm not who you think I am."

"No chance, lady. I *know* it's you."

She didn't like the predatory look in his eyes and found her hot coffee a safer place to rest her gaze.

His stomach rumbled loudly, and as much as he wanted and needed to talk, the food proved too hard to resist.

He sipped the coffee, and found it strong enough. Under the linen napkin he found three fried eggs, bacon and thick buttered slices of corn bread.

"I could warm that for you."

"I've eaten worse cold. Try beans a few days in a row. Hot for supper, cold for breakfast and happy enough to have them."

She couldn't stop her smile. It was an oft-heard complaint from men who had no womenfolk to cook for them.

"Well then, eat up. When you're done we'll talk."

"There you go again with that scold in your voice like I was knee-high."

But she didn't respond to his teasing. If anything she appeared lost in thought, or was she scheming... He didn't know. He had to keep in mind that females depended upon their emotions and usually displayed little common sense. Unlike a man.

With her distracted, he found his gaze strayed to the soft shape of her mouth. A pretty, kissable light-rose mouth. Not that he wanted to kiss her. Better to watch her eyes, green as forest pine and just as mysteriously dark. Not that he could see her eyes now, since she kept them lowered. He could admire the lovely arch of her brows and the thick, long lashes that were a shade darker than her hair.

He didn't like where his thoughts were taking him.

He ate quickly. Looking around the cabin, he had to appreciate its neatness. He could only wonder what his mother would have thought about this woman who claimed her home. Just as he had to wonder why, of all the places she could have gone to, she had come here.

Was it fate or something stronger that had led him here tonight?

Gabe had no answer for his question.

His gaze returned again to her pensive expression. She still hadn't lifted her gaze from the contents of her cup. He wanted to probe her thoughts since his own were making him uncomfortable.

He shifted on the hard bench trying to stop a most treacherous emotion unfurling within him.

She suddenly appeared fragile, almost vulnerable. Her feminine defenselessness filled him with an overpowering need to protect her.

Protect her?

The feeling grew so intense that it added to his confusion. What was wrong with him?

Maureen O'Rourke, with the bewitching green eyes, was the last woman who needed his protection.

Especially since the only one she required any protection from right now was him.

"You're ready to talk," she said in a soft voice, "and explain why you've been hunting me."

Was he?

He couldn't believe he'd asked himself that question. Hadn't he dreamed of finding her? Hadn't the thought of finally getting his hands on her driven him for over a year? Didn't he need to punish her for what she had done?

Righteous anger rose inside him and chased away every doubt she seemed to bring to the surface.

"Damn right I am."

"Lower your voice or you'll wake the children."

His words died. She was right. He didn't want to wake the children. This had to be between the two of them.

His body taut tension, he took a deep breath and slowly exhaled as he tried to relax. She couldn't run from him now. He had to remember that.

"Last fall you were in Silver Plume," he said.

"I was in a few mining towns."

"But you don't deny you were in Silver Plume."

She looked up at his face, a frown creasing her brow.

"Since you are not asking but telling me, you already know the answer to that."

"Just confirm it for me."

She shrugged her shoulders. "Yes, I was there, but not for long. There was a fire—"

"Yes, it destroyed the town," he finished for her. "Started in the middle of the night in a saloon and burned down most of the businesses before it was under control."

"It was a nightmare," she added, shivering to think about that night. "The town was helpless to fight that kind of blaze. They had trouble getting a bucket brigade set up while they waited for the Star Hook and Ladder Company to come from Georgetown. I helped the women keep coffee, food ready and see to the injured. It was terrible and not something I can forget. But what has that to do with you hunting for me?''

Maureen stared past his broad shoulder. She was leery of his questions, but not afraid. And she should be afraid of him. There was a look of barely checked temper about him and his size alone intimidated her.

''And that's all you remember about Silver Plume?''

His low question drew her from her thoughts.

She shook her head even as she answered him. ''No, that's not all. I told you it was a nightmare. People running around, injured lying in the fields outside of town, not enough of anything to do some good. Deaths being reported and being told of others missing. The horror of learning that a group of men trying to rescue three others were trapped when the building collapsed on them.

''And everywhere the stench of fire and that blaze that lit the night sky and the heat.'' She turned her direct gaze to meet his own. ''Do you need to hear any more? Because if you answer yes, it won't be from me.''

''You left Silver Plume the next day.''

His habit of stating rather than asking questions grew annoying. She cautioned herself to patience so she could get to the bottom of his reason for hunting her. The very thought was enough to send a chill slithering down her spine.

''Yes, I left,'' she said in a testy voice. ''I was free to go where and when I wanted to.''

''Was free?''

''Am,'' she snapped as her annoyance gave way to temper. ''I am free to do as I please.'' Her glaring eyes should have warned him to back down, but the moment he spoke she knew it wasn't working.

''And were you also free to take whatever you wanted with you?''

His harsh, grating voice penetrated her anger. She thought she caught a flash of pain in his eyes, but it disappeared too quickly for her to be sure.

‘‘What are you talking about? What do you think I took? I told you there was a great deal of confusion that night. And even more the next day. I had camped outside of town and went back about midmorning to offer my help again, but so many people had come from Georgetown that they didn’t need me.’’

She struggled to recall every moment of time, for he seemed to be waiting for more details.

‘‘What could I possibly have taken that—’’ She cut herself off and felt the thick, near menacing tension that came from the man leaning over the table toward her.

Maureen closed her eyes briefly, thinking again of the day as gray as the ashes that had covered everything.

She had taken… No, she had denied to herself in the next breath, it couldn’t be…

‘‘You took. You sure as hell did. Folks saw you. Some knew your name. You’re a thief of the worse kind. You stole the most important part of my life that day.’’

‘‘No!’’

She denied it again. He couldn’t be telling her the truth. He was lying. Yet even as she thought it, her own innate and strong senses were telling her that he wasn’t lying. And she had taken something with her, no, not something, but someone.

She had to look at him, had to look into his stormy blue eyes that promised revenge.

‘‘My son. You stole my son.’’

Chapter Four

"No!" She half rose from the bench to flee him, but he reached out and caught hold of her hands, pressing them against the table.

Her heart was pounding as she attempted to pull free of his strong grip.

"You took him with you. Don't deny it. I know that's the truth. That's why I've been hunting for you. I want my son back."

"I did not steal him," she declared frantically. "He was lost, alone. No one I asked claimed him and then—"

"He's *my* son!"

"Your son," she whispered in a scorn-filled voice. "And where were you when that child stood alone, frightened and crying? Where were you while he shook with terror and couldn't even speak? Some father to abandon his son! Now, let me go!"

"Lower your voice. You don't want to wake the children, remember." But Gabe let her go. He had never used his greater strength against a woman, and wasn't about to let this one goad him into doing it now.

"So, where were you when your son needed you, Mr. Channing? And how do I know you are the boy's father? I was told he was killed that night.''

Gabe scrubbed one hand over his face. ''Sit down and listen to me. I've never had anyone question my word. I am Gabe Channing and I know you have my son. Wait, don't jump in, let me finish. I was fighting the fire as every other able-bodied man in town. I was with the group when that building fell in on us. I got hit on the head and it was weeks before I remembered everything. By then you were gone and had taken Chris with you.''

''You were injured?''

Her stricken look sealed the lid on every bit of anger he had held for this woman for over a year. She wasn't lying to him. She had truly taken his son because she thought him orphaned by the fire.

He closed his eyes against her blunt question and rubbed his fingers against the bridge of his nose. He was getting another of those headaches that were a legacy of his head injury.

He dropped his hand and opened his eyes. ''Yes, I was one of the injured. They didn't dig us out until nightfall of the next day. Like I said, I didn't have any memory then. It all came back to me slowly over a matter of weeks. Then I found out what happened to my son and started hunting for you.''

Maureen tilted her head and regarded him for a long moment. She wanted to close her eyes against the painful memories he stirred, but she was no coward.

''I have done you a grievous wrong, Mr. Channing.''

''No. Now that I know why you took him, I can't blame you. In fact, I should give you a reward for saving my son. If someone less scrupulous had found him the boy might have been hurt before I could pay a ransom for him.''

''Don't insult me by offering me money.''

He paid heed to the flare of anger in her green eyes. ''All right, I won't discuss that now. But I am a wealthy man. Whatever it is you want or need, I'll see you have it. And now I want to see my son."

"That's impossible."

"Pardon me? I said I want—"

"What you want can't matter. You need to think of your son. You'd give the boy a fright he might not easily recover from. Just think, Mr. Channing. Chris was told that you were killed. I don't think he believes that, but he doesn't talk about you at all."

"Wait a minute? Chris talks to you?"

Disbelief shone in his gaze and coated his words.

Puzzled, she nodded. "Of course, Chris talks to me and my daughter. How else would I know about you or even know his name?"

"But Chris didn't talk. Not to me, not to anyone. I had him to some of the best doctors and none found a reason for it. One told me that when he was ready to, he'd talk and to leave him alone about it. And now you're telling me that my son is talking."

He buried his face in his hands and she didn't know if he was praying in thanksgiving or didn't believe her about his son. Then an ugly suspicion formed and before she thought about it, she spoke.

"Are you sure you've told me everything? I mean," she hastened to explain when he looked at her, "Chris isn't afraid of you, is he? I think I need to be sure that seeing you won't frighten him."

"Are you trying to still keep me from my son?"

"Don't take that threatening tone with me." She pushed the bench back and stood up. "I need to think about this. You should, too. If you've told me the truth and love your son, then you must see this is something that can't be rushed."

He gave an adamant shake of his head, though not in denial of her words. He was stunned hearing that Chris could talk. And the woman was right. He didn't want to frighten his son by suddenly coming back from the dead and then taking him away. He also had a strong feeling that getting Chris away from Maureen O'Rourke would prove to be a battle.

Yet he had waited so long, and no one in a long time had gotten away with denying him what he wanted. This green-eyed woman with her lack of fear and strength of spirit obviously didn't know or care about the wealth he claimed. If she had told him the truth, and he tended to believe she had, then he would wait.

"All right," he stated, rising and heading for the door. "Just until morning. Then I'm going to have my son back."

Morning came with the sight of an enchanted ice-draped forest. Sunlight sparked rainbows where icicles hung from the roof. Everywhere that Maureen looked it was as fresh and newly frosted as a Lady Baltimore cake.

She turned from the window, smiling when she heard the children's giggles and whispers as they dressed before leaving the sleeping loft. The sound forced her to banish all the dark thoughts that had plagued her sleepless night.

She dished out steaming bowls of oatmeal and added the small spatterware pitcher of heavy cream to the crock of butter and jar of apple jelly and hot biscuits on the table.

The coffeepot was still quite full. She had half hoped for, and half dreaded, Gabe Channing's presence this morning. But he was not in the barn when she slipped in before daybreak to milk the cow and collect the eggs. The chickens were as disturbed as she was by his being there, for there were only two eggs to be found this morning.

His horses were in the stall so wherever he had gone he'd walked. She prayed that he would stay away until she talked to Chris.

Guilt wormed its way into her thoughts. Gabe was out there, alone. He had never abandoned his child.

She glanced toward the window, at the bright beauty of the

snow-covered forest. She had never shirked her responsibilities. Most of the prayers she whispered through the night had been for the wisdom of how to tell Chris that his father had come for him. But she had come to love that little boy as if he were her own.

How could she just give him up? An ache spread inside her at the thought. And what would Kathleen do? Her little girl looked after Chris like he was truly her brother. All their plans for Christmas and beyond would melt away like the snow beneath the strong winter sun.

Gabe Channing had no idea of the pain he brought when he had found them.

Selfish, Maureen, a little voice whispered.

Chris is Gabe's son. He's been searching for the boy. Doesn't the man deserve your most charitable thoughts for what he's been through? What you put him through by taking the child without making sure that the man was dead.

Guilt overpowered every other emotion.

She had to smooth the way for father and son to be reunited. And she had to give Chris up without anyone knowing that she'd be tearing off a piece of her heart.

Maybe she could atone for what she had done.

Maybe…

The scrape of the bench made her turn around with a bright smile. "Good morning, you two sleepyheads."

"Morning, Mama." Kathleen ran to give her mother a hug.

They came running as they did every morning. Kathleen, braids of red hair shades lighter than her mother's, reached Maureen first. Then came Chris, a little slower, his black curly hair still rumpled from sleep. Maureen looked down into a pair of bright-green eyes that she had given to her daughter, and caught her breath when she saw how much Chris owed his blue with hints of gray color to his father.

"Sleep well and warm?" She held the children a little tighter and a little longer than she usually did. Her daughter, eight years old this past spring, was thin but very tall for her age. Maureen pressed a kiss to the child's forehead and smiled. The pale skin and freckles sprinkled across her cheeks and nose proclaimed her Irish descent. Kathleen didn't like her freckles, but Maureen insisted they were fairy kisses and only given to the prettiest little girls.

Chris always wished for a few of his own, so Maureen always gave him a few extra kisses in the morning.

"Hungry?" she asked, skimming a quick eye over their clothes. They both had grown so much over the summer that she could barely keep up with altering their clothes. But both were presentable, and warmly dressed if not the most fashionable. Lord only knew what Gabe Channing would think of his son wearing hand-me-downs.

His jeans like Kathleen's were well-worn and faded to gray. Their shirts were wool, blue for her and red for Chris.

"Mama, we can play outside, can't we, Mama? The storm's over and Chris wants to make a snow fort. I want to make snow angels. Then, please, please, Mama, can we go up to the big hill and sled?"

"Yes, yes, please say yes." Chris added his entreaties to Kathleen's.

"We'll see." She scooted them onto the bench before she sat down across the table from them. She shook her head and hid her smile behind her hand as she watched them eat. The two of them attacked their food as if it were either their last meal or the first they had had in too long a time.

But her smile left when she understood that she had to tell Chris about his father. To delay would cause them more problems.

She closed her eyes for a brief moment. Now he was a rosy-cheeked, sturdy and happy little boy, but the night she rescued him, he'd been thin and sad.

"What's wrong?" Chris asked, putting his spoon down in the empty bowl.

"I—I need to tell you something, no, that's not right. I have a big surprise for you, Chris. Bigger than anything you've ever wished for. The kind of surprise that will—"

"Mama, what's wrong? You're crying." Kathleen's spoon fell with a clatter. Both children hurried around the table to hug Maureen.

Maureen could not seem to stop crying. This was proving harder than she thought. She gathered the children close, unable to answer them.

Gabe walked inside, holding his hat by the brim, a little hesitant to intrude. He saw Maureen crying, and a little girl so like her in features that it could only be her daughter using a napkin to wipe her tears. And the boy… His heart seemed to stop, then start with a sudden pounding as his gaze fastened on his son.

"I tried knocking," he said, swallowing against the dryness that nerves brought.

But no one heard him. It was minutes before Maureen looked up and saw that he was closing the door behind him and stood waiting for some notice. She knew her time had run out.

Blinking back her tears, she forced a smile. "Stop, Kathleen. I'm all right. It's just that I have some happy news for Chris. He's about to get the best Christmas present ever. All he needs to do is turn around." She hugged her daughter tight with one arm, and with the other nudged the boy to turn around.

Gabe smiled. For the moment he contented himself with drinking in the sight of his son. But he didn't miss the boy's wide-eyed stare or the way he drew back to press against Maureen.

"Chris, come here, boy." A roil of emotion flooded his husky voice. He couldn't quite believe that after all this time he was looking at his son. For sure the good Lord had a hand in guiding him here. Gabe knew folks through the territory thought him a fool to keep believing he'd find him, but never once had he doubted that it would happen.

When his son still made no move toward him, Gabe swallowed hard against the lump forming in his throat. He fought against feeling resentment for the woman who claimed his son's devotion to the point where he ignored her urgings to go to his father.

''Chris, please,'' Maureen whispered. ''You don't want to hurt him. He's traveled so far. He needs a hug from you about as much as you need one from him. Go on. Go.''

''Lord, yes,'' Gabe affirmed, dropping to one knee. He opened his arms wide to catch his son as he finally ran to him and flung his arms around his father's neck.

Gabe closed his eyes. He held his son tight against him. His eyes filled with the burning sear of tears, but he didn't care who saw them. He finally had Chris back and nothing else mattered.

He saw nothing of the pain in Maureen's eyes, nor could he know how she chided herself for being anything but happy for the two of them.

Gabe's total focus belonged to his son. He had seen the boy's good health and the body he clasped was sturdy and taller than a year ago. He marveled at the strength in the small arms hugging him, not knowing which miracle to give thanks for first...finding his son, or that the boy was talking.

He kept imagining the first time he held a red-faced mite, wrapped tight in a soft blanket but squalling to be fed. His hasty marriage made during the drunken celebration of his first big gold strike had ended the day Chris was born. She wanted money, not the child, and he thought he had the best of the bargain.

That same wonder as the first time holding his son now filled him. He had been given a tiny life totally dependent upon him for everything, his to love and guide.

And he had a lot of lost time to make up for.

Maureen O'Rourke was right. This was the best Christmas present ever, and he'd make the holiday one nobody would forget.

Chapter Five

"Mama, is that really Chris's father?"

"Yes, honey. He's been searching for Chris all this time."

"But I thought he was dead. They said he was killed in the fire when the building fell. And now he's come to take Chris away from us."

"No!"

Chris startled all of them with his yell. He struggled in his father's arms, pushing to get away and Gabe, stunned by the protest, let his son down.

Chris ran to Maureen. "You can't take me away from them. I won't go!"

"Chris, listen to me. We have a home. I've come a long way searching for you. And it's time we got back to our lives."

"No!" Chris found a refuge within Kathleen's arms which closed protectively around the small shoulders.

"Chris." Maureen used a firm tone, without anger, but one every mother used to warn a child that it was enough, and every child heeded that warning or accepted punishment for disobedience.

Maureen was torn in her sympathies for son and father. She had a feeling the reunion Gabe Channing envisioned with his son was less than he wanted, and having her be witness to his tears of joy wasn't easy for any man, much less a prideful one. The thought helped her ignore the harsh flare of resentment in his eyes.

With a look she warned her daughter to silence, and fixed her attention on Chris.

"This has been a shock for you, Chris, but you must not speak to your father that way. It's not respectful, and I know you know better. Now, both you children sit down. Mr. Channing, please join us."

She could only imagine how ill her ordering him sat with the man, but they all needed time to calm down. Though when she saw Chris's lower lip tremble as he held back tears and his small hands clench into fists, she wanted to fight anyone, even his father, for the child.

All her protective love was in her eyes when she met Gabe's stare as he sat down. She thought of the power he commanded over them if his claim was true about owning this cabin. She could, by her interference, see her daughter put out in the dead of winter. A denial flared inside her at the thought, and she admitted to herself it was unlikely. But it didn't change her mind. Chris needed her.

She smiled at both children to show there was no anger with them and fought her instinct to take Chris up in her lap and just hug him.

"What I wanted to say was this," she began. "I'm sure your father doesn't mean to ride out this very day, Chris. Do you?" she asked Gabe.

"No. Of course, not. We'll get an early start—"

"In a day or so," Maureen finished for him.

"Another storm like yesterday and the passes will be closed. I won't be able to get him home," Gabe said in a controlled voice that held no hint of the anger he felt because of her interference. Yet he felt guilt, too. She was trying to smooth things over, and he could not fault her for that.

"Won't go. I like it here."

"You liked Denver, too. Remember our big sleigh and Mrs. Kingsley's cookies? You liked the toy shops. Your friends miss you, Chris. Not as much as I did, but they all hoped and prayed that I'd find you and bring you home."

Gabe shook his head. His grin widened into a smile. "Just wait till they hear you talking. I can't believe it myself. This will take some getting used to."

With a very serious expression, Chris remained still and silent for long minutes, then words burst forth. "They said you were dead."

"Who, Chris? Who told you that?"

"Men were yelling in the hotel. I wasn't sure. I wanted to see."

"Then you left the room, right?"

He couldn't meet his father's gaze and looked toward Maureen. "She helped me say my prayers every night that you were alive."

"You can't know how much that means to me, Chris." Gabe's voice, husky to begin with, broke a little. "I'd like to spend time with you and get to know this grown-up son."

Maureen thought father and son spending time alone was a wonderful idea. She ignored Chris's resentment when she kept Kathleen from following him. But before Gabe stepped outside, she went to apologize to him.

"I wish I could take back the moment I believed you were dead and took Chris with me."

"The how and why don't matter. Nothing matters now that I have my son. But I can see I've a hard trail to get him to leave you and I've got to get back to Denver."

He appeared thoughtful as he snapped the brim of his hat forward and buttoned up his heavy jacket. "You might think about coming with us."

Giving her no time to answer, he was gone.

"Mama, you can't let that man have Chris. He—"

"He's the boy's father, Kathleen, and that gives him all the rights in the world."

"We aren't going to leave here, are we?"

But Maureen couldn't answer her daughter. It simply might not be her choice. Yet she had the uncomfortable feeling that Gabe Channing didn't take no for an answer often.

There was only one thing to do. Maureen made soup. Like her mother and grandmother before her, anything that happened, births, deaths, fights or weddings, they made soup. And the bread making came after, for there was time to think while kneading dough. And she had lots to think about.

It was the aroma of baking that lured Gabe and his son back to the cabin. Gabe had learned quite a bit about his boy. He had taken some of that Irishwoman's stubbornness and made it his own. He would not be moved about leaving Maureen and her daughter. And Gabe was in a neatly boxed corner.

"It would be the best ever Christmas present to take them home with us. I don't want a new pony or a new sled. I want Maureen and Kathleen. They love me, Papa. They really love me."

It was then that Gabe realized that the son he thought protected from the truth about his mother not wanting him had known the truth. He hurt for his son, and as he lifted the boy into his strong arms and just held him, he knew he would do anything, give anything, to keep his child happy. He was also mindful of the great debt he owed Maureen O'Rourke and her daughter. But how did a man pay back someone for loving his child?

"I will try, Chris. I can promise you that much. But you understand that I can't force them to come with us."

"Sure you can. You can do anything."

With that praise and belief a burden on his shoulders, Gabe walked into the cabin where the luscious scents of fresh-baked bread and steaming soup were enough to make his mouth water and his stomach growl. But there was another sight that aroused a far different hunger.

Maureen O'Rourke.

A bit of flour was smeared at her temple and tiny curling wisps of hair escaped her neat coil. She appeared softer somehow with her rosy cheeks flushed with heat from the oven and a warm smile of welcome that included him.

He had not had much chance to think about the strength and courage it took her to travel with two children in this wilderness. And while he was not a religious man, he had to wonder what unseen fate had led her to this cabin, and then sent him here. He had not lived here in almost five years, and in that time been back only to make sure the cabin was snug against the weather.

His gaze strayed to the well cared for rifle hung near the door rack, much the same as his father's hunting rifle hung there when he was a child.

He listened to the soft murmur of Maureen's voice talking to the children and thought about her not asking for anything from him, other than a demand that he go gently in treating with his own child.

Gabe had a bone deep, unshakable feeling there was not a mercenary thought in her head. She had to know she could ask and receive anything, everything he had for what she had done for his son.

Strong enough for the land, pretty enough to stir a man, gentle and kind enough to love a stranger's child. Maureen, he decided, was a woman a man could search long and hard to find. When a wise man found such a woman, he could count himself lucky, incredibly lucky.

There had been women who had attracted him over the years, but none offered what he wanted. And if asked, he couldn't have put names to what he was looking for. Yet, there was something about Maureen that drew him.

He must not forget the woman had a temper. He smiled to

himself. His mother had an Irish temper that kept the house roused with betting when she'd been alive.

Cautioned by those memories, Gabe determined that keeping his promise to his son depended on planning and executing a good campaign to have his way.

There wasn't a moment to be lost if he was to get them all out of the mountains to celebrate a spectacular Christmas in Denver.

Chapter Six

Gabe had his first opportunity to be alone with Maureen after supper when the children were tucked into the sleeping loft. For a man who was rarely at a loss for words, he wasn't sure how to begin. He had seen the cool distance she had maintained all day. He thought a truthful compliment would be a good start.

"You are a mighty fine cook. Don't know when I've eaten better."

"I saw you enjoyed your supper, Mr. Channing, but I'm sure your Mrs. Kingsley takes good care of setting a fine table for you."

"Why, she does. But that doesn't mean a man can't appreciate another woman's cooking." He smiled at her, but she wasn't looking at him. "Did you and your husband have a bakery?"

"Bakery? Oh, you mean all the bread. I just like to bake."

Gabe thought he had never had a question turned aside so neatly. He decided to let the matter be for now.

"Mr. Channing—"

"Gabe, please."

"All right, then. It seems to me you've been chewing on

something all day. If something is bothering you just say so. I'm not a woman who cares to walk on eggs around a body.''

''I never meant to worry you.'' Gabe refilled his cup with the last of the coffee and set the pot aside. He glanced to where she stood at the end of the table, calm as could be.

''Won't you join me?'' he asked, indicating the bench next to him. ''This may take a while to say.''

Maureen sat across from him. Her concern focused on one thing. Would he or wouldn't he allow them to stay in the cabin? Direct she might be, but she could not force herself to ask that one question.

''I know that you said you didn't want anything from me,'' Gabe began, ''but I can't allow that. There must be something you want or need. Chris is very fond of you. He said he won't come home with me unless you and your daughter come, too.''

She did not answer, only studied the man across from her. The more she looked upon him, the more perfectly each feature of his face blended into a handsome countenance. She resisted the urge to brush back the one lock of black hair that continually fell over his forehead. And his mouth was not as stern when he smiled.

He cleared his throat and she roused herself, glancing away from him.

''Have you no answer?''

''Mr.…Gabe, did you never wonder why your son came so easily with me? Or to think how we came upon this place?''

''Of course I wondered. Chris said you found him outside the hotel and—''

''Yes, that's true. But did he tell you that he was running away? I kept him with me and Kathleen, fearing that he would run off with no one to care for him. When word came that you were believed killed, I asked if he would come with us. And it was Chris who spoke of this far-off cabin, although, I admit, he never said it belonged to you.''

''Chris was running away?''

Sympathy welled inside Maureen. Here was a father who knew little of his son. "It all turned out well and you have the boy back. But will you make a new beginning with him?"

She knew she had shocked him silent, for he sat shaking his head. The rest was for Chris to tell his father, but she could start him thinking in the right direction and give the boy she had come to love as her own a true Christmas present. One that he would have for the rest of his life. And the present would be twofold, for Gabe Channing would receive a gift that could not be bought, yet was more precious than any purchased gift.

"Chris," she said softly, "told me this is where he wanted to come. He had to see the place where you were born and grew up. He heard the tales from your father before he died and this was a dream of his. He said you refused to make the trip with him. Being a bold and, to my mind, very courageous boy, he decided to set out on his own."

"But he's only—"

"Does age matter when a dream is to be followed?"

"No. No, you're right. I had no idea he felt so strongly about this."

Maureen went with her instinct and covered his larger hand with her own. "Gabe, before you leave here, spend some time with your son. He's a very special boy, and one who loves you. But he needs to find his own way, too, and he thinks you protected him too much."

"My lord, I had no idea he felt this way."

"Now you do." Maureen rose from the bench. "I'll set a bed by the fire for you. No more talk about sleeping in the barn."

"You've given me a great deal to think about, Maureen. My mother often said things happen for a reason. Perhaps I was meant to lose Chris without harm coming his way so that I would understand that all I have is nothing without him."

Their eyes met with a silent understanding, but she found she had to be sure.

"Then you'll stay?"

"You mean for longer than a few days?"

"Yes, Gabe. Stay and spend Christmas with us There is plenty of food, and the children have so much they wish to do. It would be a simple time and one for sharing."

Backlit as she was by the fire's glow, he found himself nodding, and his son was not the only reason he agreed. There was something special about this quiet woman. Only time together would tell him if something more could come of it.

"One thing more, Gabe. All time is relative. One day may be a lifetime, a year can be forever. It is not the number of the days, but how those days are spent."

"As well as whom you spend them with."

"Yes, Gabe. That as well. Good night."

Sweet dreams, lovely lady. He only thought the words and merely echoed her wish for a good night as she left him.

Would it be so terrible to spend time here? To teach Chris and show him favorite places? Wasn't part of being wealthy being able to do as he wanted and not needed to do?

A wise woman, Maureen O'Rourke. Wise and lovely. He wouldn't find spending time with her and the children less than a pleasure.

Making his bed by the fire, he lay there with his eyes closed and thoughts filled with questions about Maureen.

She appeared a young woman who had overcome some great adversity and found peace with herself. She intrigued him.

And as sleep claimed him, he found that she filled his dreams, as well.

Maureen lay tossing in the bed she had never shared with another and prayed for sleep to come. There was no wind tonight, but it was cold. She glanced to where the moonlight streamed through the frosted window.

Shifting yet again beneath the thick down quilt, she tried to ease her mind of all thoughts and settle down to sleep.

But thoughts of how lonely she had been intruded. Loneliness and the man on the other side of the fireplace seemed to go hand in hand. She tried to deny that she found him a threat. Not his size, which was taller and heavier than herself, but he threatened this new life she had made for herself and daughter. And Chris. She couldn't forget the boy.

She wondered how bad a mistake she had made to encourage him to stay on here. He was a troubled man, and one who needed some guidance with his son. He wouldn't see it that way, she was sure, but her feelings were too strong to be denied.

One has only so much time in this life, so devote it to the people most important to you, to work you love, and leave all else. She couldn't remember how many times she had heard her papa say those words. And they were good ones to live by. Chris was someone she loved. She had to help him.

Punching down her pillow, she turned again, wishing she could deny the strange stirring inside her whenever she imagined Gabe's stormy blue-gray eyes. And the touch tonight of his hand, strong, long fingers that would both protect and soothe. Funny thought. She didn't want a man to protect or to soothe her. Maybe one to share with, but men as a rule didn't want women to walk beside them.

There would be nothing more to these fanciful thoughts. She intended to make sure of that.

Still, it had been pleasant to sit and talk over the last of the coffee with him. It boded well that he was willing to listen to her. Perhaps… But the thought was never completed for sleep came and she dreamed of a man as lonely as she.

* * *

It was the warmth that helped Maureen to wake up. In the year she had lived in the cabin she had gotten used to it being chilly until she stoked the stove and built up the fire.

But sunlight was streaming into the back room and she smelled coffee. Coffee? She sat up abruptly, clutching the quilt to her chest. Then she remembered that Gabe had spent the night in the cabin. From outside came a rhythmic thud. Someone chopping wood. Gabe again.

She dressed quickly, embarrassed over letting him take care of the children and the chores. What must he think of her? Lying in bed of a morning, lazy as could be?

There was no sign of the three of them when she reached the table. The coffeepot was on the stove and still hot. The dishes were washed, too. She poured a cup of coffee for herself and moved to the one window and looked out.

Gabe was there with a pile of freshly split wood and both Chris and Kathleen were moving pieces to the woodpile.

Maureen stared at the ripple and play of the muscles in Gabe's strong back. He had stripped off his heavy coat and worked in his shirt, sleeves rolled up to show powerful forearms as he lifted the ax and struck a clean blow to the wood. She didn't want to think about his body, but alone now with none to see her, she felt the stirring of desire. It had been a long, long time since she felt attracted to a man. Her gaze held to his hands as he struck the wood again. He said something to the children, for she saw their smiles as he stepped back and allowed them to pick up the newly split wood.

He had to feel her watching him. He turned quickly and looked toward the cabin. She almost stepped back and away from the impact of his intense gaze.

He lifted his hand to shade his eyes from the sun and she held her place, lifting the cup and smiling at him.

Kathleen approached him and he leaned down to hear what she said. It must be something serious, for Gabe crouched down and appeared to be listening with all his attention to her daughter.

The door of the cabin opened, and Maureen turned. Chris stood there, a wide smile and sparkling eyes telling her he was happy.

"Papa wants to take us sledding. We want you to come with us."

A day of playing with the children? Why not? With Gabe along, she would have someone to share the burden of climbing back up the hill.

"All right, Chris. Give me a few minutes to change."

He was gone in seconds, running back to his father, and Maureen heard the excitement in his voice along with a whoop from Kathleen.

She took from her chest the heavy twill pants that had belonged to her husband along with a woolen shirt. She stripped and redressed quickly, knowing the impatience of the children. Tucking her long hair beneath a wool cap, she paused for a moment to whisper a prayer, then hurried out to join them.

Gabe hid every painful wince walking brought to his aching muscles. It had been a long, long time since he had split wood. Yet, despite the pain, he felt good when he saw the pile of wood stacked against the cabin. He knew that Maureen had watched him, and he was thankful that she had not seen his first attempts.

He glanced back to where Maureen walked with Chris. She almost looked like a child dressed in clothing too large for her. A man's clothes. He wondered whose they were.

He knew too little about her. Where had she come from? Yet he trusted her. That in itself was unusual for him.

But what else could he do? Whenever he thought about his coming here as he did, meeting Maureen and then finding out she had his son made a man wonder if the Lord hadn't had a hand in the planning of this.

His mother used to talk of miracles. His father didn't believe that anything but hard work would give a man all he needed.

Gabe had thought himself the same, but now he wasn't sure.

He couldn't believe he'd suggested going sledding. This was play, a child's play and here he was leading the way up the gradual rise of the slope where he had sent his own sled flying down years ago.

The air, cold and crisp, had a bite to it. Without the wind the sunlight made it feel warm. He had forgotten how the woods looked with their drapes of thick snow piled on the towering pine's sweeping boughs, and icicles hanging with rainbows trapped inside. Above, the sky was blue without a cloud and nothing but the crunch of their boots broke the silence.

He looked upward, toward where the mountains lifted abruptly, ragged slopes broken by steep ledges, covered with snow. It was a lonely place, but he remembered being happy here as a child. He had the woods and his books.

''We marked this place,'' Maureen turned to say. ''All summer, the children cleared rocks from the slope. We had a few spills because of them last winter.''

The children's laughter brought his smile. He could well imagine who had done the spilling into snowdrifts.

''Well, who goes first?'' Gabe set the sled he carried down, working the runners back and forth to give him a smooth start.

''Chris should have the first ride with you.'' Maureen stood off to the side with her daughter. Gabe dropped belly first onto the sled and Chris scampered to climb on top of him.

''Give us a push. A good one,'' Gabe said.

Maureen and Kathleen did as he asked, and watched as the sled sped down the hill, Chris's shout filling the air. She wasn't sure what Gabe did, but the sled slid to a smooth stop down where it was level. Chris climbed off, and if Gabe was a little slower, it was barely noticed.

Gabe took Kathleen down next, then Maureen had a turn with each child. When she came back up with Chris, there was whispering among the three of them, but she didn't hear it as she set the sled in place for another run.

"We're all going down on this one."

Maureen stared at Gabe, her mouth open, but her protest died when she looked at the children. Still, someone had to be sensible.

"I don't think we'll all fit."

"Sure we will."

He made her sit first, with Kathleen snug between her legs and Chris on her daughter's lap. Maureen was afraid the sled would go over before Gabe got in position behind her. They were packed together like peas in a pod, warm, too, with Gabe's body cutting the cold behind her.

"Hold tight. Here we go."

Gabe pushed off with one foot and then they were flying down the hill, the children screaming with delight. Maureen hid her face against her daughter's shoulder, afraid to look. She wasn't sure who twisted to the side, but felt the sled tilt and before any of them could right the sled, over it went, dumping them into a snowbank.

It was a cold, wet, hungry group that trudged their way back to the cabin. But there was laughter, too, a wonderful sound to a man who had heard little of it from his child, and more so to a woman who enjoyed the deeper laugh of a man who had not laughed much at all.

Boots and coats dripping with melting snow were by the door as the children ran for the sleeping loft to get into dry clothes.

As if they had done this a hundred times, Gabe moved to replenish the fire and Maureen moved to stoke the stove. She made a fresh pot of coffee, and then heated a pan of milk for the children.

"You'd better change into something dry," she said without looking at him. She couldn't explain this sudden feeling of shyness that came over her. "By rights the back room should be yours. I'll bed down out here."

"You go change first," he countered. "I saw the fixings for flapjacks. That and bacon I can handle."

"You cook?"

"Don't sound so surprised. I did for myself for a long time before I had a claim that paid off. Simple grub, nothing fancy."

Maureen left him to it and hurried back to change. Her turkey twill skirt had seen better days, but its dark-brown color hid much of the mending she'd done. Her shirtwaist was once white, but repeated washings had turned it to the color of cream. A bit of black ribbon tied her hair at her nape.

The bacon was sizzling when she rejoined them. The children were seated at the table, eating the first of the flapjacks Gabe had made.

"Sit down. I'm told they are passably good. Not as good as yours, but filling just the same."

"Kathleen," she said with a warning look.

"Wasn't me, Ma. Chris said it. I like them just fine. I'll even have seconds. Please," she added quickly at a look from her mother.

Maureen watched Gabe with the children while they ate, him doing most of the talking about favorite places he had while growing up around the cabin. He had a great deal of patience with their questions, but it was the sound of his husky voice that lulled her into daydreaming.

Pleasant it was, to sit in the middle of the day with the sun streaming in through the window and the fire's warmth at her back.

She listened to the days of a boy alone finding his way through the woods, making his own discoveries from a beaver's dam to a small herd of buffalo in a mountain valley almost a day's ride from the cabin.

"Take a summer afternoon and find a meadow sweet with

wildflowers blooming and just lie there watching the clouds form. Listen to the breeze ruffling cottonwood leaves or stirring the aspens.''

''Golden coins,'' Maureen murmured, watching him with half-closed eyes.

''Just like that with the sun shining on them,'' he agreed.

''We picked berries in the summer,'' Kathleen told him.

''And see deer all the time. We even found a fawn but Maureen said we had to leave it be. She let us watch from the edge of the forest until its ma came for it.''

''You liked that, Chris?'' Gabe asked his son.

''I love being here. Up in the grove of aspens we see elk when we gather dry wood. And I get to fish. Maureen showed me how to make fish traps.''

''An unusual skill for a woman to have.''

His soft voice sent no alarm to Maureen, yet she was not so sleepy that she did not miss the question there.

''We like to eat fish. And it takes time to sit with a line in the water. Keeping the three of us fed and putting up stores for winter, the traps seemed like a good idea.''

Chris yawned and Kathleen followed with one of her own. It was catching, for Maureen put up a hand to cover hers. The sledding had been a good idea, but she was accustomed to steady work that didn't take so much out of a body.

With her elbow resting on the table she propped her head on her hand, smiling as Chris, then Kathleen each told of the adventures they had had since coming to the cabin.

''The berries were the biggest I've ever seen and Chris, well, he picked a bucketful in spite of all he ate. Then this old bear came, a big silver-tipped grizzly and treed us. We was scared. But Ma, she came looking for us near to dark. She had to fire a few shots to chase that bear away.''

That was the last story Maureen heard. To the soft rise and fall of their voices her breathing became deep and even and she made a sleepy murmur when she felt herself lifted from the bench. Someone warm and strong held and carried her, but some inner sense told her she was safe, that it was all right for her to sleep.

Gabe stared down at her for a few moments before he drew the thick quilt over her. There were faint bluish shadows beneath her eyes. The woman needed someone to take care of her. She worked hard, and he guessed she found little enough time to rest. He remembered how it had been living in the cabin for his mother, working from before sunrise to after sunset.

From a chance remark made by her daughter, he knew she had been widowed before the child was born. But the men in Colorado weren't blind. Why hadn't she remarried?

Without thought he reached out to touch the cool, silky hair, brushing a loose tendril from her cheek.

There was a danger here for him. She was making him feel things he didn't want, and maybe want something he couldn't have.

But he committed himself to staying. And there was Christmas to think about.

So while she slept, he led the children back into the forest to gather pinecones lying close to the trunks. They in turn played hide-and-seek within the shadowed caves formed by the weighted branches. They had a snowball fight, which he promptly lost, and once back inside he showed them how to pierce the cones, then string them into garlands for the tree they would have.

He found himself promising all sorts of things to his son and the less shy Kathleen. By the time Maureen woke up and joined them, filled with apologies for sleeping the afternoon away, he silenced her with his intent to stay.

''We are going to have a fine Christmas together.''

''Oh, Pa.'' Chris threw his arms around his father's neck. ''You already gave me what I wanted most. And just you wait till you've tasted one of Maureen's cakes. You are gonna love them. Love them as much as me."

His gaze sought Maureen's. Love? There was a thought. And who knew what the cold winter days would bring by Christmas?

Chapter Seven

Three days later, Maureen, with a faint ghost of amusement in her eyes, turned away from the corner where Gabe and the children were whispering. There was a lot of that these days, and she left them alone to make their plans. Gabe Channing filled a void she hadn't known was there. He had a quiet, easy way about him that drew her to spend time in his company. Her daughter adored him, overcoming her painful shyness to speak her mind whenever he urged her on.

Only last night, Kathleen confessed that she wouldn't mind having a papa just like Gabe. Maureen had been so flustered, she couldn't even remember what she answered.

She had never thought of another husband. Perhaps if she didn't have money put by she would have done what most every other woman did—remarry as quick as a fox runs.

She wasn't sure she was comfortable with how easy it had become to depend upon Gabe. He chopped the wood, he shoveled the snow from another light fall. He was up before her every morning and tended to chores out in the barn. And he took such pleasure in the work that she said nothing to him about usurping her place. He ignored her every query about the ownership of the cabin. Actually walked away when she mentioned that she would buy the land from him.

Patience, she warned herself. Lots of patience. Just as much as you have with teaching the children their sums or reading.

But it was hard to bridle emotions when the man took special care with her daughter. He was so gentle with her shy child. And Chris… Oh, she couldn't believe the change in the boy. He was full of mischief, laughing and talking and making plans.

One thing she knew, Gabe didn't have a selfish bone in his body. He was so considerate of her feelings, of those of the children that she knew it carried into everything he did. Tempting her. The man was temptation itself when he smiled at her in that special way of his, as if she were the prettiest lady in his life.

Maureen returned to mixing the thick batter for corn fritters. She had soaked the dried corn in milk with a bit of grated sugar before she added the eggs, cornmeal and flour.

"My mother always put a pinch of salt in the batter."

Maureen almost dropped the bowl. The words were whispered in her ear and Gabe was so close that she could feel the heat of his body as he leaned over her shoulder. If she moved her head a fraction her lips would likely brush his cheek. As it was she felt her pulse leap and her heart seemed to speed up its beat.

She licked her lips, ready to answer him, but he had turned away.

"I'll be in the barn until supper," he said.

"I'm coming." Chris jumped up from where he'd been reading by the fire. "Kathleen?"

"No. You go on. I'll help Ma with supper."

Maureen saw that her daughter had a dreamy expression as she stared into the fire. "Anything wrong, honey?"

"I like that man, Ma. He's so sweet to me. Wait till you see what he's— Oh, I'm not to tell you. It's a surprise."

"A surprise?"

"For Christmas, Ma. A present. And don't you go around peeking any."

Maureen laughed. Her daughter sounded like her when she warned the children against hunting for the gifts she had hidden in her chest. But Kathleen's words stayed with her and later in her room with the candles lit, she wondered what she could make for Gabe for Christmas.

She had been as amazed as Gabe when Chris had asked about his mines, naming them all. Then mentioned the ranch, and the men working there.

What kind of a homemade gift could she give a man who already had so much?

For the first time she felt the lack of money, and of being near a town where she could buy something fitting for such a man.

And she didn't like this feeling at all. She had nothing to be ashamed of, and it was more for the children to give him something nice. Something special.

She had to think quickly for the days were passing.

In the barn the same thoughts were passing through Gabe's mind. His hands were busy smoothing out the wood for a small quilting frame that Chris and Kathleen swore Maureen longed to have. All her daughter would tell him was that her mother's got broken, but wouldn't say where or when or even how. But he wanted to make her something else, a thing so special she would always remember the gift and the man who gave it. He didn't even know where this need came from, only that it was there when he finally fell asleep at night and was the first thing in his mind in the morning.

Now in the quiet night, the scent of fresh-cut wood curls filling the air along with the hay and animals, he thought of the years behind him. And of the lonely nights.

He had wealth and a fine house, a ranch and respect. He had ridden the wild country but left that aside when he married until he understood the poor bargain he had made. Now he wanted more. He wanted that house to be a home. One filled with love and laughter. And children.

He wanted more nights where the fire blazed warm and the talk flowed easy and sleepy children needed to be carried and tucked into bed. He wanted what he had found here.

But he wasn't at all sure of what Maureen O'Rourke wanted or needed.

He'd always been a direct man. Yet he found himself shying away from prying into her past, or asking about her future. She wanted the land and cabin. Beyond that, he knew too little.

He was sure she liked him. She had been lingering awhile after the children were asleep and their time was quiet, but a shared quiet that brought him a peaceful feeling. She was a woman who would always walk beside her man, rich or poor, good times and bad.

And that very kissable mouth held a temptation he was finding hard to resist.

The woman was as deep as the still waters of the pond below. She had said nothing that wasn't all polite and respectful without a bit of suggestion to tell him how she felt about him. If she felt anything at all.

Gabe might have saved himself the questions about Maureen if he had seen her slip outside to stare up at the night sky. The stars were coming out, one by one, bright and brighter still like lamps lighting the night.

She knew Gabe was back in the barn with Chris and she wondered if he ever thought about her. There was a great strength in the man, but something more, for with him she felt at ease, calm, secure and at home. There was that special something a few men have, that quiet assurance that was balm to her spirit that come what may, Gabe would stand tall.

They had so much in common. If only he would make some move, say a word or maybe…kiss her.

Lord, she thought, *I've not asked for much in this life, but if You truly brought us all together for a reason, I'd like to know.*

Gabe was born for this land. She couldn't see him living in a city like Denver. He was born of these mountains, or the tree-clad hills, and she believed this is where the home of his heart was.

A good man, a little rough, and a whole lot lonely.

Very much like her. She huddled within the thick coat, looking up at the bright north star. She hadn't made a wish on a star since she was a child. Foolishness. That's all it was. But she whispered the words and made her wish.

Her breath caught on a startled cry when she heard her wish whispered aloud by Gabe. His husky voice sent a shiver of awareness through her.

"Sorry. I didn't mean to startle you. Guess you were lost in thought. Can't blame you. I haven't made wishes on those stars since I was a boy living up here. There were times when I couldn't wait to grow tall and climb the mountaintop so I could reach out and pull one of those stars down for my own."

"Oh, I've felt the same. They seem so close to us up here. I never tire of looking at them on a clear night like this."

"But it's getting colder," he said, slipping an arm around her shoulders. "Chris is already inside claiming he's hungry as a bear. Time we went inside, too."

Once he had helped Maureen with her coat and hung up his own, he took a deep appreciative breath. "This is close to what heaven must smell like. I can taste those fritters you made topped with sugar and cinnamon."

"You're not smelling them, Pa, you're seeing them."

"Right you are, Chris." Gabe tousled his son's hair and took his place next to him on the bench. As with each meal, Maureen said grace before passing the platter of thick ham slices and cutting the loaf of corn bread.

Gabe poured cups of milk for the children. Both he and Maureen reached for the butter crock.

"You first," she offered.

"No. Ladies first, always."

Their gazes locked and for a moment or two they stared at each other. Kathleen rolled her eyes at Chris, then pushed the crock toward him.

"Oh, no, Kathleen. You heard Pa, lady goes first."

Hearing themselves mimicked, brought smiles then soft laughter and only seconds later they repeated it over the platter of fritters. There was more teasing as they took their time at the table, for these winter nights were for storytelling and Gabe had a store of them.

There were sleepy protests from both Chris and Kathleen when he ended his last one and helped them up the ladder to the loft. He was climbing back down when Maureen came around the corner holding a lit candle. The red glints of her hair against the smooth skin of her cheek drew his gaze. With each passing day he felt the stirring of desire and now, for the first time, he sensed the feeling was returned.

The space was narrow and there was no way to pass without touching each other unless she backed up or he climbed higher. He felt the need in him to touch her, and wondered if his hands would tremble if he did. The light, flowery scent of her only increased the need.

Her eyes were troubled when she looked up at him.

He saw the rapid flutter of the pulse at the base of her throat, and even a faint flush on her cheeks. He heard the small catch in her breath and found his own was uneven. When she stepped back, he wasn't fooled. She was as wary of him in this small space as he was of her.

"You don't need to be afraid of me, Maureen."

"I'm not afraid of you." *Only of myself and what you make me feel.*

"I'd never hurt a woman or be where I'm not wanted."

"But you know you're wanted here," she said with an impish smile as she took his words to heart. He wouldn't hurt her, nor would he force her into any decisions until she was ready to make them.

"Go on to bed, Maureen. I want to take a look around outside before I bed down."

"Has Chris told you yet why he was running away?"

"He told me."

She saw pain and denial in his eyes and touched his arm. Her move brought the candle closer to his face.

"Was your boy unfair?"

"No. He told the truth as he saw it. I was busy, too busy building wealth to leave to him so he'd be free to do whatever he loved."

"He loved you best, I think," she said softly, then smiled. "He has a great deal of courage. All he wanted is you. And he said he had dream of coming here. I guess you told him about the place often enough. He never once faltered in his directions. Uncanny how we all came to be here."

"Maybe it was meant to be," he said with a smile of his own.

She shied from committing herself in any way. "Maybe."

"Sweet dreams, Maureen."

He pressed flat against the ladder to allow her passage and watched her disappear into the back room. But it was a long while before he found sleep. He had heard two Christmas wishes whispered in his ear tonight from Chris and Kathleen. They were not exactly presents he could put beneath a tree or hang on the branches. He was not even sure he could make their wish come true.

Chapter Eight

Gabe ran his fingertips over the wood roof of the dollhouse he and Chris were building for Kathleen. He had found most of his father's old tools stored up in the barn loft and wondered why they had been left behind. Not that he wasn't thankful. The time he was spending with Chris helped him understand his son. They shared laughter and quiet talks.

"Kathleen's gonna love this, Pa. She's been wanting one for a long time. Guess with them moving around so much there wasn't room for her to have one. Four rooms, too. Only she ain't got nothing to put inside."

"We could make some furniture, Chris. Think she'd like that?"

"Guess she would. Women set a store by having things don't they?"

"Some more than others. And son, some women set a store by having gold to buy more than they will ever need."

"Maureen's not like that. She thinks this place is as close to heaven as a body can get. You know she's happy 'cause she hums and sings all the time she's working."

Gabe ran the plane over the edge of the roof, then followed with his fingertips to be sure it was smooth.

"Pa, how come you never worked with wood at home?"

"Wasn't a need to."

Chris stood back to admire the house, but shook his head when his father glanced at him. "Don't understand that, Pa. You're as happy as Maureen when she bakes up a batch of cookies and knows me and Kathleen are gonna snap them up quick as can be. Don't seem right a man should have pleasure in a thing and then not do it."

"And just when did you get to be so wise?"

"Maureen figures all that time I wasn't talking much I looked and listened and was just storing things away. Being quiet, she said, gave me lots of time for thinking."

"She must be right. It can't be anything I taught you. But I promise you, Chris, that won't ever happen again."

Gabe held his son's gaze with his own. "I love you, son. You're more important to me than anything else in the world. I don't ever want you to think you need to run off. You come tell me when something's bothering you. And I want your promise about that."

"All right, Pa."

A wide grin split Chris's face and Gabe's matched it.

"You know Pa, Maureen would sure like an angel for the tree. Said when she was little they went to some fancy lady's house and they had candles on their tree with pretty ribbons. And right on top was an angel."

"Chris, you're talking about carving skill and I don't think I—"

"You could try, Pa. You could. I know—"

"All right. All right. I'll try. Anything else?"

"Well, you got to think about the wishes me and Kathleen told you."

"Chris, you start trimming off that round from the log for a tabletop. And those wishes, well, son, to tell you the truth, it's not an easy thing to happen. Folks either have feelings for each other or they don't. It isn't something that can be forced, Chris. You understand that? Maureen's a woman with her thoughts and feelings. Her own wishes for what she wants her life to be like, too."

"But you're a fine man, Pa. I heard Mrs. Kingsley say many a time what a fine catch you'd make for some woman. Only you ran awfully fast. Didn't you ever—"

"Chris—"

"No. You said you'd listen to me. Sometimes, Pa, I'd get so lonely I wanted to cry. And sometimes I'd see a look in your eyes like you was lonely like me. I just figured you like Maureen a lot. You're smiling more. Never seen you smile as much as you do here."

"Oh, Chris, you make it all sound so easy. But, son, grown people need love before they promise to share their lives together."

"Did you love my ma?"

"I thought I did. I wouldn't have married her if I didn't believe that. But she was looking for riches and I was too quiet for her. So she wanted to take off for back east, and I paid her way. Gave her a good settlement, too, when I divorced her."

Gabe caught hold of his son and hugged him. "You were what I wanted to keep."

"And I want to keep hold of Maureen and Kathleen. Can't do that without you, Pa."

Gabe didn't answer. He couldn't. But he wondered if Kathleen had schemed with Chris to bring this about. How did Maureen feel?

Maureen at that moment was holding her daughter close and thinking about what she said. How could this child know of a woman's loneliness? But that's what Kathleen said she saw in her mother's eyes. She knew her child missed having a father and a home after all these years spent moving from one place to another. She tried to explain that a woman should marry for love, for the need to share life with that one special man, but all Kathleen said was that Gabe was a fine man and that she loved him a little. And she never wanted to be without Chris, for she thought of him as her little brother.

To her daughter it was all so simple. Maureen wished it was. Now, she wondered if she hadn't made a terrible mistake by insisting that Gabe and Chris stay on.

It didn't take great wisdom to understand what Chris and Kathleen were scheming.

The thing was, she did not know if she should talk to Gabe about it.

Waiting a little might help her reach a decision.

But waiting, when two determined children were around, proved a sore trial for Maureen and Gabe.

Christmas day grew closer and there was much to be done, and much of it with whispers broken off, or warnings not to go there or peek somewhere else. They had spent a day in the woods scouting out the perfect tree, but Gabe shared his worry about the lack of snow.

''Seen one year like this. Had some light snowfalls and then nothing. When the next one came in, we could barely keep a path shoveled to get to the barn.''

Maureen with her daughter's help spent every free moment in her room. She had a finely tanned hide that she cut into game bags for Gabe and Chris, and sewed with strips of thin rawhide. There was just enough rawhide left to thread through holes to form the initials of their first names.

All four of them worked together at night snipping then flattening the tin from the canned goods. Maureen drew patterns of stars and diamonds. Gabe cut them out and the children punched holes for hanging with bits of string Maureen had saved. It was a quiet-talking time, a good-feeling time with teasing and hints of presents to come. And each night Maureen lingered a little later for private talks with Gabe as they spoke of their pasts and their dreams.

Maureen's tale wasn't unusual. She was born in Ireland to a tenant farmer who wanted a better life for his family. She was three when they settled in Pennsylvania and her father found work in a mill. It was hard saving money, for everything was bought on credit at the mill-owned store and there never seemed to be extra. Her mother earned a bit with her lace making and the stories of free land in the west lured her parents to try farming. But drought took the crops two years running, and then her mother died.

''Da, he headed for Oregon, for they said the land was rich soil with trees big as ten men around. For a while it was good there. I married young and then Da and my husband were killed in a log jam on the river. I sold off the farm not knowing that I carried Kathleen. I've been moving ever since looking for a place to settle.''

''And then you found Chris and he led you here,'' Gabe finished for her.

''Yes. I felt as if I had come home.''

He reached across to hold her hand. ''I know. And I forgot how much the people inside make a place a home.''

She squeezed his hand, feeling no need to add to that and they sat watching the flames, content to share this quiet time.

Maureen caught him yawning and started to rise, but Gabe tugged her hand to keep her sitting near him. He reached out and smoothed her hair back from her cheek.

''Maureen, I… Oh, no sense in saying anything.'' And he kissed her.

Surprise held her still in those first moments, and then the very gentle touch of his warm lips on hers lured her into staying. She had dreamed about Gabe's kisses, wondered if he would be gentle or rough. But here was a sweet tenderness that took only what she gave until need asserted itself and passion demanded a bit more.

His hand cupped her chin, tilting her head as his lips met hers for a deep, searing kiss. Her hands curled on his shoulders, clinging to him. The passion he had sensed was there. Her arms slid around his neck and she kissed him back.

Her nose bumped his as she slanted her mouth beneath his and he pulled back as she caught her breath. She was awkward, most endearingly as if she had little experience with kissing. Tenderly then, he tempered his kiss with gentleness, smoothing her hair back away from her cheek.

Maureen heard the soft moan that escaped her lips. She went willingly into the arms that pulled her tight against Gabe's chest. This was wrong. She knew it was wrong, but the desire rose strong inside her, stronger than she had ever felt. She had to stop. A few seconds more, then she would.

Something of her thought had communicated itself to Gabe. He didn't pull away. He held her, one hand stroking her back, his lips breaking the kiss only to move to her delicate ear where he felt the shudder of her response. He tasted the smoothness of her skin, breathed in her scent and knew he had to stop. Now. While he could. But still he held her, listening as their breathing slowed, two heartbeats steadying from rapid drumming. He rested his forehead against hers, waiting for the fever to pass.

"Don't ask me to apologize, Maureen," he murmured. "I can't be sorry for kissing you." He leaned back then to see her. Her eyes were dazed, her mouth soft and damp by the light of the fire. And he wanted to kiss her again.

"I'm not sorry," she whispered. In spite of what she said, Maureen rose from her place and without another word she left him.

She waited until she was snug in bed before she would allow herself to think about what happened. A kiss. His kiss. More than she had dreamed it would be. There still lingered the fluttery warmth that began with the first touch of his lips on hers.

Sweet. Sweet and tender and ever so gentle. She had never thought that a man could be so gentle, as if she were some small, fragile thing. It wasn't a weakness in Gabe, for she knew him to be a strong man, strong in spirit as well as physical strength. But that kiss…ah, that kiss had stirred awake the very desire she feared.

She had to remember her own promise that she would never again marry without love.

Gabe Channing said nothing of love, nothing about a future.

What would a wealthy man like him want with the likes of her? She was building daydreams with less foundation than a cloud to hold them.

What did she know of love? What she felt for her daughter and Chris was love. She loved her parents and thought she loved Conn when she married him. But their time together had been too short. Seven months from their meeting to marriage followed by his death.

Conn was a young girl's love. There was no way to know if what they had would have grown into a deep and abiding love.

But that was what she wanted.

Only it took two to turn attraction into love.

With a deep, heartfelt sigh, she punched her pillow.

He shouldn't have kissed her. A moment later, she amended that and knew she hadn't wanted him to stop.

She remembered her wish on the star and thought of this special Christmas season. A time for love and a time for miracles. A time of giving and a time for dreaming of the impossible.

She had to trust to the Lord that He would make His reason clear for bringing them together. She just had to.

A light snow had fallen during the night. By the morning the sun was shining and the temperature rose until it was warm. Gabe kept looking at the sky, muttering that he didn't like the looks of the clouds piling over the far mountain.

"Maybe," he said, as they finished their soup and biscuits at noon, "we should go cut our tree now. We'll bring it up close to the house, set it in a bucket of water and if it freezes, the tree will be fresh when we bring it inside.''

Maureen looked up at him. So attuned to his masculine presence she noticed the worry in his eyes though he spoke lightly of his intent. She wanted to ask him what was wrong but the children, as usual, were crowding close to him, both trying to top the other about the places where the best of the trees could be found.

''Maureen, we'll take your team with us to drag the tree home.''

''You three go ahead. I've a few chores to do. And if I can,'' she added over the children's protests, ''I'll make spice cookies.''

As Gabe harnessed the team he kept thinking back to the winters he spent here. He thought of things his father said about the snow and the possibility of slides. He had picked the spot for the cabin after two winters of checking the mountain behind to make sure there would never be a slide coming down to bury them.

But the warming weather alarmed him. He thought about leaving the children behind, then shrugged off his worry. They weren't going to be gone long. He, too, remembered a few good spots where some young spruce grew.

Hoisting his ax, he led the team out and Chris and Kathleen fell in behind him. Camp robber jays flitted in the trees, their landings sending a flurry of snow to fall.

The children sang, and he joined in as they steadily climbed the slope.

They startled an elk from a thick stand of aspen and stood watching as the huge animal with its massive rack of antlers trotted through a clearing.

''Just over the other side of that stand of trees is the place where we'll find our tree.''

''But Pa, I know a good place.''

''I do, too.''

"Do not. Girls don't know the same as boys."

"Do, too!"

"Enough," Gabe said with a laugh. "We won't fight about it. Since I'm the eldest, I get to pick."

Chris stuck his tongue out at Kathleen, but behind his father's back.

"Boys!" Kathleen hurried ahead to walk beside Gabe.

Far off they heard a thundering sound. Standing in the middle of the clearing, Gabe brought the horses to a stop. When Chris started to speak he hushed him.

"Listen! What you hear is snow coming off the mountain."

Something in his voice kept both children silent.

The sounds died away. Wary, Gabe waited a few minutes longer, then hurried the horses across the clearing and into the trees. There was an old Indian trail here, kept clear of brush by the game that followed it. Gabe pushed along, every sense alert, instinct telling him to hurry.

He spotted the stand of spruce before they were clear.

The children ran ahead, exclaiming over the thick, lush growth. Each quickly found first one, then another tree that was perfect.

Gabe came along with the horses, but he looked toward the mountain with its ragged peaks. Off a ways was a gorge that curved toward the west. If what he heard was the beginning of a slide, chances were good that was where the snow fell. But there was no accounting for the trail it would follow.

He listened a moment or two to the good-natured bickering between his son and Kathleen. She was a fine girl and he had grown fond of her. From thoughts of the daughter came thought of her mother and the kiss they had shared last night.

He had dreamed about Maureen, dreamed about kissing her and then making love to her until the passion he sensed in her and the desire he felt left them both breathless.

But there was so much more to the woman. He liked her quiet ways, enjoyed talking to her, something he had rarely done with a woman. Her laugh was a sound he carried inside him, it was that warm and inviting.

"Pa! Pa, you ain't listening," Chris yelled, tugging on Gabe's jacket sleeve. When he finally got his father's attention, he turned and pointed. "Kathleen and me found it. Maureen's gonna love this one. All you gotta do is cut it down."

"Let's take a look." Gabe looped the lead reins over a limb and followed his son through the stand of spruce. He inhaled deeply, loving the scent of the evergreens, even the crisp cold air. It was a lonely place, but where both man and child had room to grow and learn.

Kathleen stood guard on the tree they had picked out and Gabe stopped, looking it over.

Nearly ten feet tall, and half as wide, it was much too big. Before he opened his mouth to say so, he looked from her smiling eyes to his son's.

"Isn't it grand?" Kathleen asked. "Ma will love this one. Won't she, Chris?"

"You bet. Right, Pa?"

Gabe nodded, walked around the tree and saw that they had picked a good one. The trunk was straight, he saw, parting the branches to look. He could easily trim it down.

"I'll get your ax, Pa."

"You do like it, don't you?" Kathleen asked, her cheeks flushed with the same excitement that brightened her eyes.

"It's a fine one you two picked. But I doubt we'll have enough to decorate all the branches."

"Oh, I know that. But it will fill the corner and make the cabin smell so nice. My ma always wanted a big tree. We had a little one last year. It was all we could cut down. But this year will be the best Christmas ever."

"You bet," Chris added as he came up to hand over the ax to his father.

Gabe made short work of cutting down the tree. He labored

to drag it through the thick growth and hitched it to the traces on the team.

The day was suddenly clouded and there was a sharp drop in the temperature. He started them moving toward home.

Chris ran ahead for there was little snow on the ground. The way was a little muddy from the melt. Kathleen stayed beside him.

Impulse made Gabe reach out to take her smaller hand within his. Her smile made a warm feeling spread inside him.

"If I had a pa, I'd want him to be just like you."

"That's the nicest thing anyone's said to me in a long time, Kathleen. I imagine it must get lonely for you and your mother."

"Sometimes. It's been real nice having Chris with us. I think of him like he's my brother. Do you think I'm silly to do that?"

"No. Not at all. What you and your mother did was a fine thing, taking in Chris. Your mother's a special woman."

"Pretty?"

"Very."

"Do you...do you like her?"

Kathleen covered her mouth with her free hand, and the flush on her cheeks deepened. "I'm sorry. I shouldn't have asked."

"No, it's all right. I do like her. Like her a lot."

Gabe looked ahead and there was no sign of Chris.

"Where's that boy got off to?"

The words were no sooner spoken than the sound of thunder came to them. Gabe caught hold of Kathleen with one arm, holding her close and gripped his rifle with the other. He yelled at the horses and they started trotting, dragging the tree behind them.

"Hold me tight, sweetheart. We need to run. Chris!" he shouted. "Chris, get back here!"

The thunder swelled louder until it seemed to be everywhere. Gabe couldn't find Chris. *Lord,* he prayed, *please help me. Don't let me have found my boy only to lose him.*

"Chris!" he called again, and Kathleen added her own cries to his.

The horses were entering the trees. He hurried to get to them, afraid they'd be caught. He couldn't stop calling his son, but heard no reply. Kathleen shook in his arms, but she, too, kept yelling for Chris to answer them.

Beneath Gabe's feet the ground trembled, and a heavy rumble sounded behind them.

"Slide, Kathleen. That's a snowslide coming our way."

"Put me down. I can run. I can beat Chris running."

Gabe didn't answer, nor did he set her down. He saw the horses free of the woods and running full-out. He made for a shelf of rock with boulders and a towering pine to one side. It wasn't much of a shelter, but running with that snow coming down would surely get them killed.

"Pa! Got the horses!"

He heard Chris's yell, and he spun around, off balance carrying Kathleen in one arm and holding the rifle out in the other. He never saw the patch of ice. He felt himself falling, and managed to twist his body so he took the brunt of the fall on one knee.

Pain lanced him, but he struggled to his feet using the rifle as a crutch and got Kathleen tucked under the rock shelf. He turned halfway around and saw the snow filling the clearing they had just crossed, crushing the trees before its massive weight. It wasn't a wide slide, but carried every tree and rock debris in a thirty-foot path down the slope following what might have been an old water course.

He hunched protectively over Kathleen's huddled body and watched the snowy splashes flying high as if a gale force wind had taken hold. The thundering sound roared until it was all he heard as the slide plunged down gaining in speed. He knew the ravine below would be filled before it was done. His vision took in the riot of rock, broken trees, ice and masses of snow that hurtled in flight.

And when it was done, there was such a silence that he was almost afraid to breathe.

And nowhere did he hear the sound of his son's voice.

Chapter Nine

The day darkened and the wind came up when Maureen noticed the first snow flurries. She was not worried, for Gabe and the children had only been gone about two hours. It would take time to search out the stands of trees. But several times she slipped outside and saw that the flakes were big, thick wet ones, the kind that stick and the sky was darker.

She lit the lantern and hung it outside the door, worry building inside her until she restlessly paced from fire to window.

She was outside when she heard the far-off rumble of thunder and knew it for what is was—a snowslide.

And there was no sign of them returning. Three hours now, she reckoned. Surely they would be on their way back.

She banked the stove and added water to the soup pot. A worrisome feeling took hold of her. She forced herself to remember that Gabe had lived here, that he knew these mountains and the perils of snowslides. He wouldn't let harm come to the children.

But the slow-passing minutes increased the urge for her to do something.

She was dressed warmly before she thought about it. Taking another lantern, she stepped outside. The snow appeared a solid curtain, blanketing everything with its whiteness. She struggled against the wind. This storm was going to be what the old-timers called a howler, for the wind was strong and the snow thick and steadily falling.

Not too far off she heard a wolf howl. Before she neared the corner of the barn, she turned around and headed back to the cabin for her rifle.

One thing Maureen knew. She must not panic. If they were hurt they would need her. As she passed the barn she thought of the horses, but the way the snow was drifting before the wind, the horse would have more trouble finding a way up the slope than she would walking.

She called out every few feet, swinging the lantern from side to side. The wolf howled, only now his voice was joined by another.

Every step of the way she blessed the knowledge her father had passed on to her, to know the mark of the land. She had no fear of where she walked, but only for those who were missing.

A gust whipped snow into her face. She paused near the trunk of an ancient tree, calling out and once more swinging the lantern wide around.

At first she thought she imagined someone calling her. Hurriedly, she stepped out.

"I'm here! Can you see the lantern!"

She heard the horses before she saw the dark, massive shapes form out of the falling snow.

The cold was intense. Maureen started forward when she saw the small form leading the horses.

"Chris! Are you all right?"

Within minutes he stood in the circle of light and told her through lips near blue with cold of the snowslide. "I was too far ahead and scared to go back."

Maureen had to get him back to the cabin. She had to trust that Gabe would care for Kathleen. She only prayed that they were not hurt, for the snow had changed in these few minutes to icy particles that stung her face.

She handed the boy her rifle and then the lantern and blessed every hour of hard labor that had strengthened her body as she lifted Chris onto a horse and led the way back to the barn. She sent Chris to the cabin while she unharnessed the horses and rubbed them down with rough sacking. The cold worked its evil on her, for she could barely catch her breath as she made for the cabin to make sure Chris was all right.

He was putting on fresh socks when she came inside.

"I had some soup to warm me up. I'm coming with you to look for them."

Maureen opened her mouth to argue, then shut it. She could not leave him here alone, and if Gabe and Kathleen were hurt, she would need Chris.

"You mustn't worry. Pa's got woods savvy. He won't be far."

"Chris, get the sled. I'm going to fill this canteen with some of the broth. They'll be cold when we find them."

When, not if. She kept repeating those words as they hiked up the slope, the wind so sharp and cutting they could not call out. It was a struggle to place one foot in front of the other. Everything was buried deep under the drifted snow.

Maureen searched with care as they came to a stand of trees. Chris was sure this was where he stood when he heard the first thunder of the slide.

It was shelter of a sort beneath the snow-covered branches. But Maureen knew they dared not stand and wait here. The howls of the wolves were closer and they had a clearing to cross. From the little she could see, the wind had swept the south end clean of snow. She pointed out the way to Chris and they started off.

From the corner of her eye Maureen saw the dark shapes closing in on them. A wolf pack! She handed over the lantern to Chris, her gloves making her hands clumsy as she thumbed back the hammer of the rifle and fired a shot in the air. She did not want to kill them, just chase them away. It took another shot before they backed off, but she knew they had not gone far.

She thought that they should go back, that maybe Gabe and Kathleen had already reached the cabin, but something held her to search a little longer. How much longer, she did not know, for the cold numbed her feet. The only thing to be thankful for was that the snowfall lessened. They trudged onward, heading for the next stand of trees.

When she heard the piercing whistle, she thought the wind was playing tricks. But Chris knew what it was and whistled back. Within minutes they saw Gabe and Kathleen, hobbling toward them.

Such joy burst inside her that she could barely contain it. The fear she had held close drowned under that gladdened joy of seeing Gabe and her daughter, safe. And when they came together at the edge of the clearing, not a word was spoken, but they huddled and hugged. The lantern light showed the sheen of tears and beyond them, the relief that they were together. It was only as they started out that Maureen saw Gabe limp. He refused the sled, gesturing the two children to get on. Still using his rifle stock for a cane, with Maureen leading the way, they made their way home.

Tired, cold and hungry the four of them looked upon the lighted window with smiles. Home. A word slipped from lips chapped by cold and wind. Home. Warmth and shelter, and togetherness.

Maureen heated buckets of water. Some went to reduce the swelling on Gabe's knee, part to the animals for the creek was frozen. How the house pump worked, she did not know, but she was thankful for it.

She tucked the children into her bed and returned to Gabe.

“I’ll bathe your knee again. I…was afraid for you and Kathleen. I surely prayed hard.”

“Maureen.” He said her name and no more as she came to kneel on the floor beside where he made his bed. He took hold of her hand as she reached for the blanket that covered his legs. “Wait.”

He looked into her green eyes and liked the way the firelight brought out the red glints in her hair. She had been rushing around taking care of them and the animals and he saw the weary droop to her shoulders, but she smiled at him, and that smile made him feel as if his heart had turned over.

“There’s a thing I wish to say. Out there, I, too, was afraid. In those minutes of watching that slide destroy all in its path, I thought of my son and my leaving him to you. And I knew I could never find anyone better to have the guiding of him to grow to manhood.”

“Gabe, please, I did not do so much.”

“Hush. Let me finish. I also thought of you and the children here alone. Christmas is a short time away and I want to give you a present. I want you to have title to this land. I want to know that it is yours. And if… Well, there is Chri…” His voice trailed off, and he stared at the fire.

“Stop this. Nothing is going to happen to you. It is the brush with death that brings such thoughts.” She sat quietly beside him, waiting, for she sensed there was more he had to say. After long minutes passed, he spoke again.

“You have a rare quality, Maureen, to listen and wait for a man to form his thoughts into the right words. But they don’t come easy.” He glanced around the cabin and thought of how bare it had looked the last time he had been there. “You’ve made this into a home again. It is a fine place to raise a child.” He reached out and cupped her chin so his blue-gray eyes met hers. “A fine place for a man and a woman, a child or two or more.”

Her heart felt as if it stopped then returned with a stronger, harder beat. "Gabe, please, it is the loneliness that makes you talk like this."

"True. I'll not deny that. But I find that the day begins brighter when I see your smile. And your laughter brings the need within me to laugh with you. You've given me something these last few days that I didn't know I had needed. Happiness, Maureen. You're a caring, warm woman and a man would need to be a fool to let you go. Have you no feelings for me?"

The memory of his kiss flared into her mind and she saw within his eyes that he remembered those few moments of passion, too. But there was more. He talked of a man being a fool to walk away from her, but she knew she could not find a better man than Gabe.

She brushed the lock of hair from his forehead as she longed to do so many times. As they looked into each other's eyes, she sensed that he read of her deeper feelings as she did his. Sometimes it was too hard to put those feelings into words.

"Think about sharing your life with me, Maureen. I'd try to be a good husband to you, a good father to Kathleen. Do you. . .do you think you could come to care for me?"

But she answered with a question of her own. "And you, could you love me?"

He drew her down and whispered her name in a voice suddenly heavy with need. Yet his kiss was a tender cherishing of passion held in check.

Holding her beside him, he thought of what she asked.

"Love? How can a man define love? I know the love I have for my son. There was an emptiness inside me that grew into unbearable pain for every day that I searched and didn't find him. I love having a good horse beneath me and the feel of a fine weapon when trouble comes. And I love this land that demands a man's strength and courage to tame it.

"But truth told, Maureen, I know little of the love a man feels for a woman. I don't know if I have the right words to make you understand. I see you as a beautiful woman that makes my blood run hot and heavy. I hear your voice and know that I can reach out to share some small sight or a thought with you. Your silence is a comfort, too, for I never feel alone. I admire your strength and your courage.

"There is pride in you, Maureen," he whispered in his husky voice as he brushed the hair from her cheek. "And there is the woman's softness all men and children crave and need as they need air to breathe. These things," he said, struggling to turn on his side so he could see her, "these are the things I have come to love. The passion in you, for life and giving. And for loving a man. Yet, more than the strong desire I feel, I can lie beside you and am filled with completeness.

"Is this love I have when you are always in my thoughts and in my dreams? Ah, Maureen. Don't cry. I'll not press you to answer me."

He leaned closer and kissed her lips, then skimmed her flushed cheeks before he tasted a tear.

"Just think of what I've said. I really believe that our coming together was meant to be. It's said that this season of Christmas is always one filled with love. Can there be a better gift to give each other?"

She saw that he believed what he said, and she wanted to. No man had ever bared his heart to her like this.

Here was the answer to her wish. Here, held within the circle of strong arms, with gentle lips taking her tears. But there was more, for here was a man who spoke from his heart, so strong that his gentleness was another kind of strength.

"I've not courted you properly, Maureen," he murmured, his lips warm against her ear. "But I will. That I promise you."

"Gabe, I—"

"Hush, now. No answering me tonight. But stay with me. Just let me hold you."

"Let me tend to your knee."

He pulled back a bit and looked down at her. "All right. But only if you'll stay."

"I'll stay."

Chapter Ten

The days flew by as winter blanketed the land and soon Christmas would be celebrated. Maureen smiled a lot, but Gabe managed to avoid any serious talk between them. He teased her a great deal, and made the children giggle with his talk of a surprise come Christmas morning. It needed all four of them to get the great tree inside, and even then, Gabe had to trim down the branches to make it fit into the corner.

In the evenings when chores were done and the snow fell, Gabe told stories, those he remembered his mother reading to him, while Maureen and the children popped corn to string for the tree. The dried berries had been hung and their tin cuts shone in the candlelight among the thick green boughs. The scents grew tantalizing with baking of cookies and more than a few mock battles ensued over the stealing of them.

When Gabe's storytelling was done and the children tucked into bed to dream their Christmas dreams, Gabe would draw Maureen to stand before the tree, for each day they added some made or found decoration.

She loved the birds' nests he had found, and told him her belief that they would bring them all good luck. And tucked into the branches awaiting the rock candy she had hidden were the carefully broken and washed eggshells with their little yarn handles.

It was the sweetest time of the day, this quiet they shared, and then he would turn her within his arms and kiss her. There was yearning here, and the heat of passion for throughout the day the lingering glances each had cast had built to a sensual anticipation.

Sometimes she would break away first, and sometimes it was Gabe who was stronger to send her off to bed before temptation took hold.

It was a fine line to walk being mother and a woman who was courted. He never pressed for an answer and she cherished that about him, for she wanted the moment to be right when she spoke it.

She spent many a minute staring at nothing and thinking of the small acts that a man does that spoke more of love than any grand words. Getting up first in the morning to stoke the fires and make sure the stove was lit with coffee nearly ready by the time she joined him. Every day, he managed to take the children off to work or to play for a few hours, giving her time to complete her gifts and see to the baking.

There were always treasures found, a bit of rock broken from the ice-covered stream, tiny pinecones found hidden beneath thick-piled needles and boughs of fragrant pine to hang around the cabin. For her the treasure was the smiles in the children's eyes and their laughter, and Gabe, always there, snaring her glance and holding it with his own.

Love. It shaded every hour awake or sleeping, colored her voice as she hummed about her work, touched her hands as she cooked and brought a bright sparkle to her eyes.

Two days before Christmas the angel appeared on top of the tree. Breakfast had long been over, yet they had lingered about, giggling and whispering with a great deal of head shaking when she glanced at them.

Gabe finally took her over to the tree. "I've been hearing

from a wee Irish lass that there is a thing you've been longing to have, Maureen. Will you not open your eyes and see it?''

She poked among the branches, and saw nothing new. Chris and Kathleen said she was giving up too quickly.

''You've got to look lower, Ma.''

''No. No,'' Chris piped up, ''definitely higher.''

Maureen stood with her hands on her hips bunching her apron. ''And you, Mr. Channing, where do you suggest that I look?''

''At me?''

''Yes, Ma, do. Can't you see he's shaved every morning?''

''And polished his boots,'' Chris added.

Maureen felt heat creep into her cheeks as they kept on with their teasing, then threw her hands up.

''Enough! Now, tell me what I'm to look for.''

''Up!'' The three of them crowded around her and pointed.

''An angel,'' she whispered. ''Wherever did you find an angel?''

''Gabe—''

''Pa—''

''I made it for you,'' Gabe said over the little ones' shouts.

''It's lovely.'' She turned back to look again, seeing the raw wood with its reddish grain mixed with a creaminess from the heart of the wood he had used. It wasn't very big and there were no painted features. The wings spread out to the sides as if to take flight, but Gabe had used rawhide ties to keep it in place at the top of the tree.

Her hand sought and found his waiting and she smiled at him. ''I've wanted an angel on my tree for a long time. But maybe I've had my wish answered another way. Could it be the Lord sent me a real angel in you?''

''Not unless heaven's crowded this year. I already know He's sent me one.''

They had slowly drifted closer, so close their breaths mingled and had not realized they were in each other's arms until Chris spoke.

"Are you gonna kiss her? Are you, huh?"

Kathleen grabbed hold of Chris's arm and pulled him away from the tree.

"Wait. I wanna see if he's gonna kiss her."

"You can't. Only a silly boy would want to watch. I know better."

"You saw them kissing?"

She drew him around to the table. "Promise not to tell," she whispered.

"Promise."

"Last night."

Eyes round, Chris gulped. "You mean it's gonna happen?"

"Shush. I don't know. But when a man kisses a woman he respects you can bet he's thinking about marrying."

"How come you know so much about it, Kathleen?"

"'Cause I'm older than you. And a girl. And girls are smarter about these things."

Chris offered no argument. "So, when is it gonna happen?"

Since they were sheltered from sight by the tree, Kathleen dipped into the crock and pulled out two cookies. Trying to appear serious and thoughtful, she shook her head.

"I imagine he'll go down on one knee and take hold of her hand. That's when he asks."

"Just like that story Pa told of Ivanhoe kneeling before the king?"

"Just like that, Chris. Now, hurry up and eat your cookie before Ma comes."

"Aw, she don't get mad. She only pretends."

Kathleen, knowing better, wisely held her tongue and carefully, but hurriedly ate her own cookie.

When the children's whispers reached Gabe and Maureen, they had trouble holding back their laughter.

"So, should I kiss you and make Chris happy?"

Gabe's murmur went no farther than her ear, but she felt his smile against her cheek.

"What about me kissing you and making me happy?"

"You're a tempting woman, Maureen O'Rourke. Mighty, mighty tempting." He looked into her green eyes. "There's nothing of the angel in you now, woman. Pure devil's mischief cooking—"

"And you'd like a taste," she finished for him. But it wasn't the kiss he envisioned, only a chaste peck on his cheek. "That will keep you until later."

Only later, Gabe found that Maureen had talking on her mind.

"I'm scared, Gabe. I've never had so much happiness and I'm afraid to believe it will last."

He dropped the load of wood he had brought in for the night and sat beside her in front of the fire.

"Why would you think it can't last between us?" He slipped his arm around her shoulders and drew her near.

"It's too good, too perfect, Gabe."

"And I've nothing but promises to make that I will do everything I can to keep you happy. As happy as you are now. I guess that's what it comes down to, Maureen. Do you trust me enough to believe me?"

She turned to look at him, studying the craggy features that had become so dear to her heart. Strangely there was no fear left, not when she looked into his eyes and saw the love he felt waiting there.

She took his hand within her own smaller one and lifted it to her cheek. "I believe you, Gabe. And I'll make a promise, too. I will do everything I can to make us be as happy as we are right now."

He didn't move, almost didn't want to breathe. He had needed to hear her say that, needed it so badly that he cast the thought to the far corner of his mind. And this was part of loving a strong woman, that she needed him to make her happiness complete.

He brushed his thumb over her trembling lips. "I love you, Maureen."

"And I love you."

He saw the moonlight through the frosted window and took her mouth with his. Holding her, warming her with his big hands, soothing and inciting the passion that simmered between them.

"And you'll marry me as soon as we can get back to Denver?"

"Yes, oh, yes, Gabe. I want to be your wife."

From the darkened corner of the cabin there came a smothered sound that quickly became a whoop. Chris rushed toward them, Kathleen only moments behind. They came together in a tangle of arms and legs, shouts and kisses until Gabe sorted them all out.

"I knew you would, Pa! Kathleen told me so."

"Kathleen! How could you—"

"Ma, you've been making calf eyes at him and blushing something awful when he's looking at you. 'Sides, I saw you kissing him. And I wished so hard that he'd be my pa, too."

"And I was wishing to have you keep on as my mother."

Maureen opened her arms to the two of them, hugging them tight. Behind her, she felt Gabe's arms reach around to hold them all. It was a good feeling, this happiness filled with love.

Up before dawn Christmas morning, the children made breakfast a noisy affair. They all ate heartily of the flapjacks, eggs, bacon and ham, biscuits and sweet rolls. Last night, Christmas Eve, they each told a part of the Christ child's birth, and this morning, they knelt to pray and sing hymns.

But childish excitement could not long be contained. The stockings were quickly emptied to shouts and exclamations. Chris loved his new pocketknife and harmonica. The checkers set, a much read copy of *From the Earth to the Moon* by Jules

Verne and the fishing hooks were things she had traded her baked goods and sewing to have for him. And Kathleen proudly showed off her new hair ribbons and hair combs. She had books, too, *Vanity Fair* and *Little Women,* along with two new outfits for her rag doll. The clothing matched the skirt and shirtwaist that Maureen had made and Chris loved his shirt, cut down from an almost new saved one.

They shared gifts, too. An almost new box of Jack Straws she bought for eight cents, and a set of dominoes, and a tattered copy of the third volume of John James Audubon's *The Birds of America.* And there was candy, peppermint sticks, rock candy and candied ginger.

But before the presents hidden beneath sacking could be opened, they dressed warmly and went out to the barn where the horses and cow were given their Christmas treats of apples and carrots. It was a clear day, but cold, and soon the cabin filled with the delicious aromas of roasting turkey and baked apple pie. Potatoes were simmering, ready to be mashed, onion corn bread and light yeast rolls. Peas and bacon and carrots sweetened with honey.

Then they opened the special gifts. Gabe and Chris loved the game bags Maureen and her daughter had made. And Kathleen spent rapturous moments exclaiming over her dollhouse. For Chris, Gabe had fashioned a pair of snowshoes and, of course, there was the small quilting frame he made for Maureen.

Quite unexpectedly, Chris and Kathleen stood up.

"Pa, there's a thing you need to do. To do the right way."

Bemused, Gabe repeated what his son said.

"You've got to get down on one knee and hold on to Maureen's hand and ask her proper. That's what Kathleen said."

"Ah, I see. Very wise of Kathleen," Gabe said with a wink for the blushing girl. Down on one knee he went and took hold of Maureen's hand, then motioned Chris beside him. "Come on, son, down you go alongside me. This is a two-man proposition. And you, young lady, stand here beside your mother.'' As soon as she had, Gabe lifted her hand and laid it over her mother's.

''Now, Maureen, will you do me the honor of becoming my wife and Chris's mother? Wait now. And you, Kathleen, will you do me the honor of becoming my daughter and a sister to Chris?''

Maureen grinned at her daughter. ''Be sure now, lass. If you say yes, we'll be together for a long time. And Chris might not be the only brother.''

''Oh, Ma, I like the sound of that word, *together.*'' She smiled at Gabe and took hold of Chris's hand. ''This is the best Christmas ever.''

''I agree,'' Maureen added. ''*Together* is a wonderful word and a beautiful Christmas gift.''

''Woman, would you say yes so I can get up and kiss you proper?''

''Yes, oh, yes, love,'' she answered with a laugh in her voice.

And he kissed her, not as passionately or as long as he wanted, but a satisfying kiss nonetheless.

''Gabe, can we come back here? We have found more than a miracle here. We found love.''

''We'll come back. I promise you that, and what we found we will have forever.''

* * * * *

Tender Romance™
6 brand new titles each month
...love affairs
that last a lifetime
Available on subscription every month
from the Reader Service™
GEN/02/RS2

Medical Romance™
6 brand new titles each month
...medical drama
on the pulse.
Available on subscription every month
from the Reader Service™
GEN/03/RS2

Sensual Romance™
4 brand new titles each month
...sassy, sexy
and seductive.
Available on subscription every month
from the Reader Service™
GEN/21/RS2